The Arthurian Relic

Andrew Clawson

**Get Your FREE Copy of the Parker Chase story
A SPY'S REWARD.**

Sign up for my VIP reader mailing list,
and I'll send you the novel for free.

Details can be found at the end of this book.

Chapter One

Tangier, Morocco

A moped crash saved Harry Fox's life.

He had been sitting in the shade under an awning, outside an anonymous café in the heart of Morocco's cultural center. Dusty air choked his throat. He'd been there for an hour, his back to a wall, studying the river of humanity flowing around him, waiting for a man who wanted to buy the metal case resting against Harry's foot. For a million dollars. If he showed.

Harry had paused, a cup of tea halfway to his lips, as one of the city's ubiquitous speeding scooters veered out of control. It was whizzing around the traffic with reckless abandon as the driver pushed his luck and finally went too far. The bike wobbled, the engine roared in protest, and then rider and machine went down, metal screeching on asphalt as the bike smashed into a parked car a short block away from where Harry sat.

The car's driver got out, cursing in Arabic, while the moped operator stood up from the ground, dusting himself off and checking himself for injuries. Harry's eyes narrowed and he looked more closely at the irate driver.

That's him. The man he was supposed to meet. The buyer willing to part with a small fortune for Harry's artifact. They'd seen each other only once, during a streamed meeting for Harry to prove the

1

artifact was genuine. When the buyer had balked at meeting in person, Harry had threatened to scuttle the sale. He didn't care if the guy didn't like it. Plenty of other people would buy what Harry had. The buyer had relented, promising to meet Harry in Tangier to complete their transaction.

That had been three days ago. The buyer had promised to come alone, same as Harry. Same parameters Harry set for every buy. You don't like it? Find the one-of-a-kind merchandise Harry sold somewhere else. The buyers never could, so they always caved in the end and agreed to Harry's demand of coming in person and alone. Which is why Harry's heartrate picked up when another man appeared from inside the damaged car. A big, bearded guy, thick with muscle. A couple of quick steps took him to the moped driver, who never saw it coming. One second moped guy was arguing with the buyer; the next, he was on his back, courtesy of an uppercut from the beefy passenger.

The passenger vanished into the crowd. The driver, Harry's buyer, headed for the café. Harry gulped his tea and his body tensed. *They're setting me up.*

He looked right, then left. No sign of the bearded passenger. People filled the street in front of him, a half-dozen languages dancing in his ears. Morocco's city center offered a perfect place to get lost. The colorful blanket of possibility and fresh starts covered a ruthless side, where a man could easily find himself cornered with no way out. Harry wasn't about to let that happen to him.

He suppressed the urge to reach for the empty spot at his back where he normally carried protection. He couldn't risk smuggling a gun into Morocco. Getting caught with a firearm was a sure ticket to jail, where the cops would soon figure out the contents of his case had more question marks than answers. Harry's only weapons were his fists and a keen desire to stay alive. They would have to be enough.

Harry didn't stand as the buyer approached. He considered the man from behind his sunglasses, and found himself reaching for the amulet dangling from his neck, an Egyptian piece made of gold and a bluish-green ceramic called faience. A new habit, something he did without realizing it. The amulet helped to calm his nerves.

The buyer's light skin stood out in Morocco, marking him as a Westerner in this land historically controlled by the Portuguese, English and Spanish. The man's white linen suit looked brand new, practically sparkling in the sunlight.

"Mr. Smith," the buyer said. He stood across from Harry, not yet taking the seat in front of him. "You have it?"

Harry had given a fake name, of course. Just as he knew the buyer's name wasn't real either. "Mr. White. Have a seat."

The aptly named buyer did as asked. "You didn't answer my question."

Harry removed his sunglasses and glanced at the ground. "It's here." A look to either side found no sign of the bearded man. "Did you bring payment?" Mr. White reached into his jacket pocket. "Easy," Harry said. "It's crowded here. Don't make a scene."

Mr. White hesitated, then displayed only the top of a small bag. Black velvet, cinched at the top. "They are all here."

"You came alone?"

Mr. White pursed his lips. He opened his mouth, closed it, then tried again. "As instructed," he said.

A bead of sweat glistened on Mr. White's forehead, and he removed a handkerchief from his pocket – white, of course – to wipe it away. He cleared his throat. "I trust you're alone as well?"

"Of course," Harry said.

Harry let Mr. White wait as his mind raced. Where had the bearded guy gone? He could have looped around to come at Harry from the near side. With traffic grinding past not ten feet away and a steady stream of pedestrians on the move, Harry had little hope of making the guy in time. "Let's finish this," Harry said. "You'll want to inspect the merchandise."

Mr. White leaned forward in his chair when Harry lifted the case to their table, glancing toward the street as he did. Harry twisted the case away so Mr. White couldn't see him punch in the code. An electronic lock beeped, and Harry lifted the lid. "Be careful. It bites."

Mr. White inhaled sharply. Whether from momentary fright at the serpent looking his way or the sheer surprise at how impossibly beautiful the Egyptian pharaoh's crown ornament looked up close, Harry couldn't say. Harry took a moment to savor the familiar effect. He'd reacted nearly the same way when he first saw it.

"Fantastic." Mr. White leaned closer. He didn't try to touch it. "A golden Uraeus. The rearing cobra." A Germanic accent clipped his words, Harry noticed now. "Granite eyes, a lapis lazuli head."

"The rest solid gold," Harry finished. Mr. White had gawked enough. He could be playing for time, all the shock and awe an act giving bearded man a chance to get the drop on Harry. "From the eighteenth dynasty, which included King Tut. More than three thousand years old. A steal for what you're paying. Satisfied?"

"Oh, yes." Mr. White's face fell when Harry snapped the case shut.

Harry reached into a pocket, keeping his hand beneath the table. "Let's see the payment."

A waiter came over as Mr. White removed the small black bag, asking in Arabic if Harry needed anything else. Harry responded in the same language, then looked over to Mr. White. "You want a drink?" he said, still speaking in Arabic. No reaction. "Hey, I'm talking to you. My friends are going to ambush you in a second and steal those diamonds." Again, no response. If Mr. White spoke Arabic, he did a fine job hiding it.

Harry turned to the thoroughly confused waiter and switched to English. "I'm fine. Maybe my friend needs a drink."

The waiter turned to Mr. White and spoke in English, though Mr. White waved him off, glancing over Harry's shoulder as the waiter departed. "You will find the payment is in order." Mr. White reached into the bag and removed an explosion of light. Harry squinted as sunlight bounced off the single cut diamond. "One million dollars in untraceable stones." The rock disappeared back into the velvet bag. "As agreed."

Mr. White was for real. Harry locked the case, making sure Mr. White saw him do it, and then replaced it on the ground beside his chair. "Put the diamonds on the table," Harry said. "I'll take them with me and leave the case. You stay here. I'll call you in five minutes with the keycode."

Mr. White lifted his eyebrows. "You do not trust me?" Again, he looked past Harry's shoulder, toward the street. "I am a businessman, Mr. Smith."

"You're buying a looted Egyptian artifact with diamonds," Harry said. "I don't trust you. Now put the diamonds down and push them toward me."

A car horn blared. Mr. White's hands didn't move. His mouth, however, did. "You are intelligent, Mr. Smith. Know I am very sorry to do this. You will pass the case over now."

Cool steel touched Harry's neck. "Don't get up," Mr. White said quickly. "My associate is a nervous man."

Harry twisted his head, looking up into the glistening, curled beard of the man holding a pistol to his neck. The guy could barely see Harry's face through all that hair on his chin. Harry played a hunch and spoke rapidly in Arabic, low enough that only bearded man could hear. "Whatever he's paying you, I'll double it."

Bearded man fired back in Arabic. "Stop talking." The pistol pressed harder on his neck.

Harry swiveled his eyes back to Mr. White, who was frowning. "I only want the artifact," he said. "Not to kill you. If you struggle, though, it will be necessary." Mr. White's elbows found the table. "Now, the case."

He'd only have one chance. Harry leaned over, shoulders hunched forward, eyes down as he lifted the case and set it atop the table. He turned to bearded man and continued in Arabic. "I'm giving it to him. Get that gun off my neck before it goes off by accident." Though the man glared in response, his pistol moved back a fraction. Harry turned in his seat, moved his weight forward slightly so he was perched on the chair's edge, weight on the balls of his feet. Mr. White stared at the case. Bearded guy did too. Harry pushed the case forward and knocked his tea setting to the ground. The metal serving tray flashed as it fell.

Harry sprang up and twisted, corkscrewing around to put everything he had into a punch aimed at bearded guy's chin. The knuckle dusters he'd slipped on moments earlier did their job. Bearded guy fell back, bounced off a parked car and thudded to the ground. He wasn't moving when Harry turned to find Mr. White frozen in place.

"I thought we were here to do business." Harry lowered his hand beneath the table, out of sight. With his other hand, he slid the case the rest of the way toward Mr. White, then stuck his hand out. "The diamonds. Now. Or I leave and you never see this Uraeus again."

Mr. White never blinked, looking from Harry's hand to the case and back again. Harry cocked an ear for any sound of bearded guy getting up. Fighting that guy on even terms was a suicide mission. Harry counted to three. "That's it." He snatched the case back and made as though he were about to get to his feet. "Time's up. My other buyers will be pleased to hear it's still available."

"Wait." Mr. White pulled out the velvet bag, offering it with a shaking hand. "We still have a deal."

Harry sat back down, leaned over and picked up the diamonds. Bearded guy was moaning. Harry turned and glanced at him. Still down. He turned back to Mr. White, who reached for the case and gave it a tug. Harry didn't let go of the handle.

"One more thing," Harry said. Mr. White had both hands on the case now, and Harry pulled it back toward him, bringing the man closer. "I don't give second chances."

His right fist shot out from under the table and landed square between Mr. White's eyes. Glasses broke, cartilage shattered, and Mr. White was out cold before he hit the ground. Harry gritted his teeth. Those damn dusters *hurt*. He slipped them off and shoved them back into his pocket along with the diamonds, scooped up the metal case and jumped to his feet. As the café's patrons stared, he leapt over the bearded guy, intending to make a break for the moped he'd stashed down the street.

But suddenly bearded guy's hand shot up and grabbed Harry's leg, sending him stumbling into a parked car. His sweat left damp streaks on its dusty window as he nearly fell, catching himself just in time. An immensely strong hand held one foot. Harry kicked once, twice, then felt his leg go free. He took off in earnest now, twisting and turning and caroming off the café's brick wall before getting his balance and accelerating.

The sidewalk was only half-full, leaving enough room for Harry to dodge between people before he came to an intersection and had to pause. A look back found bearded man coming full steam, not bothering to dodge anybody. Even if the guy hadn't been a head taller than everyone else, Harry could have pinpointed him from the trail of shouting pedestrians, sent flying when the big man ran them over.

He looked back at the traffic. Cars and bikes battled for space on the road. A sliver of daylight opened between two cars, enough for Harry to leap between them, sliding on his backside across the hood of one before he hit the ground and dove for the far sidewalk. A horn blared as the vehicle zipped past, the hot air in its wake filling Harry's mouth with sickly-sweet exhaust. The damned bearded man was still coming; he was in the road now, plowing over a slow-moving moped and causing a pileup as he doggedly made his way across.

Harry swore as the case banged off his knee. Holding it made it tough to run, to keep his balance and stay ahead of the big bastard on his tail. The guy could *move*. Harry was fast, a necessity when you were average height and trouble often found you, but he wasn't getting away. The sidewalk opened up in front of him. His moped was barely two blocks away, but even if he could get to it, the big guy would be close. Too close. A side street opened up to Harry's right. *Time to improvise.*

He turned, pushing through a crowd around one of the street stalls, and ran past narrow rowhouses that leaned over him, crowding the sky out with their overhanging stucco gutters and clotheslines crisscrossing from windows, laden with clothes drying in the heat. Until the next block, when one side of the street fell off a cliff. Literally.

A five-story retaining wall stretched to the ground below. On the opposite side, weather-beaten houses in every shade of faded paint looked over the valley. He'd been down here, trying to find a good hiding spot for his moped hours before the meeting. The vertical drop made his groin tense as he ran past with nothing more than a waist-high metal fence stopping anyone from falling ass-over-elbows to their death below.

A pair of switchback stairways attached to the retaining wall allowed pedestrians to descend to the bottom of the wall far below, though who in their right mind would do that was beyond Harry. The sounds of bearded guy gaining echoed off the aged walls. Harry sucked in hot, dry air and accelerated for the closest set of stairs, hidden behind a public drinking fountain. Two boys now splashed water at each other around it, their laughter jarring as he ran for his life. He had one shot at this.

Harry slid across the sidewalk, going low so he dropped out of sight between two parked cars. Bearded guy couldn't have seen him toss the metal briefcase under one of the cars. At least he hoped not. The two boys stared with their mouths open as a crazy man slid past them onto the first landing, popping up to descend the switchback stairs three at a time. He picked up steam when a rough voice shouted above, commanding the two boys to move. Bearded guy.

Every other run of stairs was set away from the retaining wall. Half the time you were against the relative safety of a stone wall; the other half, you walked above nothing but air. One wrong move and you could topple over the pathetic safety railing and end up splattered on the street below.

Bearded man thundered down the stairs now. Harry didn't stop to think. He leaned over the railing, reached around to grab the underside of the stairs he had just descended and slipped over, leaving himself dangling twenty feet above the landing below. Any mistake and the best he could hope for was a broken ankle. Get unlucky and it was four stories to the street below.

Bearded guy pounded onward. Harry's hands vibrated as the big man moved. He ignored the rough metal digging into his palms, twisting so his chest faced the staircase where his adversary would soon appear. Harry brought his knees up, feet aimed out. He waited.

The man's feet came into view first. He slowed, his torso now in sight, and then he nearly stopped. The guy had to be wondering where Harry went, because he should be able to see him right now. Bearded guy looked down, leaning *away* from Harry. The railing stopped at his waist. *Now.*

Harry put his whole body into the kick. Both feet smashed into the man's backside, throwing him against the railing and hurling his upper body over the edge. For an instant, it looked like he might recover. Bearded man grabbed wildly for support that wasn't there. A beat later he flipped over the railing headfirst and tumbled into space.

Harry crashed to the stairs, thankful to have made it over his side of the railing and back to safety. He scrambled to his feet in time to see the man crash-land on the roof of a passing car below. Metal crunched, horns blared, and the man's body flew off the car roof, landing right in front of the wheels of another moving car. It didn't stop in time. Harry winced and looked away.

Damn. Blood seeped from cuts on Harry's hands, dust caked his throat, and in that instant Harry had never felt more alive. Nobody had ever tried to kill him before, *really* tried. The guy would have done whatever it took to find the case, then kill him. His stomach rebelled, twisting in knots. Harry leaned over the railing, drawing in deep breaths to push the nausea down. Then he remembered the case.

Those kids. Panic crept into the edge of his thoughts as Harry ran back up to street level. They couldn't have—

The two boys stood there, open-mouthed, staring at what had transpired below. One of them, a skinny kid about nine years old, held Harry's briefcase. He held it out to Harry without saying a word.

Harry took it gently from his hands and actually looked closely at the boys for the first time. Ragged sandals. Unwashed faces. Stained shirts with holes in them. Kids born into a hard world.

"*Shukraan lakum,*" he said. Arabic for *thank you.* The boys took a step back as Harry continued in their native language. "You found my briefcase. Please, take this."

Their eyes narrowed and they continued to edge away, ready to run, as Harry reached into his pocket. Then their eyes widened and they nearly fell over when Harry handed each of them a large diamond.

"Do you have parents?" he asked. Each boy nodded. "Take these to them. Go!"

The looks on their faces were worth every penny, he thought, as they raced off. Harry wiped sweat from his forehead, checking that the cord holding his amulet still hung unbroken around his neck. It did.

The city noise covered him with welcome anonymity as he walked back to his moped, feeling for the first time in a long while that he'd done something good, helping those kids. And he could resell the Uraeus. Now he just had to convince his boss it was a win. A high-stakes proposition. You didn't want to make the man angry.

Harry sighed. The challenges you faced when your boss was the head of a Brooklyn crime family.

Chapter Two

New York City

The ground rumbled beneath Harry's feet.

The G train, only ten minutes behind schedule. Dependable as ever. The street light ahead turned green and Harry darted across.

Three days had passed since his trip to Tangier. Three days spent wondering if Mr. White had managed to get a lead on Harry's true identity or where he lived. Levels of anonymity were a requirement in Harry's line of work, and until their meeting at the café Harry's dealings with Mr. White had been at arm's length. Online, with no real names attached. A middleman had helped Harry to find a buyer for the artifact he'd acquired, eventually putting him in touch with Mr. White.

Harry stopped at another intersection. Other pedestrians filled the spaces on either side of him, close enough that he could hear the tinny music beating from their earbuds. All acting exactly like native New Yorkers, which meant ignoring everyone. The light turned green, the amoeba of humanity burbled onward, and Harry kept his eyes open. Chances were, if Mr. White was angry enough to find out Harry's true identity, he'd also discover Harry worked for a man named Vincent Morello. Once he knew that, if Mr. White had any sense, he'd write off the million dollars in diamonds as a learning experience.

Vincent Morello, Vinny to no one, had arrived in America as an infant during the early years of World War II. At a time when Italian immigrants often found themselves treated as Mussolini's cousins, Vincent Morello's father had staked his claim to a piece of real estate in Brooklyn, using old-world connections to figure out who truly ran the Italian community. The underground one, where *mafioso* touched everything and you always gave the don a cut of your profits.

Vincent's father rose through the ranks, taking the hard path. Broken bones, cement shoes, the whole bit. At the end he came out on top, establishing the Morello family as one of New York City's most formidable organized crime outfits. He ruled with an iron grip until the day an old adversary got the drop on him, putting two bullets in the don's chest. The old don was dead, long live the new don. Vincent Morello exacted revenge, then in a move emblematic of how he differed from his father, brokered a truce between the city's five largest Italian families.

Now Vincent led them all, a de facto *capo dei capi* who adamantly opposed the idea of having a role in leading rival factions. However, it kept the peace, so he offered guidance when the other families came to Vincent for his help in settling disputes, brokering agreements and generally keeping them from killing each other too often. Harry had never met Vincent's father, having been born several decades after the old man's murder, but he could see streaks of the legendary ruthlessness in Vincent on occasion. It wasn't unheard of for someone to anger Vincent more than necessary and suddenly go missing, though Vincent, now an old man himself, didn't enjoy that side of the business.

Harry zigged down a series of side streets, past food stands and storefronts offering the freshest tomatoes this side of Sicily, until he stood in front of the century-old building where Vincent Morello ran his operation. He exhaled, long and slow. Mr. White faded from his thoughts. Vincent lived in and worked out of this massive brownstone, which had been two private residences until Vincent remodeled them into one oversized home. Situated on a quiet corner in the heart of Morello turf, Vincent was as safe here as anywhere in the world. It helped to have half the neighborhood on your payroll. Considering the police precinct covering this area had mostly home-grown recruits, Vincent also enjoyed an unofficial layer of security from them.

A passing woman nodded to Harry, the stroller in front of her rattling as she walked. He smiled, and she returned one, a look he didn't always get from people around here. Harry stood out among all these Italian Americans. His Pakistani-American heritage didn't exactly allow him to blend in.

Harry found his hands clenched into fists. For reasons he didn't fully understand, Vincent had treated him like family since the day they'd met. That didn't mean Harry wasn't cautious around him. *Quit stalling.* He touched the amulet around his neck for luck and walked up the stairs, briefcase in hand. The old man had liked the Uraeus, so seeing it again should put a smile on his face.

A familiar figure sat inside the front door, standing from a chair as Harry walked in. A massive hand thumped on Harry's shoulder. "Harry Fox, back from the desert. How ya doing?"

"I'm good, Mack. I was near the water, where it's nice. None of that desert nonsense for me." Harry steeled himself as the big man thumped his shoulder again. "How's my friend Mack these days?"

"I thought the desert was in your blood," he said with a straight face. He couldn't keep it long. "I'm just messin' with you, you know that." With Vincent's soldiers, Harry couldn't always tell. Mack, though, was always busting his chops with glee. He and Harry both gave as good as they got. Mack spared Harry's shoulder another pounding and looked to the briefcase. "Hear you made a helluva deal. Can't imagine all the gold coins you must be carryin' around now."

Harry rolled his eyes. "You could say that. I'd rather it had gone as planned, though. A quiet sale is better than a fight. And they don't pay me in gold."

"Ask for it next time, and keep a couple in your pocket. Those heavy things are good in a fight if you're stuck." He tapped the side of his head. "Always think ahead, Harry." Mack gestured to the door. "Go on ahead in, Harry. I heard what you did to that fella out there and I don't want no piece of you. End up hit by a car if I'm not careful."

"Very funny."

Mack rumbled with laughter as Harry went past. Through one open doorway, he found the inner door to Vincent's private office ajar. Though he moved silently, a voice called out at his approach.

"Harry, come in."

Harry couldn't see the old man yet, but no doubt Vincent had tracked his movements since he had approached on the sidewalk. Cameras kept watch over the entire complex, with every feed going to a monitor on Vincent's desk. Overseeing the Italian mob in New York shortened a man's lifespan if he didn't take precautions.

"Mr. Morello." Harry slipped into Vincent's office, standing just inside the door. "Thank you for inviting me here today."

"Please, Harry, come here." Vincent stood from a sleek Herman Aeron chair Harry always found incongruent with the old man's battleship of a desk. Vincent's shock of white hair practically glowed as sunlight from the window fell on it. "I am glad to see you unharmed."

Moving with a light gait belying his nearly eight decades, Vincent came around to Harry and clasped his face between both hands. He didn't have to reach up far, even though he was shorter than most. He planted a kiss on each of Harry's cheeks. "You worry me like my own son."

Harry accepted the personal greeting with ease. Outside of his immediate family, Vincent never greeted anyone this way. "It's good to be back, Mr. Morello."

"It's Vincent, to you. Please, Harry, you know this. Now have a seat and tell me about your trip." The wrinkles around his eyes deepened when he looked at Harry, making him appear more like a concerned grandfather than a mafia boss.

Harry's father had taught him to show the old man respect in every way, no matter what. It was a lesson Harry wouldn't forget. "I'm afraid I let you down, Vincent. The buyer tried to double-cross me. I didn't see it coming until almost too late."

He detailed how he'd located the buyer through Rose, their standard intermediary. The buyer showed up with another man, the bearded one who got the drop on Harry at first. Vincent smiled when Harry described clocking Mr. White, then the foot chase through Tangier. Vincent touched his own chest when Harry told him he'd kicked his pursuer over the railing.

"*Grazie al cielo.* Thank heavens, Harry. I cannot imagine losing you." Vincent looked to the ceiling for an instant, then leaned forward. "And we will find another buyer for the artifact. Is it still in your case?"

The case went up onto Vincent's desk. Harry unlatched it to display the golden Uraeus, which Vincent studied for a moment but didn't touch.

"I also took these from the buyer," Harry said. "Figured it was only right, considering he tried to steal from you." Harry hadn't told anyone about taking the payment, and true surprise crossed Vincent's face as he opened the black velvet bag holding a million dollars in cut diamonds. "I gave a small finder's fee to two boys who watched the artifact while I dealt with that guy." He briefly relayed that part of the story as well. If the old man were going to be upset with any of it, this would be the part. Vincent hadn't gotten this far in life by giving profits away.

Vincent sat back in his chair, holding the diamonds. "You are a good man, Harry. There is a place for you behind St. Peter's gate. It's my hope you changed their lives."

An invisible pressure lifted off Harry's shoulders. "I hope so too."

"Now that you are back, I set up a meeting for you. Rose is expecting you at her office in one hour. I suspect she already has a new buyer lined up for the piece. Are you able to go see her?"

You didn't decline Vincent's suggestions. "I'll head over now," Harry said. "Same price for the Uraeus?"

Vincent smiled. "I trust your judgment, Harry. You are like your father: a good man." Vincent again looked to the ceiling. "May he rest in peace."

"I appreciate that, Vincent."

"I consider you my other son," Vincent said. "It is the least I can do after what your father did for me." A creaking sounded from behind Harry. "Speaking of my son, here is Joseph."

Harry stood and turned to face a younger version of Vincent. Joseph Morello looked every bit the Italian prince as he entered the room and stopped beside his father's desk.

"Harry. Good to see you're safe." He didn't offer his hand.

"It's good to be back. I just finished telling your father about my trip."

"We can still sell the piece, so no harm done."

"Better than that." Vincent tossed the velvet bag to his son. "Harry kept the payment *and* the artifact."

"A million bucks worth, if I remember." Joey pulled out one choice stone, held it to the light. "I can take these straight to the bank deposit box."

"Joey, give that stone to Harry. To show our thanks."

Harry put his hands up. "I couldn't accept that, Vincent."

"Now, Harry." Sunlight bounced off the gold cross between open buttons on Vincent's shirt as he took the stone from Joey, then walked over to Harry, his hand outstretched. "I insist."

Harry pocketed the stone without further argument. "Thank you, Vincent. I won't forget this." He turned to the door, then paused. "I do have one question." Vincent and Joey didn't move. "It's about Rose. She set up the Tangier deal. I have to ask." Harry found his throat had gone dry. He swallowed, which didn't do a thing. "Do you think we should use her again?"

Vincent finally blinked. "Rose worked with your father. She has never let us down. I am certain this was a terrible accident. Nothing more. We are fortunate you proved so resourceful." End of conversation. One olive-hued hand touched the small of Harry's back.

Harry promised to keep both Morellos updated on selling the Uraeus as he left. At the front door, he found Mack perusing the sports section.

"Done already, Harry?" He peered over the paper's top edge. "Hope they're sending youse somewhere sandy again. You blend in those places better than I would."

Harry kept a straight face. "Mack, the only place you blend in is an Italian restaurant or the horse track."

Mack snorted. "Got me there, Harry."

The man's laughter chased Harry out onto the sidewalk, leaving him surrounded by quiet once the door clicked shut. A breeze warmed his cheeks, bringing the scent of grilled meat to Harry's nose as he headed for the subway. It didn't pay to keep Rose Leroux waiting, especially when Vincent Morello had made the appointment.

Fifty minutes later Harry stood outside the Upper East Side address where Rose Leroux conducted business. The building was a stone's throw from Central Park, and Rose had run her operation out of it for decades. Likely ever since she'd come to the States, though Harry had no idea when that had been. Rose's accent told him she hadn't been born in the U.S., though other than that, he had no idea about her past. Based on how little he'd learned about her from the few times he'd inquired with his father or among the Morello crew, no one else did either.

Harry pressed the buzzer. A moment later, the lock *snicked* open and Rose's unmistakable voice sounded through a speaker. "Right on time, Mr. Fox. Do come up."

The front door opened and Harry let himself in, stopping outside the inner door for a moment until it too clicked open. Rose Leroux may not have had any avowed enemies Harry knew of, but given that black-market antiquities deals were routinely completed in this building, extra security seemed appropriate. The interior door he passed through looked capable of withstanding a battering ram.

Harry closed the door behind him. Rose stood inside it, one hand on a hip, the other holding a martini glass. Lunch hour had not yet finished. "Ms. Leroux."

Rose Leroux's office mirrored its owner. Sharp angles, minimal fuss, elegantly appointed. Harry wondered if anyone ever touched the furniture. Rose came right up to him, her heels clicking on the marble floor. She did not put her martini glass down as she touched his face. "Harry Fox. My dear boy. I am so sorry."

Now the glass went on a table and Rose leaned down, wrapping her arms around him. Rose easily stood six feet without shoes.

"It's fine, Rose. All turned out for the best."

"So Vincent told me. Please, sit. Would you care for a drink?"

He considered. It had been a rough couple of days. "Why not?"

"Wise choice." She sighed, though her eyes were mirthful. "Beer again?"

"You know me too well."

She gestured to a small refrigerator that looked nothing like one. "Come, sit with me." Rose settled into a chair of leather and steel, motioning for Harry to sit in an identical one across from her. Only after he settled in and took a long pull from the excellent Scottish pale ale did she speak. "Vincent told me you had a close call."

He gave her the short version. Rose didn't blink when he described kicking a man to his doom. But she froze when he mentioned the diamonds. "You acquired payment *and* retrieved the artifact?" Her drink settled on the table. "How marvelously capitalistic of you. Well done."

He set his beer down. "I'd have preferred the deal go smoothly. Now there's no telling if Mr. White will show up looking to collect his diamonds from me. Plus interest."

Rose had been around too long to fall for that. "Never mind him." She waved one hand, pushing the concern away. "He is small-time. If he were dumb enough to try, it would end as soon as he realizes you work for Vincent Morello." She paused in the act of lighting a cigarette, looking at Harry over the flame. "Also, I wouldn't let that happen to you. No son of Fred Fox will be killed if I have anything to say about it."

Harry voiced his appreciation. "Still, our world isn't a large one. People know people. It wouldn't be hard for this Mr. White to find out who the Pakistani-American seller is and send another goon to collect the stones."

"You speak like an American, resemble a Middle Easterner, and think like a thief." A compliment coming from Rose. "I doubt he could find you so quickly. Remember, you have Vincent and me looking out for you." She drained her glass. "Now," and she turned the page on his concerns, "about the Uraeus. Is it in there?" She pointed to the metal briefcase by his leg, and he nodded. "Excellent. Any damage?" He confirmed there was none. "In that case, I have another buyer. Same price."

Harry looked at her over the top of his beer. "Any chance this sale will be less interesting than Tangier?"

She blew a thin stream of smoke to the ceiling. "You won't even have to attend in person. I have a long relationship with this buyer. I will handle the transaction personally."

Rose's connections stretched to every corner of the black market. It wasn't unusual for her to handle deals on Harry's behalf. He had no concern about her cheating him. Not because of him, of course: it was Vincent Morello she'd fear crossing.

"Then I'd say I owe you a drink," Harry said.

Rose barely acknowledged him, though her eyes never left his face. She sat with her legs crossed; the red soles of her shoes were like roving sharks' eyes reflected on the white marble floor. She held his gaze for so long Harry started to fidget.

"Is everything okay?" he asked.

"I received an interesting phone call," Rose said. Her empty martini glass went on the table to one side. "From a source who has proven impeccable in the past. He's heard about an artifact no one has seen for eight hundred years."

Harry leaned forward, elbows on his knees. "You have my attention."

"Before I tell you any more, you must know that more than one man has disappeared searching for this particular piece over time."

"A cursed artifact. How original."

Rose lifted her eyebrows. "Perhaps you won't feel so after you hear the story." The tip of her cigarette burned bright orange before she blew another stream of smoke into the air. "What do you know about Geoffrey of Monmouth?"

"Factual knowledge?" Harry shrugged. "Geoffrey was a British cleric around the turn of the millennium. I know he wrote *The History of the Kings of Britain*, which is likely almost entirely fictional, though for a long time people thought it was based in fact. By the time historians figured out the stories were mostly made up, a legend had been born."

"Geoffrey was Welsh, not British. He lived in the early twelfth century, serving as a cleric at various locations across Britain. Beyond that, not much is known about the man other than his famous book purporting to detail British history. Given the first person he references as having settled Britain is from Greek mythology and supposedly the son of the goddess Aphrodite, it's likely most of what he wrote isn't accurate."

"Brutus of Troy, wasn't it?" Harry asked, and Rose said it was. "Descended from Aphrodite and the Trojan hero Aeneas. Or is Aeneas Roman? He was supposedly related to Romulus and Remus."

"The twin brothers who settled Rome," Rose said. "You are correct. Geoffrey's story traces Britain's history through various kings, many of whom actually lived, though their exploits are likely fiction. The most notable king in his book is one every child knows to this day."

"King Arthur." Armored knights and generally helpless damsels flashed across his mind's eye. "Lancelot, Guinevere, the Round Table. One of the better myths, in my opinion. It sure has lasted a long time."

"A book of myths." Rose finished her cigarette with one long pull. "Though what was in the true first edition, it's hard to say."

Harry narrowed his gaze. "What aren't you telling me?"

"No one has ever located a verified first edition."

"The only way you'd know it was a first edition is by matching the writing to Geoffrey's, which means you'd need to compare the writing in what you think is an authentic first edition with some type of personal writing from Geoffrey. Some verifiable way to tie it directly to Geoffrey as the author."

"Such as a page from the original manuscript with Geoffrey's writing on it." Rose stood and walked to the bar to refill her glass. "If such a piece surfaced, it could authenticate a true first edition." Rose speared an olive with a tiny plastic stick and dropped it in her glass. "The table beside you. Open the drawer."

A cool hand grabbed Harry's chest. Rose hadn't brought him here for a history discussion. She clearly had something on her mind, a topic sensitive enough to broach only in person. Rose was a businesswoman and shrewder than even Vincent Morello. She'd brought him here for a reason. He was about to find out why.

"It's not booby-trapped, is it?"

"My dear boy, if I wanted you hurt, you would never see it coming."

Not quite reassured, Harry slid the drawer open to reveal a large manila envelope. He glanced up to find an inscrutable expression on Rose's face. He picked it up. Judging from the weight, there wasn't much inside. Harry took a deep breath. What about Rose put him on edge? The woman had never been anything but professional. So why did his nerves tingle?

Stop it. The whole Tangier thing had been nothing more than a good deal gone bad. What Rose said was true: if she had wanted him dead, he wouldn't have had a chance. Harry flipped the folder open.

"Whoa." The vibrant colors and thick, blocky text were instantly recognizable. "An illuminated manuscript." He lifted the oddly heavy piece of paper, protected by a thick plastic sheath that crinkled under his touch. He leaned over it, his nose nearly touching the clear cover. "Latin, but based on the text I'd guess this is Middle English." Rose confirmed it. "Which dates this to sometime after the Norman Conquest in 1066."

He could read Latin better than write it, but it still took him a minute to figure out this was the opening of a chapter. Damn, he was out of practice. No, not a chapter. A *book.* "Hold on – this is Book Nine." He looked up. "What about the eight before it?"

"Keep reading."

His eyes dropped back to the page. Harry found it in the very first sentence. "*Uther Pendragon being dead.*" He looked up. "Uther Pendragon is Arthur Pendragon's father. The same mythical Arthur from Geoffrey of Monmouth's..." His words trailed to nothing. "You think – you think this is genuine."

Rose twirled her glass. "I don't *think* it is genuine. I *know* it is. You are holding an original page from a first edition of *Historia Regum Brittaniae.* Geoffrey of Monmouth's chronicle detailing two millennia of supposed British history and the kings who lived it. That is not just any book, Harry. It is the first page of Book Nine. Arthur Pendragon's book."

The enormity of it all would have knocked him down if he hadn't been sitting. "This is the beginning of Camelot." Harry reverently set the page down. "If this is real, it's worth a fortune."

"It is real."

The tiny part of him not enthralled with possibility shouted for attention. "How can you be so sure?"

Rose came over to sit beside him. The acrid scent of cigarette smoke followed in her wake. "Radiocarbon dating puts it in the twelfth century. The ink composition analysis matches as well, and so does the illumination." She outlined the oversized *U* that began the tale. "This page was found hidden in a verified copy from several decades later, in the late twelfth or early thirteenth century. Science and circumstance align. It is authentic."

"Hold on," Harry said. "This page was found in a later edition of the *same* book?"

"Sealed between the cover and first page," Rose said. "Given how thick the cover was, the owner found it by accident."

Now Harry's internal alarm bells warmed up. "How do you know all this?"

A clock on the wall chimed gently. "Get another beer," Rose said. "Let me tell you a story." He did, Rose waiting until he sat again to continue. "In 1885 a collector in England *obtained* this later edition from the library of a parish church."

"He stole it," Harry said.

"As far as I know, yes. He was a minor nobleman who fancied himself a gentleman adventurer. Given the book's tie to the Arthurian legend, it's no surprise such a man would want it, but the nobleman had no idea he'd actually stolen one of the earliest copies ever discovered. The book must have been kept at the church for centuries, buried with other texts, essentially forgotten. The nobleman discovered this within the stolen copy." She tapped the manila folder. "Hidden behind the front cover. Flip the page over."

He'd been so engrossed in the front, Harry had never considered the reverse side. He turned it over and saw tight script, much like that on the other side. No artwork this time. He squinted. "Is that a note along the top?"

"Not a note," Rose said. "A *message*."

At first glance he thought the words scrawled above the text were a reader's notes, remnants from a long-dead owner. Then he looked closer, translating the Latin to English as he read aloud.

Whichever valiant soul receives these words, know they come from Theobald, servant to the most Reverend Geoffrey. Upon his deathbed, Geoffrey entrusted me with the truth. Upon God's honor, all is true. Geoffrey's words are a path to divine knowledge, concealed where he rests eternal. The path remains open for those most valiant. First, my lord's final home, then seek the mortal carriage of Dux Legionum Castus to reveal the door to find the gospel of our Savior.

Harry looked up. "You think this is important? My Latin's rusty, but I've never heard of *Dux Legionum Castus*."

Rose lit a new cigarette. "*Dux Legionum* is a Roman military rank. It roughly translates to 'Leader of Legions'. An important role in the Roman military structure."

"What about *Castus*?"

Rose blinked. "We will come back to that. First, the other parts of what you read."

As a man who made his living acquiring and selling historical artifacts on the black market, Harry knew his history. Rose, however, was on a different level. He wouldn't tell her anything she didn't know.

"How about I ask questions and you give me answers," Harry said with a touch of levity. "Faster that way."

Rose pouted. "Not up for my test?"

"The sooner I figure out what this is, the sooner I know if I'm interested." He held the sheet up. "You say this is cursed. Two days ago, a guy in Tangier tried to kill me. I'm not sure *cursed* is what I'm after right now."

"Really, you are no fun. But as you insist." The room went dark for a beat as a lone cloud covered the sun. "The nobleman who stole the book died shortly after discovering this hidden page. I believe he came to the same conclusions that I have about the message."

Harry started playing along despite himself. "If we take it at face value, Theobald was Geoffrey of Monmouth's servant. Which puts him in a perfect place to get his hands on a first copy of Geoffrey's book. And radiocarbon dating doesn't lie, so the timeframe is correct. Any idea if Geoffrey actually had a servant named Theobald?"

"Nothing directly ties Geoffrey to a servant named Theobald. However, church archives in Monmouth list a man with that name living in the town at the same time as Geoffrey."

"Towns weren't huge back then, so it's possible." Harry shrugged. "As close as you can hope for."

"The next question is what would Geoffrey have told Theobald about the story of Arthur? I do not have that answer, though Geoffrey went to some lengths to ensure Theobald memorialized his wishes for later generations."

Harry tapped the final line. "Sounds like Geoffrey and Theobald tell you where to start looking; first *his lord's* final home and then the *mortal carriage of Dux Legionum Castus*." Harry pointed to Rose. "Which you've already done."

Rose didn't even protest. "Before I share, what about *savior?*"

Harry smiled. "Geoffrey was a religious man. My guess is *our Savior* does refer to the pride of Bethlehem. I've lost count of how many legends supposedly tie to Jesus's time on earth. I'll worry about finding the rest of this first edition. If there's a connection to Jesus along the way, great." When Rose frowned, Harry rolled his eyes. "Come on, you can't be serious. You think Geoffrey truly had a line on anything tied to Him? A thousand years later?"

"The Uraeus you are selling is three times as old," Rose said quietly. "The passage of time is not a disqualifying factor."

Harry grunted. "Fair point. Who is *Castus?*"

"Castus is a Roman surname, not overly common. Only one Roman military leader in particular is still spoken of today. He was a commander named Lucius Artorius Castus."

Harry's ears perked up. "*Artorius?* Sounds like—"

"—Arthur." Rose's gaze bored through him. "That is not all.

Lucius Artorius Castus is considered by some modern historians to be an inspiration for the legend of Arthur. For more reasons than his name alone."

Excitement tingled in Harry's chest. "I'm starting to think you're on to something. We need to figure out what he means by *lord's final* home, and also where Castus is buried. Assuming *mortal carriage* means what I think it does."

"His mortal remains," Rose said. "I agree. However, there is more to the story. The nobleman who found this page came to the same conclusion as we did. The man who sold this to me provided the nobleman's private journal, in which he details 'recovering' the book, locating this page, and researching Theobald's handwritten message."

Harry leaned forward, now sitting on the edge of his chair. "This nobleman went after Geoffrey's *lord's final home*. Did he find Geoffrey's house?"

"He did. However, he did not just look for Geoffrey's home. In Latin home can mean a house, or it can also indicate a location. Where you are, for example."

"If it's literal, he means Geoffrey's final, permanent home. He's talking about Geoffrey's grave."

"Correct," Rose said. "The nobleman hired two men to locate Geoffrey's grave. According to his journal, they succeeded and went there to investigate." Rose paused. "Both men were found stabbed to death a day later. There is a newspaper article confirming this."

"Unsolved murders?"

"Yes. The nobleman followed their trail." Her lips pursed. "He died the next day, stabbed less than half a mile from where the two men were found. His murder is also unsolved."

The cool tingle in Harry's chest chilled considerably. Nothing like three bodies to change your mood. "Hold on. By my count at least four people died related to this page. That's only three so far."

"Fast forward one hundred years to 1967. The nobleman's book collection was auctioned to the highest bidder. A single collector bought everything, which included the journal and this page from the first edition."

"And that collector eventually tried to locate Monmouth's grave," Harry guessed.

"Before leaving his Boston home the book collector told his teenage son it was a business trip related to the nobleman's estate. He was murdered two days later."

"Don't tell me," Harry said. "Stabbed to death. Perpetrators never identified."

"No." Harry started at the word. "The man who stabbed this book collector was caught. He was arrested, but refused to talk. After being booked into jail, he somehow escaped before ever being identified. His fingerprints yielded no match. The man was a ghost, escaping without a trace."

Harry filed that tidbit under *Leave This Alone.* Then he ignored his own advice. "You never mentioned how you got your hands on this book."

"A few months ago, a contact of mine heard there was a supposedly cursed book for sale with ties to Geoffrey of Monmouth. I made inquiries. The murdered collector's son sold it to me for practically nothing. He had no interest in hearing more about the story behind it."

Harry finished his beer and walked to the window. A row of gray clouds heavy with the promise of rain hung on the horizon, blocking the sunlight. Four dead men, a vanishing killer and nothing but conjecture and circumstance across a millennium. This was a fool's errand at best. A potentially fatal one. He should get out of here before the rain started.

"I'm interested." Harry turned around to face Rose. "Are you selling the book or is this a freebie?"

"I thought you might be intrigued," Rose said. "Consider it my apology for nearly getting you killed. We will discuss a price if you find anything."

"Where is Geoffrey of Monmouth buried?"

Rose stopped with her lighter halfway to a fresh cigarette. "He was buried not far from his birthplace in the town of Monmouth, Wales. You only need to go to St. Mary's Priory Church to find him." Tobacco flared as she inhaled with relish. "Do not forget your armor, Harry. That church can be a dangerous place."

"No worries." Logistical concerns flashed in his head. "I need Vincent's approval first. Not sure if I'm overvaluing myself, but I don't know if he wants me going to Wales after I almost died in Tangier. Too much trouble is bad for business."

Rose laughed. "Vincent would never force you back in harm's way after what your father did for him."

A blessing and a curse. As usual, he let the reference slide. None of the people who knew what his father had done for Vincent ever gave him a straight answer when he asked, but he could do worse than having a man like Vincent in his corner. "I have to clear it with him."

"Of course." Rose waved her cigarette, leaving a smoke trail in the still air. "There is another opportunity closer to home I could offer if Vincent does not approve Wales."

Harry pushed aside his prep plans for a moment. Rose didn't offer anything but quality chances. "Which is?"

"A Greek manuscript from the third century B.C. Currently stored in a bank vault. My source at the bank cannot confirm the seller's identity. If you are interested, my bank associate is willing to assist us in obtaining it, for a fee."

"How much?"

"One hundred thousand dollars."

"For a Greek document that may not lead to anything?" Harry shook his head. "I can't justify that expense to Vincent. How would your associate even get me into the vault?"

"Safe deposit boxes are not as secure as you may believe," Rose said. "By *accidentally* identifying this box as one that is past due on payment, the bank is entitled to open the box and send any contents to another storage facility. When the owner discovers their box is empty, the bank states it was a mistake on their part. The safe deposit contract limits the owner to recovering no more than ten times the stated value of the contents. This particular box is listed as having contents worth ten thousand dollars."

Harry shook his head. "Bankers are some of the biggest thieves out there."

"And the smartest."

Harry reached for the amulet under his shirt, warmed by his skin. It was all he had left of his father. Fred Fox had been killed in Rome while on the trail of an ancient Greek artifact tied to Archimedes. Fred had given the amulet to Harry before leaving for Rome, with a promise that one day he'd share the story behind why the amulet meant so much to him.

The amulet reassured him, as though Fred spoke to him through it. Take the risk close to home, or head across an ocean? Easy choice. The Welsh path didn't involve breaking into a bank.

"I appreciate the offers," he said to Rose. "If Mr. Morello agrees, let's find out what's so dangerous about a church in Wales."

Chapter Three

Brooklyn

Vincent studied Harry with kind eyes, the same eyes that occasionally sent men to their doom. For Harry, though, they radiated fatherly concern.

"Do you feel comfortable taking this project so soon after Tangier?"

The heat and danger of Tangier felt worlds away as he sat in Vincent's office sipping espresso. Harry forced himself to feel the metal steps ripping his skin, the sweat running down his back as he hung from the underside of a staircase, waiting to kick a man to his death.

"I do," Harry said. "I failed. Let me do this to make it up to you."

"Harry, my boy." Vincent set his cup down. "You have never disappointed me. Every situation is a chance to learn. An opportunity to improve yourself. My only concern is you are unharmed."

"Thank you, Mr. Morello."

Vincent *tssk tssk'd* with a finger. "Vincent. Call me Vincent." He leaned forward, palms spread across his desk. "Now, you will go to Wales? I have never been to Wales. Is it cold there?"

Harry nodded. "Their cold season hasn't started yet. I'll probably find a lot of rain waiting."

"Next time, ask Rose for a project in Italy. The sun always shines there." Vincent looked to the wall behind Harry, to a black-and-white photo of Vincent's childhood home in a small town near Naples. A

31

young mother with small children gathered in front of her, their father to one side. Harry had never asked which little boy was Vincent. "But Rose does not concern herself with our comfort. Such is life." He blinked, pulling himself back to the office in Brooklyn. "What do you need for this project?"

Harry had also shared Rose's offer to steal the Greek document from the safe deposit box. Even with an inside man, Vincent had agreed with Harry's instinct that it involved too much risk. Financial institutions had the one thing that kept authorities on their side: money. Stealing from a bank was simply bad business. Harry laid out his request list.

"You will be careful while you find this book, won't you?" Vincent asked. Harry said he would. "Then it is settled." Vincent rapped his desk. "Find the book, bring it home, and we will celebrate your success over a meal together." A sadness came across Vincent's face. "I only wish Fred were here to join us. What I owe your father can never be repaid. He is the reason we are both here today." The old man shook his head. "Taken far too soon."

Another vague reference to how Vincent had come into their lives. A story never shared; one Fred had never wanted to discuss. Harry kept silent, his normal response in this situation. His father's memory followed him like a beloved spirit; so close, yet impossible to touch. Less than a year had passed, hardly long enough to figure out how he felt. All he knew was it hurt.

"We both miss him," Vincent said. "You are a good son, like my Joey. You both make your fathers proud."

"Thank you, Vincent. I'll do my best to keep it so."

"Watch your back. I cannot say who may come after you, though recently my friends say the damned Albanians are showing ambition." Vincent's hands clenched into fists. "That will not be tolerated."

Harry tilted his head. "You think the Albanians will cause trouble? I didn't know they were interested in these kinds of projects."

"Lowlifes, all of them. They will leech onto any part of my business." Vincent's hands unclenched. "However, it could be talk, nothing more. Who knows, you may get along with them better than I do. Albania is filled with Muslims."

Harry didn't remind Vincent that even though he was part Pakistani and looked it, he hadn't entered a mosque in decades. "I'll keep that in mind." Vincent had a simple view on religions: you were either Roman Catholic, or you weren't.

"Good boy." Vincent stood and walked to the heavy wooden bar tucked into one corner, beneath a tall window Harry knew was bulletproof. Leafy trees made darker by the clouds overhead stretched for several blocks outside. "Have a drink. We toast to your success."

Harry joined him at the bar, accepting a glass. Red wine, something expensive from the nose on it. Not that the old man ever drank anything but the good stuff.

"You know, Harry, I do not consider your trip to Tangier a failure. It would have been a disaster had you not returned. If you had lost the artifact without being paid, it would have been disappointing, nothing more." A hand lined with age rested on Harry's. "Success is not always about winning and losing. Very little is black and white. Did you learn a lesson in Tangier? I say yes. You learned your life is worth more than artifacts. Nothing is more important than family, than being there for those you trust. For the people who trust you." A gnarled finger tapped Harry's chest. "That is what matters. Your father knew that. I believe you do as well."

Harry had no idea what to say. "Thank you, Vincent. You have no idea how much that means to me."

Vincent's hands cupped Harry's cheeks. "You are your father's son. You make him proud." He raised his glass, and Harry did the same. "To your success, and safe return." Glasses clinked, expensive wine vanished, and Harry headed out the door.

Neighborhood sounds hit him as his feet found the sidewalk,

people venturing back out as the worst of the clouds had moved on, their promise of rain unfulfilled. The sidewalks grew increasingly full as he walked, people in parks and on porch steps, in shop doors and running along the street. Harry dodged between a group of boys kicking a soccer ball against an apartment building wall before he turned a corner and stopped.

One hand went to his amulet. A gift from his father, albeit one his old man had never explained. Ever since Harry was a boy, his dad had always worn it around his neck. It was a circular piece of crafted gold hanging from the same worn leather cord that Fred had used. Harry was sure it had a story. But his father had taken the mystery to his grave.

A shoe scuffed the sidewalk behind him. Harry spun around, hands clenched and in front of him, ready to swing. Instead of an Albanian gangster, he found a woman pushing one of those shopping carts that doubled as walkers coming his way, her gray hair beneath a plastic cover. She didn't even look up as she passed.

Easy, Harry. There weren't Albanians around every corner. But Vincent's warning had stuck with him, put him on edge. He took a deep breath. No reason to get worked up, not with everything he still had to do before leaving town. The materials he had requested from Vincent would arrive at his apartment tomorrow, after which he would board the next flight to England. If Vincent was right and the Albanians did somehow get a bead on Harry's search and decide to interfere, he'd have a good head start. Vincent had promised Harry pictures of the Albanian gang members. Maybe that was going overboard, in truth, but you didn't refuse Vincent's offers of help.

Vincent's mention of his father had brought memories. Not only of Fred Fox, but also of Harry's mother, Dani. He had no direct memories of her, only stories, as she had died when he was little. An accident, Fred had told him in the rare times he spoke of it. Fred did tell him, though, that she had always worn a matching amulet. Their way of staying connected even when apart. Now Harry's amulet connected him to both parents, two people who had come from opposite parts of the world to make a life together.

Until the world had ripped them apart.

Chapter Four

New York City

The man moved rapidly along the sidewalks on the Upper East Side. He slipped between other pedestrians, hurrying his pace between intersections. Twice he stopped to suddenly browse at store windows, never going inside. If someone happened to be watching, they might have thought he was strange, or at least unpredictable. In either case, they would be correct. Stefan Rudovic hadn't stayed alive by being anything but cautious.

Every sudden stop, ostensibly to window browse, was a chance to check for pursuit. Each time he sped up or slowed down seemingly without reason was an opportunity to force a tail into the open. Moving fast then slow, doubling back, or stopping in the middle of the street, all served one purpose: to be certain no one was following him. Stefan did this every time he came to this building, one of the few places his enemies knew him to frequent. Falling into a routine would be easy. People did it every day. It could define a person, make them as predictable as the rhythms of the seasons. It could also get them killed.

Satisfied he hadn't been followed, Stefan ran a hand through his bristle-like shock of hair and rang the bell, looking up at the camera lens mounted above the door. The lock *snicked* open. He slipped through, careful to close the door tight behind him. Who might come after him was hard to say. More than a few faces came to mind, none friendly.

The harsh scent of burning tobacco hit his nostrils. A blend he could place anywhere, as he'd breathed in those fumes for three decades now. Only one woman he knew smoked it. She stood in front of him, a hand resting on the short bar.

"Good evening, Rose." Stefan Rudovic bowed his head a fraction. "Good to see you."

Rose beckoned him closer. "How are you?"

He accepted her quick embrace, didn't back away when she touched the hair on his chin. "You really must shave. To hide such a handsome face is unnecessary."

"I did," he said. "I can't help my genes, you know that."

"Balkan men have many struggles," Rose said. "Sit down. Have you eaten?"

Only Rose Leroux would ever ask in such a way. "I have, thank you."

She frowned. "A drink, perhaps?"

He waved a hand. "No. I don't have time."

"As you wish," Rose said. "To business. But first, be a dear and shake this for me."

Stefan stood and rattled the steel tumbler until his hands were ice. Only after her martini glass had been filled to the brim and she was seated across from him did Rose speak.

"You asked for information on the Morellos' activities. You spoke with Altin as well?"

Stefan laid a thick envelope on the table. "Your fee," Stefan said. "Now, what do you have for me?"

Rose didn't touch the envelope. It had likely never occurred to Rose that someone would try to shortchange or cheat her. If they did, it would only happen once. "First, tell me how you intend to use this information. For profit only?" She puffed at the cigarette.

"As long as no one gets in the way, we have no interest in harming anyone." Stefan's elbows found his knees. "I'm only here for information."

"Which I trust you will use to make money," she said. "And nothing more." He didn't respond, and she continued. "Harry Fox left here several hours ago. He is traveling to Wales in search of a relic tied to Geoffrey of Monmouth." Stefan didn't react, and Rose sighed. "Geoffrey of Monmouth created the legend of King Arthur." She laid out how Geoffrey had written about Arthur Pendragon and created the Arthurian legends.

"It's all fake, right?" Stefan crossed his arms. "You say this guy made up all these stories. One of them stuck, is still popular today."

She sighed again. "How much do you think an original copy of the very first edition would sell for?"

He grunted. "To the right buyer? Good point. What else?"

Rose detailed the supposed cursed nature of the book, and this grabbed his attention.

"Hold on," Stefan said. "You think those deaths are all related? They happened over a century apart."

"I could not say." Rose sipped her martini. "In my experience, coincidences are discounted at your peril. Men keep dying searching for this book. The question to ask is not why, but who?"

"As in who's killing them." Stefan looked to the ceiling. It offered no answers. "Either way, the book is valuable."

"Valuable enough to send you across an ocean in search of it, with the Morello family's antiquities hunter also on the trail. Perhaps you are trying to make money. Or you have other motives."

Stefan looked down from the ceiling to find Rose studying him. She was looking for a reaction. Trying to figure out why an underboss in the Cana family gave a damn about a book, though in truth she knew why. The Cana family wanted to expand their turf. How a book no one had seen for centuries fit into that plan was another question. One he didn't mind answering.

"It's about money, Rose. You gave Harry Fox intel on an artifact. He makes money for Vincent Morello every time he steals or sells one, which keeps Vincent rich. Money keeps him in power. Some people think Vincent Morello's time is nearing its end, and one way to make that end come faster is to cut off his funding." Stefan snapped his fingers. "It won't happen overnight, of course, and the money isn't everything. People respect Vincent, even fear him. But if, all of a sudden, his guys aren't succeeding, aren't getting what they're after, then he looks bad. That happens often enough, people will start losing respect, stop being afraid of Vincent Morello. When that happens, things can change."

A lighter flashed as Rose lit another cigarette. The falling sun threw long shadows across the room, her diamond earrings glinting like fiery stars in the light. "Altin Cana should be careful. He is not strong enough to take on Vincent Morello."

Stefan tamped down the retort in his throat. "Perhaps," he said after a pause. "Altin is no fool. *If* he had any interest in moving on Morello turf, he'd be careful."

Rose didn't blink as she spoke. "Stefan, you are a smart boy. Do not let Altin's ambition hurt you."

Stefan's jaw grew tight. *Easy for you to say.* People came to Rose and they paid her for information she got from every dark corner of the world. She hardly had to leave the city. Not everyone had it so easy. "I work for Altin," he said, forcing himself to keep a level tone. It was Rose, after all. "Altin gave me a chance when no one else would. I'm Albanian too, like him. We watch out for each other. If that means going to Wales to steal this book so he makes money and Vincent Morello doesn't, then I will."

Rose spoke into her drink. "Albanian heritage is different than growing up there."

Stefan slapped the table. "I know," he shouted, losing it for a moment. He took a breath. "It doesn't matter. Altin looks out for me. He always has."

"He's not the only one."

Stefan frowned. "I realize this. I'm grateful to everyone who's helped me along the way. Including you." Now he stood and walked over to Rose, resting his hand atop hers. "I'm not the one going to Wales to secure the book. One of my men will handle the retrieval."

"All the better," Rose said. "This man of yours, is he even-tempered?"

Stefan considered. "He will be if I tell him to be."

"Then do it," she said. "I did not give you this information to see anyone die." Now she grabbed his hand. "Promise me."

He could hardly refuse. "All we want is the book. I'll make sure Harry Fox dying isn't part of the process." He could keep the guy alive. But keep his man from knocking Harry around? Not so much. A broken bone or two would give Harry Fox something to think about. More importantly, it would let Vincent Morello know he wasn't the only game in town when it came to the antiquities market. Altin Cana wouldn't be ignored any longer.

Stefan looked to his watch. "I have to go. When did you say Harry Fox was leaving town?"

"I did not say."

It was worth a shot. "I'll be in touch." He wrapped his arms around Rose quickly, then backed off. "It's always good to see you."

"You too, my boy. Come back soon."

Stefan left Rose and hurried outside, back toward the Cana headquarters. It was several dozen blocks and a world away from the Morello house in Brooklyn. They shared the same borough, but the two operations couldn't be further apart. The Cana family organization hadn't existed twenty years ago when a tough Albanian had arrived in New York City with no English on his tongue and a ruthless desire to make his name known. Even back then, the Morellos had run Brooklyn. Today they still quietly ran most of the city, Vincent at the helm.

And today, twenty years later, Altin Cana had succeeded. The Cana family was knocking on the door of New York's supposed "big five families," this raucous outsider family demanding to be let in. Feuds had been born, but overall Altin Cana had played it right, smart enough not to pick the wrong fights yet vicious enough to stamp out any lower competition.

Stefan Rudovic had been with Altin Cana every step of the journey, starting as an errand boy. Without a father in his life Stefan had found guidance in the form of Altin Cana. Now, Stefan Rudovic was the youngest Cana underboss and the man Altin turned to when he needed results. Like giving Vincent Morello's reputation a bloody nose.

Horns blared as Stefan crossed the street and stopped by a subway entrance. He fired a text off, then descended the stairs to a subway platform, emerging a half hour later in Brooklyn. His man stood outside the Cana family headquarters, a renovated apartment building. Altin Cana had bought it years ago, then remodeled it to suit his needs, which consisted first and foremost of security. You'd never know from the outside, but this place was rock solid.

"You ready to travel?" Stefan asked.

"Of course," Gabe said. Sunlight turned the diamond studs in his ears to kaleidoscopes. He followed Stefan inside, heading for a room in the far back where Stefan had a leather messenger bag waiting. Inside it was everything he had requested via text earlier before he got on the subway, everything he thought Gabe needed to come back with Geoffrey of Monmouth's book. If the damn thing even existed. This could all be a waste of time, but Altin Cana had waved away any concerns about that. Find the book, he'd said. If you can't, be sure the Morellos don't find it either, and let them know we're here.

Stefan tossed the bag to Gabe. "Ever been to Wales?" he asked.

"No," Gabe said. "What's there?"

Gabe didn't balk at a possible overseas trip. He did as he was told, did what was necessary to help the Cana family. Same as Stefan had, and look where it had got him. Do what Stefan told him, and good things happened.

"A book, but that's not the most important part. You need to deliver a message from Altin. We're putting the Morellos on notice."

Stefan pointed to the bag. "Cash, credit cards and gold coins. I reserved a car for you at Heathrow. You'll have to handle hotels on your own."

Gabe flipped through the stack of British pounds and euros. He picked out a gold coin and flipped it once. "Why the gold?"

"Bribes. Hopefully you won't need them, but in case you do, use it. Altin gave the go-ahead to spend it all, as long as we send a message."

Gabe didn't blink. "How serious is this message?"

"He should be able to walk away from it," Stefan said. "Don't kill anyone if you can avoid it. I'm serious. I made a promise."

Gabe shrugged. "Whatever you say, boss. Who are we going after?"

"Let's talk about the *what* first." He ran through an overview of Monmouth's *History*. Only when King Arthur's name came up did recognition dawn on Gabe's face.

"Got to be an old book," Gabe said. "How do you know it's there?" Stefan told him. "A lot of dead guys around this book," Gabe said. "Need to keep my eyes open."

"Don't add your name to the list. Here's the Morello guy you're looking for."

Gabe opened a folder to find a glossy, color snapshot of Harry Fox staring back. Altin Cana's men kept tabs on the other families in the city. It paid to know your possible enemies, even if they weren't yet officially on the list.

"Doesn't look like a wop." Gabe pointed to the dark hair and olive skin. "This guy's a raghead."

"He's part Pakistani," Stefan replied. "Don't let it fool you. He's Morello, through and through. His old man was tight with Vincent Morello, and now Vincent treats Harry like one of his own. It's possible he has protection with him. Find Harry, tail him and see if he's alone. Don't do anything before you know what you're up against."

"He will never see me until I want him to." Gabe closed the folder, which disappeared into the bag. "Where in London do I find him?"

Stefan shook his head. "Not in London. I don't know how Harry's getting there, but I know he's going to Monmouth. The book is supposed to be somewhere in that town. Fly to London, get the car, and go straight to Monmouth. It's not big. Find Harry, figure out if he's alone, then worry about the book."

Stefan fell silent for a breath. "Monmouth is where all of those other men were murdered. This is serious, you understand? Tell me you do." Gabe said he did. "Watch your back. I like you, Gabe. Don't get yourself killed."

"Do not worry," Gabe said. "Get the book, bust up Harry Fox, and stay alive. I can handle it."

Stefan clapped a hand on Gabe's shoulder, thick with muscle. "Good man. Altin is anxious to hear of your success. Send a message to Vincent, but don't kill Harry. If you have the book afterward, even better. We'll talk about more responsibility when you get back. The Cana family needs men like you."

Stefan wrapped his arm around Gabe and the two men thumped each other's backs before Gabe departed, bag in hand. A twinge passed through Stefan's gut. He liked Gabe, truly. The man was ambitious; he followed orders and didn't get queasy if things got rough. All qualities you looked for in Altin Cana's gang. Except for the ambition part. That, Stefan wasn't so keen on. In their world, you moved up the ladder when the rung above you emptied, often ascending to find blood still on that next step. An ambitious guy like Gabe might do whatever it took to keep moving, to stay ahead. If luck didn't favor Gabe on this trip and he ended up in the Monmouth town morgue, well, that was one less person trying to take Stefan's place.

Chapter Five

Harry slept the entire flight from JFK to Heathrow. Vincent Morello had told him to fly first class, and who was he to argue with the *capo dei capi?* No reason to show up tired to a trail already littered with corpses.

With the bag from Vincent slung over one shoulder, Harry grabbed his carry-on and headed for the car rental desk, picking up keys for an Audi sedan and heading out. The car came with GPS, a life-saver given that all of Harry's attention was focused on not driving like an American. Twice within five minutes he nearly turned into oncoming traffic, earning a few blaring horns and one double-barreled bird before he found the highway heading west and gunned it. He'd have preferred to take the train, but it took twice as long and required transferring to a bus. Plus, he had no idea where he might go next if the book wasn't in Monmouth.

The thought made his chest tighten. *Damn you, Rose.* She'd given him the page with Theobald's note, basically a riddle. Nothing like traveling across an ocean to find something that probably didn't exist, with only a thousand-year-old Post-It Note as your guide. Harry downshifted, accelerated and sank into the seat as the Audi jumped ahead. He calmed down a sizzling mile later. *Okay, think through this. One step at a time.*

First, this was more than a random riddle. He trusted Rose, who had carbon-dated the sheet to Geoffrey's time, even confirming the writing on it was very likely from Geoffrey's personal assistant. As good as you could hope for after so long. Second, Harry wasn't the first to go after this. Others had come to similar conclusions, independent from Harry and Rose. That they'd all ended up stabbed to death was secondary. Harry's lips creased in a grim smile. *Worry about that later.*

Third. Well, he didn't have a third. What he had next was a bunch of circumstance, conjecture, supposition and plain wishful thinking. Yes, if this true first copy of *History* still existed, Geoffrey of Monmouth's home town was the most likely spot. But Harry had to figure out the missing piece. What had Theobald meant by *concealed where he rests eternal?*

The *he* mattered most. Was it Geoffrey? Context suggested so, but that wasn't proof. Theobald was a cleric, after all, so it could easily reference a biblical person, Jesus most likely. It could also be part of a code or message that only made sense to someone in Geoffrey and Theobald's time. Did a section of the message connect to shared experience in the twelfth century? If so, Rose and Harry had missed it.

These thoughts ran through his mind during the drive beneath overcast skies. Rain seemed a foregone conclusion, though his wipers came on only once in nearly three hours, and when Harry passed a sign for the Monmouth town limits, one fact in his thinking had come back to the forefront again and again. The dead men. Coincidence didn't explain it. The dead men had one common bond: pursuit of Monmouth's *History.* It could mean Harry's chances of joining them as casualties of this search were distressingly high. He slowed for a turn and his eyes fell to the bag beside him. Thank goodness for Vincent Morello.

He had provided Harry with a false passport in the name of Daniel Connery with Harry's face on it, the better to cross national lines anonymously without being found. Also thousands of British pounds and euros, the first-class plane tickets, and a satellite phone so he'd have connection no matter where this search took him. And his hardened polymer knuckle dusters were tucked in a side pouch. Lightweight and invisible to metal detectors, they'd made the journey home from Tangier to Brooklyn and on to London undetected by airport security.

A white-flecked river ran alongside the highway as Harry entered and passed a school where children ran around a fenced-in playground. A green field stretched for acres to his right as he motored down the quiet street. Low-slung gates and rough brick walls fronted homes along the main road into town. He passed a manicured soccer pitch before entering the town center.

A young woman crossed in front of him, pushing a stroller before her. She glanced at him as she walked, and the smile on her lips nearly faded for a moment before coming back. Harry waved and returned her greeting. Chances were, these townsfolk didn't see many people who looked like him. She cleared the road before he motored onward, the moment fading like so many others. He had bigger worries ahead.

Timing was on Harry's side, and he pulled into a street parking spot in front of the sign identifying St. Mary's Priory Church.

The engine clicked after he turned it off. Harry sat and stared. Rose's research suggested he should begin his search at St. Mary's. The foundations dated from 1075, at least a decade before Geoffrey of Monmouth was born. If there were any place in town with ties to Geoffrey, this was it. Harry slung the bag with all his resources over one shoulder and got out. Bracing Welsh air was a tonic for his nerves as he breathed deeply, filled with a natural cleanliness he hardly recognized after a lifetime in New York. It actually tasted good.

A sandstone wall fronted the church grounds, the spiked metal fence running atop it a regal mix of threat and stateliness. You wouldn't want to climb over that thing if you could help it. Harry stepped to one side as two elderly nuns passed him on the sidewalk, one of them mumbling what sounded like words, though any meaning was buried in the thick accent. For no other reason than they were likely headed inside, Harry followed them. His hunch paid off when the nuns took him to a side entrance. The metal gate stood open, and although his attention went to the tallest structure in town, Harry's nose told him the pizza shop up ahead sold kebabs as well as slices. Seems the outside world had found its way into Monmouth after all.

Bells began to clang. Sonorous, powerful, they rattled his chest with each strike. They stopped shortly, the hours noted, and movement at the corner of his vision made Harry start. He twisted, fists clenched, and found himself facing a man not much taller than him. As the man walked out of St. Mary's gate, he pulled a yarmulke from atop his head and nodded to Harry. Instinctively Harry returned the greeting, and then the mustachioed man passed. Harry relaxed. *Focus, man.* Stop worrying about bells and kebabs and the air or you'll end up like those other guys. Dead.

Vincent's warning came back to him. The Cana family kept tabs on the Morellos' activities; that was no secret. If they had somehow found out Harry had brought back a million dollars in diamonds without parting with the Uraeus, it was possible they'd put a tail on him, try to steal whatever he was after next. Good thing this information on looking into St. Mary's Priory had come from Rose. She stayed true to one thing. Money. And Vincent Morello had the most of it.

The sun snuck out for an instant, glinting off a gilded weathervane several hundred feet overhead at the spire's peak before the clouds coalesced to snuff it out. A good omen? Harry shrugged. Right now, he'd take it. A wooden door darkened by age barred his path at the top of the steps, though it fell open silently with a touch. Harry glanced over his shoulder, found no one paying him any attention, and darted inside, stepping quickly to one side of the door and stopping. White stone pillars supported curved archways, which in turn kept wooden beams high overhead afloat. Two rows of lengthy pews on either side of the nave led to an altar, also of white stone. Dark, brooding windows looked down on the pulpit where the main priest gave sermons, numerous unlit candles surrounding it on all sides.

If the sun came out, this would be a nice place. Not that Harry was qualified in the least to judge, given he'd spent about as much time in churches as he had in mosques. Or synagogues, for that matter. Thankfully the place was empty except for a black-robed priest to one side and a smattering of congregants scattered in the pews either with their heads down or eyes on the man nailed to a cross hanging above the altar. Harry did not send out a prayer for guidance. If anyone happened to be listening, they probably wouldn't like his plan.

Which was pitiful. *If I was a dusty skeleton, where would I be?* He'd considered it on the way over, and the best idea he'd come up with had been tied to the age of this place. Harry's research indicated the town cemetery hadn't come into existence until the eighteenth century, so Geoffrey wasn't there. The only place still around from the turn of the first millennium was St. Mary's Priory, and the best place to find skeletons in old churches? The crypt.

He circled the chapel, bowing his head when he passed the altar and then turning to circle back. A devout man, appreciating the paintings and memorials displayed around the church. Or at least he hoped people thought that, because he was really looking for a staircase going down. First step, find the crypt. Second, the graves.

The first staircase he passed had a sign for *Church Offices*. No luck there. The second one had more promise. It was stone, smooth with age, and it descended nearly straight down. Only after congratulating himself on his shrewd thinking did he notice the lettered sign next to the staircase. *Crypt & Antechambers.*

"They need a bigger sign," he said under his breath, then glanced behind him. A new congregant had appeared, seated at the very back of the church with his head bowed and hands clasped in prayer. The man wasn't paying him any attention, and nobody else seemed to be either. A pillar stood between him and the single priest, blocking Harry from view. He grabbed the handrail and stepped down. Cooler air snaked up his pantleg with each step. The stone beneath his feet had been worn smooth over the centuries, and he kept a tight grip on the polished wood handrail as he descended to an underground level.

The steps ended in a stone passageway with curved walls and a low, rounded ceiling. Alcoves cut into the walls stretched down either side of the passageway, the limits of which were swallowed by darkness too dense for the watery light cast by the rows of overhead bulbs. Perhaps the effect was intentional, a somber reminder that whoever walked this hallway stood in the presence of so many gone before them; Harry counted over a dozen alcoves on each side before the light grew too dim. Each contained at least one tomb; some held two.

He started down the corridor and stopped to glance down another hallway that opened to his right. This one was short enough that he could see the end, and the handful of doorways indicated only offices or storage closets. No tombs that way.

A creak sounded above and behind him at the top of the stairs. Instinctively, he put his back to the wall. Here he was, standing in plain sight for anyone to see. Was the public allowed down here? Even Vincent Morello's influence wouldn't get him out of a Welsh prison. He turned to the nearest alcove and stepped inside the opening, listening and looking back at the stairs. For now, it seemed no one else was coming down.

The alcove walls were all of cut stone, though the rear wall of this one was old brick, with the mortar crumbled in spots. A single tomb of gray stone sat within it. Carved letters on the top told him this was the final resting place of James Curtis, dead since 1742. Harry shook his head. This man had died before the American Revolution, one of who knew how many buried beneath this small-town church in the

English countryside. The lineage of history was much longer in England.

Interesting, but Harry didn't have much time. He needed tombs almost seven hundred years older than this one. He stepped out and looked toward the staircase; no one to be seen. The next alcove held two smaller tombs side by side. A husband and wife who had died in 1848. A century later than their single neighbor. As he moved farther down the passage, it became apparent the tombs weren't organized in a sequential manner. The oldest death date was 1577, still a half-century too late. The passageway turned sharply, and Harry's heart beat faster when he rounded the corner to find another series of tombs, though the hallway ended not far ahead. These alcoves were cruder, the curved sides more roughly hacked from the stone than carved, with the tombs themselves smaller than the ones he'd examined before. He pulled a penlight from his pocket, flicked it on and stepped into the closest alcove. A layer of dust coated the tomb's lid, thick enough to hide the faded letters carved across the top. He brushed a hand over it. Dust filled the still air.

Harry sneezed. A gunshot would have been less noisy in the near-perfect acoustics of this small, rounded enclave. After his hearing came back, he looked at the inscription. Nerves sang up and down his body. *This person died in 1204.*

William Rogers had lived to the age of forty. Practically a record back then. His tomb had been repaired over the centuries, resulting in rough stone alongside smooth, fresher patches. The oldest parts had been crafted within a century after Geoffrey had likely died. Harry noted how small this tomb was – about half the size of more recent ones, and small enough that two other tombs fit in behind William's. Both bore female first names and the same last name: Rogers. William's two wives, judging from the two death dates.

The two remaining alcoves in the row had tombs from the same decade William had died, while the three behind him were slightly more recent. None belonged to either Galfridus Monemutensis or

Galfridus Arturus, the two names Geoffrey had been known by during his lifetime. Harry stepped back from the last grave and flicked his light off. One hallway left.

He backtracked toward the staircase, moving on the balls of his feet. A glance up the stairs found them still empty, though he knew his luck couldn't hold forever. The first crypt on the far side held a woman who had died in 1802. He frowned. If Geoffrey was here, chances were he'd be way at the back. The hallway became a murky shadow as he jogged ahead, each light overhead seemingly less powerful than the last. The same type of sharp turn waited at the end. He took it and nearly ran headlong into a tomb.

This offshoot of the main hallway was even smaller than its counterpart. One alcove to each side, both holding three aged tombs. However, a single tomb had been placed in front of him where the path ended. Stones dark with age stood behind this final tomb, and it was here he went first, flashlight coming to life as he stepped toward it. Dust flew as he swiped a hand over the tomb's cover, feeling for any sign of writing. So faint he missed them at first, the letters had faded to near-invisibility. He leaned over and squinted until he could make out the years inscribed on it. *1102 – 1168.*

The century when Geoffrey of Monmouth died. Harry's throat tightened as he rubbed dust from the name. *Sarah Forwin.*

A woman's grave. He checked again, outlining the letters with his finger to be sure. They were faint, but without a doubt that was the name. Harry smacked the tomb. *Ouch.* Shaking his hand to get the worst of the sting out, he checked the tomb to his right. Same timeframe; a man's name this time. Not Geoffrey. He turned to the last option and readied himself with a long, slow breath. *This is him.* He didn't want to consider what would happen if it wasn't.

The sound of approaching voices filtered in from the hallway. Harry snapped the light off and stepped to the corner, dropping to one knee and putting his shoulder against the wall. Two voices speaking English, though he couldn't make out much of it. One grew louder as the first person came into view, popping out of the stairwell coming down from the main floor. Harry's eyes narrowed. A man, mid-thirties with dark hair, talking to someone still on the stairs, though he wasn't looking back. No, he was looking down the hallway, directly at Harry. Harry fought the urge to move back, instead staying immobile. The human eye tracked movement better than color or shapes. From this far away in the gloom, the guy couldn't see Harry, even though he was looking right at him.

Harry's instinct proved correct as the man turned around to look the other way, deep into the darkness stretching ahead. Now he recognized the man: he was the lone worshipper who had come into the chapel after Harry. Internal alarm bells sounded, though not at full volume. It could be a coincidence, nothing more. The man he was speaking to appeared now, revealing himself to be the priest from upstairs.

The priest's voice rose in volume when the other man started walking down the hall, headed away from Harry. The dark-haired man stopped, then turned and went back to the priest, who gestured toward the hallway in front of them, where Harry had spotted office doors and storage closets. The dark-haired man lifted one hand, gesturing for the priest to lead on. The priest took two steps before the dark-haired man closed on him.

Harry struggled to process what happened next. One second the priest was leading the other man down the hall; the next he was sprawled on the ground, knocked down courtesy of a heavy blow to the head. The dark-haired man had some kind of short club in his hand, which landed alongside the priest's head, hard enough to drop him at once, though Harry suspected he'd eventually get back up. Harry was trapped in a basement hallway with an armed intruder.

Maybe the guy wanted to rob the church. Any money would likely be in the offices down here. For a moment, this seemed to be exactly the situation: the intruder grabbed his victim beneath each shoulder and dragged him into the closest alcove, depositing the unconscious man out of sight. Then everything changed. The assailant didn't go toward the offices; instead, he crept out of the alcove, weapon at his side, and started checking the other alcoves one by one, walking in Harry's direction.

Harry pulled back from the edge. *The guy must have seen me come down here.* That was the only thing that made sense, given he was checking each alcove, looking behind the tombs before moving on. The man wasn't here to steal anything. He'd come to find Harry.

Vincent told you this could happen, dummy. Why didn't you listen?

Too late now. The guy had to be halfway down the hall. The hairs on his arms rose as Harry slid the strap of his bag over his head, quietly removing the knuckle dusters before setting it out of sight behind the closest tomb. If this went south, there was a chance the man wouldn't see the bag, which would leave Harry with the funds from Vincent. If he survived, that is. As seconds passed, an idea took shape. Harry backed himself farther into the alcove, then pulled the bag's strap out far enough that someone looking closely would see it. He left the strap in view and raced on tiptoe across to the opposite alcove, ducking behind the stone tomb inside it. His heart thudded as he strained to hear any hint of his assailant's approach.

Nothing. No footsteps, no sounds of breathing, no sign the guy even existed. The stone tomb was cold against his back as Harry slid toward one corner to get a better view. His father's words echoed in his ears. *Stay quiet, move fast, hit first and hit hard. A fair fight is for fairytales.* Infinitely more comfortable using his words for battle than his fists, Fred Fox had imparted valuable lessons to his young son during their training sessions together. *Fighting is a zero-sum game. Don't take the risk.*

Harry poked one eye out from behind the tomb and found himself staring directly at the other man.

Or rather, at his backside, because the man was reaching for Harry's bag strap, leaning over so his balance would be off as one hand held the club and the other inched closer to the visible strap. *I'll be damned. It worked.* Harry balled his hand into a fist, seeing it all happen. Two steps to close the gap, first shot to the knee, which brings him down. Second to the nose, disorienting him. Finish with a knee to the groin, putting him out of commission for a few seconds at minimum. Enough time for Harry to get his club away and secure the wrists with a belt. Most guys didn't have much fight left after a knee to the junk.

The man bent over to grab Harry's bag. Wait for it. Wait… *Now.*

Harry didn't yell as he jumped up, didn't make a sound. It still wasn't enough. With one more step to go, the man must have heard something, sensed the air moving. Dark-haired guy turned at the last moment and Harry's fist hit nothing but air, momentum carrying him forward to crash into the man and smack him off the tomb. Hot pain exploded in Harry's back on the way down as the club smacked below his shoulder blade. Harry rolled, looking for space to breathe.

The guy hadn't looked so big standing farther down the hallway. Up close, he had four inches and fifty pounds on Harry. The guy growled something in a language Harry didn't understand. Harry feinted low, then pulled back, and the club whizzed by his head, just missing as Harry came in behind and landed a glancing blow on the man's chin. Not solid enough to put him down. The man charged again, and Harry rolled to one side and bounced off a tomb. Harry quick-punched, popping the guy's nose hard enough to stop him in his tracks. Harry slipped smoothly past and kicked at the guy's knee. The shot landed, dark-hair screamed, and then Harry's foot caught on something.

Dark-hair had gone down to one knee, but managed to catch Harry's shoe as he fell. Harry stumbled, arms pinwheeling, as he failed to catch his balance before bouncing off the tomb and landing on his back. He sat up as dark-hair charged.

Fighting his natural reaction to move, Harry got his feet under him and waited the split-second for dark-hair to hit him. The man must have sensed something was wrong and seemed to slow, but it was too late. Harry used his oncoming momentum to flip the guy up and over as he rolled onto his back. He used both feet to propel dark-hair into the wall behind him, grunting as he kicked hard enough to flip himself over and end up on his feet.

Harry twisted, fists up and ready. The man lay unmoving. A quick check of his neck found it wasn't broken, and he still had a pulse. Blood leaked from a gash across his forehead. The guy was out cold but would be fine, eventually. But for now, he was out of commission.

There was a grating sound and Harry leapt aside as a falling brick nearly clipped him. Where had that come from? He checked above him; nothing. Then he looked a bit lower and spotted it. A hole in the wall. A brick had fallen out where dark-hair had slammed into it. Others around it had been pushed inward.

Jeez, I didn't throw him that hard. Harry examined the wall more closely. Sure enough, it had caved in, away from the tomb. That should have been impossible.

Unless there's an opening behind it.

Harry studied the single brick. Rough-hewn, with toolmarks creasing every edge, including the front, which was scarred. His thumb traced the groove on the front. It wasn't a toolmark. It was a *letter.*

G.

Harry moved closer to investigate. The fallen bricks had left an opening large enough for his fist to go through. His assailant was still slumped over, unconscious. Harry stepped back to him and secured the man's wrists using his belt, then dragged him behind the tomb where his bag had been laid as a trap. That priest the guy had hit wouldn't be out for much longer, and Harry had no desire to have to explain any of this when he got up.

Harry flicked his light on and aimed it into the darkness of the wall opening. Air dusty with the passage of centuries tickled his nose when he leaned close. He played the light up, across, then back. A stone block came into view. Then another. Two rectangular blocks with what looked like lines running along the top, as though a lid covered the bottom portion of each. The dim decorative carvings atop both confirmed it. Two more tombs had been hidden behind this wall, a wall with the letter *G* carved into it.

Turning an ear to the side, he listened intently for several seconds. No noise, no footsteps, no raised voices. That couldn't last, so he reached into the newly created hole, touched a brick, and pulled. Nothing. The wall held tight, as it had for so long. He leaned back, putting his weight into it, and it gave way. The second brick he grabbed put up a fight as well, as did the rest, but a minute of muffled destruction created a hole big enough for him to squeeze through.

Without waiting to think, Harry crawled through the narrow opening and lifted his light for a better look. The tombs weren't more than five feet away, side by side. A low-slung roof stretched not far overhead. His light played over the tops of both tombs as he stood between them. One tomb was half again as tall as the other, the bigger one reaching to his waist. An elegantly carved cross decorated the top of this taller tomb. Dust flew as Harry leaned over and blew, creating a storm in the still air that obscured any writing atop the grave for a moment. When it settled Harry saw the inscription.

Galfridus Monemutensis
1095 – 1155

Chilled air met the sweat still beading Harry's forehead, the icy contrast going unnoticed as he stared. *Geoffrey of Monmouth.*

The second tomb also had a cross on top, albeit a much smaller version tucked into an upper corner. Beneath it, a name.

Theobald Miller
1104 – 1172

Theobald, the faithful scribe, still with his leader. Which meant that if his interpretations were correct, the prize should be here as well. Harry knelt down to inspect the lid on Geoffrey's tomb. Judging from the dust and dirt caked along the opening, it hadn't been touched for centuries. A glimmer of hope in his chest burned hotter.

Harry stuck the flashlight under an armpit, worked his fingers into the opening until he got purchase. Bent at the knees, nose scraping the tomb's edge, he pushed up with all he had and the top gave an inch. This thing was *heavy*. He tried again. The lid creaked, grinding as he pushed until it slid halfway open with a grating sound that could reach the river Styx.

Harry collapsed to his knees. Several gulps of horrid air later, he stood on shaky legs and aimed his light into the tomb. Ragged cloth covered part of a skeleton, draped between ribs and pelvis, the bone a dull white under his light. The cloth had a smattering of embroidered designs left around the neck and shoulders. Evidence of a prosperous man, one who had left his mark on life. A single desiccated shoe covered parts of one foot, though the toe bones lay scrambled at the bottom. These details flashed through Harry's mind in an instant. Then he focused on the book, which lay beside the skeleton.

Thick, heavy, made to last with leather binding and metal corner pieces. Harry picked up the book, handling it with a soft touch as he stepped through the opening back into the hallway. The book went into his bag before Harry crept to the corner and peered around. The priest lying down the hallway hadn't moved. If Harry could get upstairs and into the chapel without anyone noticing him, he was free. On his way in he'd noticed one camera above the chapel entrance facing the altar, and another outside the entrance aimed to the street.

Now he crept down the hall, moving past the motionless priest. He paused at the stairs to listen and heard nothing. Harry moved up to the first step and—

"Help." The weak voice of the injured priest stopped him cold. Silence, then it came again. "Help me."

Harry turned to find the old man up on one elbow, an arm raised to Harry in supplication. Harry couldn't ignore him.

He went over and dropped to a knee, taking the priest's outstretched hand in his own. "*Hal 'ant musab?*"

The priest looked at him with a bewildered expression. Harry had asked, in Arabic, if he was hurt. He repeated the question, this time in Italian. "*Sei ferito?*"

The same confused look. Which was what Harry wanted. The priest might later remember that an olive-skinned man had been down here, one who spoke two different languages, neither of which the priest could understand. Anyone asking questions about Harry would end up with more of those than answers.

Harry switched to broken English, putting his best Middle Eastern accent to use. "I get help. You help." Making the universal sign for *stay here*, Harry turned and moved up the stairs at speed, leaving the door ajar. No one was nearby except the two elderly worshippers who had been there when he entered. Time to go. The priest's cries would soon be heard through the open door.

Harry walked at full speed out the chapel door, ducking his head low all the while. A warm breeze rustled his hair as he headed for his car and jumped in. The messenger bag went on the passenger seat as Harry fired the engine, waiting for a car to pass before he pulled out. Fighting the urge to gas it, he signaled before turning into traffic and headed back toward the highway.

He stood on the brakes when a man bolted in front of him, darting out of a side street only to disappear through the gate into St. Mary's. He recognized the runner. It was the mustachioed Jewish man he'd passed when he entered the chapel less than an hour ago.

Chapter Six

Athens, Greece

Lambs bleated as a small truck entered the compound, passing through a gate in the defensive wall that had stood for centuries. Whitewashed and blinding in the sunlight, the wall was ten feet high and had saved countless lives in its time. Now it was considered by most to be an inconvenience that should be reduced to rubble. If it weren't for local laws designating it a site of historical importance, it likely would have been pulverized years ago.

Several buildings were clustered together in the center of the interior courtyard. Occasionally a man or woman would emerge from one and hurry into another. Even at the tail end of the summer season it was uncomfortably warm outside, and the dusty breeze did little to encourage lingering. However, one man stood on a balcony overlooking it all, hands clasped behind his back as he considered a phone call, recently ended. Despite his neutral expression, his thoughts whirled. For the first time in his professional life, Aaron Shephard had just been called into action.

The conversation replayed in his head. A man from America, unknown to him, calling with news he had waited a lifetime to hear. The tightness in his gut was either fear or excitement. He didn't know for sure.

"*Yeia.*" The truck driver parked and slowly got out, waving a hand to Aaron. The breeze lifted his hair, white with years.

Aaron responded in the truck driver's native Greek. "Hello." The man's family had sold meat and dairy to this unremarkable compound on the outskirts of Athens for as long as Aaron could remember. Whatever else his complaints might be, and they were few, discontent with the menu wasn't among them. More importantly, the relationship secured what Aaron and his team desired most of all: trust. With the local population, with each other, with their contacts around the world. Aaron's entire existence was predicated on security and trust. People didn't sell out the ones they trusted, and Aaron's team would be most effective if they remained an anonymous force, silent until called upon.

Aaron's desk phone rang. He went back into his office and connected the call on speakerphone, answering in Greek. "*Nai?* Yes?"

"It's Hiram." His partner was out of breath. "I'm in Monmouth," he continued in English.

Aaron grabbed the phone and pressed it hard to his ear. "I'm listening."

"One of our ongoing surveillance targets is St. Mary's Priory Church. I stopped in to check with the priest today. He called me not ten minutes after I walked out the door. Someone assaulted him."

For hundreds of years, Aaron and the men who came before him had kept watch over a number of religious facilities around the world, waiting for any developments related to their mission. Aaron and his two brethren had been hand-picked to carry on the holy mission of those who came before them. A mission they believed could save the world from itself. A mission that came with a fair share of false leads.

"Is the priest recovered?" Aaron asked.

"He is. I went back and found the man who attacked this priest lying unconscious near a tomb. Some of the tombs underneath St. Mary's Priory date back a thousand years." Aaron perked up. "A wall behind one tomb had been knocked down. A stone wall, likely there for as long as the graves. Turns out there was a tomb hidden behind the wall."

Aaron's knuckles grew white as he clutched the edge of the desk. Hiram wouldn't waste his time with just any grave. "What else?"

Hiram's words softened. "It's him, Aaron. We found him."

The floor seemed to drop from beneath Aaron's feet. He looked up to the lone decoration on his bare walls, a wooden cross one of his forebears had carved at the same time William the Conqueror had led the Normans at Hastings in 1066. "You're certain it's Geoffrey?"

"His name is on it. Theobald is there too, in a smaller tomb beside Geoffrey."

Aaron fell into his desk chair. "All that time wondering where it could be. Turns out it's right where you'd expect."

"Geoffrey's tomb was open," Hiram said. "Opened by whoever took out the guy who attacked my priest friend."

"Did you see who was near the tomb?" Aaron asked. "Check the security footage. That church must have—"

"I'm already on it," Hiram said. "There are cameras inside and outside the main church entrance. Whoever did this is on those tapes. The priest is downloading them for me now."

A lifetime of secrecy made Aaron frown. "Can we trust the priest?"

"He's been on our payroll for decades," Hiram said. "With two different handlers before me."

"What did you find in the grave?" The only question that mattered.

"Bones. Ragged clothes. Nothing else."

Chances were, Aaron knew, whoever had opened the grave hadn't stumbled on it by accident. They had suspected what Aaron and his partners already knew: that Geoffrey's grave contained more than just the bones of a long-dead cleric turned storyteller. Much more.

"I'll call Mo," Aaron said. "He's in Cairo. He'll want to come back, but we can't have all of us in the same place. It could be someone trying to draw us out."

"Agreed," Hiram said. "We stay separated." A muffled voice came from the background. "The priest has those tapes ready. I'll call you back."

Aaron set the phone down. They'd actually *done it*. Geoffrey's grave had been empty, but even so, they'd found him. Decades of searching, now over – but with a new mystery to replace the old.

Frowning, Aaron picked up the phone and dialed their third partner. Mo Gaber answered on the first ring. *"Marhabaan?"* The vibrant sounds of Cairo filled the background.

"Hadha 'ana." Aaron repeated himself in English. "It's me."

Mo switched to the same language. "Yes?"

"There's been a development in England." Mo didn't say anything as Aaron ran him through what had transpired. When he finally spoke, it was to the point.

"Once Hiram gets the security tapes and finds whoever was there, we'll track him down. He can tell us what was in Geoffrey's tomb."

"You think there was anything to find?"

"I want to think there was more in there than Geoffrey's bones," Mo said. "Something to tell us his grave truly is a marker. But what I want and what's true may be two different things."

"This may connect to the first edition of Geoffrey's book surfacing not long ago. Hiram was checking our suspected locations in England for any links."

"The first thing we worry about is who attacked the priest," Mo said. "He's in custody?" Aaron confirmed the Monmouth police had him. "We'll see if he has ties to the first edition sale. Then we go after the man who opened Geoffrey's tomb. If we have a clear shot of his face, he won't be able to hide for long."

"Hiram's on it," Aaron said. "Don't go to Wales. Finish your work in Cairo and then we'll regroup."

If needed, Mo could get on a flight to wherever he was needed. Until then, he would carry on with the Cairo visit, looking into the unexpected appearance of a first edition of Geoffrey's book.

Aaron leaned back in his chair. The compound around him had stood for hundreds of years, but that paled in comparison to how long those before him had scoured the globe for the truth. Geoffrey of Monmouth had died over nine hundred years ago. A year after his death in 1155 A.D., one of the most important gatherings of faith to ever occur took place in Athens, when three men arrived from different corners of the globe. Three men whose faiths had been at war since Muhammad began preaching in 613 A.D.: Pope Adrian IV, Shlomo Yitzchaki – known today as Rashi, and the pre-eminent Jewish scholar of his era – and Al Muqtafi, the Abbasid caliph descended from the prophet Muhammad and who was the most powerful religious leader in the Islamic world at the time.

What had brought these men together on the heels of the Second Crusade? A threat to their very existence. A threat that had made the three leaders form an alliance. Each leader had designated one man from his ranks to work within this alliance to find and secure an artifact that had the power to destroy them all.

In 1156 A.D. the order that Aaron, Hiram and Mo served today had been founded, funded, and set loose on the world. Today, nearly a millennium later, that search continued. Unless Aaron and his team could locate the man who had uncovered Geoffrey's tomb, the faith of over three billion people would be at risk.

Aaron realized his jaw hurt from clenching. Now they knew Geoffrey's bones had been in St. Mary's Priory in Monmouth. One man had uncovered them first. A man whose luck had now run out.

Chapter Seven

Harry pulled off the road thirty minutes after racing out of Monmouth, having made it to the town of Gloucester. Driving at an inadvisable rate of speed had taken him out of Wales and into England in short order; fate had clearly been smiling on him, as no police had pulled him over. His plan of claiming kilometers-to-miles-per-hour ignorance thankfully hadn't had to be tested.

The A40 highway ran past open brown fields lined with towering trees before it dropped him onto Gloucester's main street. A central cathedral watched over the town, exuding a stately, gothic aura, like something out of a Harry Potter movie. Enough cars buzzed past in either direction that the weight bearing down on him since escaping Monmouth dissipated, leaving only fatigue, as though he hadn't slept for days. If cars hadn't passed him with horns honking and motors humming, he could have fallen asleep in an instant.

Harry rubbed his eyes and looked to the messenger bag Victor had given him. The heavy book from Geoffrey's tomb lay inside it, making the seams bulge slightly. He needed a safe place to examine it. Across the street a meter maid passed by, the ticket-printing device looped over her neck as she checked for parking violations. He had to get somewhere quiet. Gloucester was big enough he shouldn't stand out as a stranger, and Monmouth was far behind. No one could have tailed him. A vehicle would have been obvious given how fast he had driven to get here.

He felt safe. For now. But where to go? Harry drummed his fingers on the steering wheel while the meter maid printed out a ticket, stuffing it beneath some poor sod's windshield wiper. She moved on, revealing the street sign behind her. Harry's eye's widened. *That works.*

He turned the key, the engine fired, and two turns later he entered the Gloucester Public Library's parking lot. Two stories of tan stone, peaked roofs and tall, narrow windows offered assurance that if your local library happened to come under attack by an invading army while you were inside, incoming cannon fire would be safely held off until your task was complete. The place was a fortress.

He found one of the street-facing entrances and walked inside, keeping his head down as he passed the security cameras. The glass doors swung closed behind him as he studied the rows of open shelving that stretched in every direction. Arched columns painted vibrant shades of red, purple and orange stood in direct contrast to the stone exterior. Computer terminals abounded. Harry moved to the farthest corner, choosing a small wooden table where he could keep his back to the wall and his eyes on the entrance.

Metal wheels squeaked as an employee passed, pushing a cart loaded with books. She offered a welcoming smile, which Harry found surprisingly comforting. He waited for her to turn the corner before opening his bag and gently extracting the heavy leather book.

The metal pieces at each corner showed little rust despite their age, while the leather binding had cracked but protected the book well inside Geoffrey's tomb. A metal clasp held the cover shut. He carefully opened it and turned back the front cover. The pages were vellum, and the only ornamentation was the single charred letter on the rear side of the cover, right at the top – G.

He began to turn the pages, slowly and gently. Dense Latin covered each one, a thousand-year-old version of the language he couldn't quickly translate. Block script, heavy on the ornamentation, all of it with thin red lines running underneath the letters. Guidelines to aid the scribes who created these books.

He turned back to the first page. A single line of script ran across it. Harry pulled his phone out, connected to the library's Wi-Fi, and pulled up a Latin translation page to double-check himself. He keyed in the line of text. *Historia Regum Britanniae*, which translated as *The History of the Kings of Britain*.

A first edition, or *the* first edition? Harry couldn't tell; he would have to wait until he returned to New York, where one of his trusted experts would confirm or deny it. If it turned out to be written in Geoffrey's own hand, well, Harry planned on taking a long vacation to someplace warm, preferably where no one wanted to kill him.

Metal squealed behind him. Harry jumped from his chair and turned with one fist raised. The teenage girl with the book cart shrank back and yelped.

"Oh my. I'm so sorry." Harry sat back down. "Forgive me. I didn't hear you coming."

The girl's hands were at her mouth, and though she lowered them, her eyes didn't get any smaller. "It's okay," she said. The young lady took a breath, then grabbed the book cart's metal handrail. "I'm sorry I startled you."

"You're really good at being quiet," Harry said. He winked, she laughed, and the only injury was his pounding heart as she pushed her cart away, giving Harry a wide berth. Still, he took a check of the surrounding tables and shelves before looking back down. No one set off his radar.

The heavy first page turned with a crackle. A brilliant illuminated letter *K* dominated the upper left of the next page, smaller Latin letters filling the space beside it. The beginning of Geoffrey's history of kings. The cover page's rear side should have been blank, but it wasn't. Handwritten notations filled the page, the script more readable than the ornate text of the main story. These letters were more flowing. More *personal.* "Like author's notes," Harry said to the still air.

He entered the Latin into the translation site on his phone, taking no chances. The quiet library faded away as Harry read it. It was a message from Geoffrey to Theobald.

Theobald, my faithful servant. Forces beyond us conspire to destroy the truth behind these writings. If you cannot retrieve what has been lost, leave this, my story, as a marker for future generations.

If you, reader, are not Theobald, know this. A cloaked enemy has been unleashed on the world, with no one to stop it. Too late did I uncover the truth regarding this illusory malady which threatens to consume humanity. For all those you love, I beg you, retrieve what has been hidden and share it with the world. Seek Emperor Diocletian's Palace east of Flavian's Amphitheater. The true man behind Arthur's legend points to a sacred message. To find it, follow Mordred's seduction to the one true sword.

But beware. Three forces conspire to end your quest. Do not trust those who come with saving grace, no matter their savior. They are the reason you must travel this path, for I could not risk allowing the truth to fall into their grasp. Follow my markers to complete the journey where I could not.

Godspeed,

G.

Harry read the note once, then again. On a whim he turned to the very last page. Perhaps Geoffrey had left an additional clue on the only other blank page, the back of the final one. Lightning arced up Harry's back when the page flipped over. *There's more.* Only it wasn't writing. He angled his head. *Is that a grid?*

A series of dots, empty circles drawn in precise rows, the sum of which formed an incomplete rectangle. The two longer rows had ten dots, while one of the shorter sides had only three, and they weren't connected. The other row across the bottom was a solid line. It appeared as though an opening of some sort had been deliberately placed in the top row of dots. Sandwiched between the two rows of ten was a single square, close to the completed shorter line. Inside this square, a cross.

No words, only the empty circles, a square, and the cross inside. Harry leaned closer. Not every circle was empty. One had been filled in. He checked again, looking at each dot in turn. Yes, one of the circles wasn't empty. Geoffrey had colored this one in. And next to it, two letters.

EX

Was it a code of some kind, a cipher he could use to understand what Geoffrey needed his servant Theobald to know? If so, the meaning eluded Harry completely.

He blinked twice. *You can do this.* His father's voice materialized from the air, a sound only Harry could hear, urging him on. Same Fred Fox he always had been, no matter what. Harry's rock, the only constant in his family life for so long. Gone now, which meant Harry had to do this. His father would expect nothing less. *Then I'd better not let him down.*

But how to figure this out? Harry sighed, leaned back in his chair and closed his eyes. First, leave the strange puzzle or drawing or whatever it was alone. Focus on what he could at least partially understand. The message from another time, written by a man he'd never met. A glimmer of light appeared. *Start with what you know, what you can confirm, and go from there.* He'd get as far as possible before calling in reinforcements. Not that he wanted to trust anyone else with this. You lived longer that way. Harry went back to the first line of Geoffrey's handwritten text and read with fresh eyes. Geoffrey had addressed this note to Theobald, which made sense. His closest companion, his trusted scribe, the one man he could count on. Except Theobald had never solved the mystery, or else this wouldn't have ended up in Geoffrey's tomb. A real confidence booster.

No matter. Clearly something had been lost, though Geoffrey never spelled that out and only told Theobald to leave the book behind so that hopefully some future adventurer would decipher the riddle. Leaving the only clue inside his coffin, hidden behind a brick wall in the basement of a small-town church might seem odd, but Geoffrey clearly had an ego and may have expected his grave to become a destination for others, one of whom might be the explorer he needed. Harry had Geoffrey's book now, the *marker* for navigating this search.

First part down. Next, the *cloaked enemy*. Did Geoffrey mean an actual cloak? Or was he being figurative, as in hidden or obscured from sight? This could mean two very different things. He filed that away for later. On to the *illusory malady* threatening all of humanity. Dire, vague, and to Harry's eye basically incomprehensible. He drummed his fingers against the table. It could mean almost anything, yet Geoffrey expected a person he'd never met to retrieve whatever had been hidden and broadcast it to the world. An idea? A treasure? It didn't say.

The next phrase provided actual intelligence if you knew how to read it. *Seek Emperor Diocletian's Palace.* Harry's spirits lifted as he considered that line. Real directions, and Harry knew where to start. He knew Diocletian had been emperor of Rome several centuries after Christ died. Good thing he was in a library.

A quick walk to the non-fiction section of the long shelves and soon Harry had a stack of books detailing the rise and fall of Rome. The imagined sights and sounds of a long-distant past threatened to draw Harry into their grasp, but he stayed the course and focused on Geoffrey's message. Diocletian's Palace, located due *east of Flavian's Amphitheater.* Or, as most knew it today, the Colosseum.

Harry pulled up a map of Europe on his phone. *Found you.* If he traced an easterly line from Rome, where the Colosseum still stood, his finger crossed the Adriatic Sea and ran aground in modern-day Croatia, specifically near a town named Split. Which was where Diocletian's Palace was built in the fourth century and which remained standing to this day. Harry needed to get on a plane and on the ground in Croatia.

Hold up. He put the phone down and looked around, soaking in the solitude. Yes, Geoffrey clearly pointed to this town in Croatia, but Harry suspected he might not yet have accomplished everything he could here in Gloucester. Three parts of this strange message remained. The *true man behind Arthur's legend*, or King Arthur, a subject that Harry knew had never been settled. He'd tackle that next, though he had an idea of where to start. Next, *Mordred's seduction.* That he understood. Geoffrey meant a woman, one who was part of the original Arthurian legend, a beauty who in Geoffrey's telling had been left in the care of Arthur's nephew Mordred while Arthur went to battle. Mordred had promptly seduced the woman, proclaimed himself king, and eventually battled Arthur. The lady who had brought this ruin to Arthur's life? Guinevere.

Parallel to that he had to consider the possible inspirations for King Arthur. If anything in those fragmented histories tied back to Diocletian, Harry had a real lead. A path forward.

He hopped up, crossed back to the non-fiction shelves, and returned to his table with more reference books. Ten minutes later he punched the air and earned a concerned look from the young librarian he'd nearly socked earlier. After taking several pictures on his phone, Harry placed Geoffrey's book back into his bag, stacked the library books neatly up on his table, and hurried out to his car. With the bag and its precious cargo stowed securely in the passenger seat beside him, he pointed due east out of town, toward London and Heathrow Airport, and beyond that, the Croatian town of Split.

One of the prime historical suspects behind the mythical King Arthur was the Roman military commander Lucius Artorius Castus. Castus had served Rome during Diocletian's reign. An interesting coincidence, though what sent Harry racing to the airport was that Lucius had been buried in Diocletian's Palace, in a tomb that remained intact today.

The engine whined as Harry veered onto the highway, gaining steam so quickly he almost missed his phone buzzing. He glanced to the dashboard. A New York number popped up, one he recognized.

Joey Morello. Harry reached for the phone, and then paused.

Things had changed between Joey and Harry. Not long ago they had gotten along well. Friends, almost, but after Harry's father was murdered, Vincent Morello had begun spending more time with Harry. Which meant he wasn't spending as much time with his own son Joey. At first Joey had supported Harry, mirroring Vincent's concern over the loss. Over time, however, that had changed. Vincent began treating Harry as the heir apparent to Fred Fox, the new antiquities man for the Morello family. Joey's growing resentment didn't stem from that; his own position in the Morello organization was secure. One day he would take over the entire Morello operation, making him Harry's boss. Rather, Joey had soured on Harry because of the time Vincent Morello gave to Harry at his son's expense. Joey would never say anything to his father about it. He wasn't wired that way. But Harry had soon gleaned that Joey Morello felt quite differently about him now than he had when Fred was still alive.

Harry also couldn't do much about it, so he ignored it. He knew he'd eventually work for Joey. Maybe things would improve then. Harry connected the call. "Joey, I was about to call you. You'll never guess what I found."

"My father wants to speak with you," Joey said. Muted conversation, then Vincent came on the line.

"This will have to wait," Vincent said. "There is a man here now and he is demanding to speak with me. I do not know what it is about."

Harry frowned. No one *demanded* anything from Vincent Morello. "Is everything okay, Mr. Morello?"

"Joey will be in touch," Vincent said. "Until then, be wary."

Vincent clicked off. As the tires rumbled below him, Harry couldn't shake the nagging sliver of fear in his gut. Nobody demanded to meet with Vincent Morello.

He pushed the gas pedal closer to the floor and picked up the phone again, dialing as he drove. Moments later, English spoken with a possibly French accent filled the car.

"Yes, my dear?"

"Rose, it's me. Harry."

"A pleasure to hear your voice," she said. "Where are you?"

If there was anyone who could help him with deciphering Geoffrey's message it was Rose. "I'm en route from Monmouth to London. I found it."

She kept silent while he relayed his journey. First St. Mary's Priory and the tombs below, then the attack. "Based on Geoffrey's message, I think the next step is in Croatia. Beyond that, I'm not confident." He veered around a slow-moving box truck. Clouds had started filling the sky. "Any ideas?"

"Bring the book home and let me sell it for you. We will make a fortune."

"Later. You're my favorite fence, you know that."

"Your only one," she said. "But you must survive whatever awaits, and to do that you need to know the danger. Who could have attacked you? Has anyone threatened you recently?"

"Other than the two guys in Tangier?" He considered. "Not that I – *damn*. I forgot." The photos Vincent and Joey had given him before he left jumped to mind. "The Cana family is trying to move in on my – on *Vincent's* – antiquities market. Vincent gave me a bunch of faces to look through when I left, guys to watch out for. I forgot about it until now."

"Did you recognize the man who attacked you in Monmouth?"

"Hold on." He moved into the slow lane and started driving the limit as he pulled out the photos from his bag. "There are maybe fifteen or so." One at a time, he flipped through the snapshots, keeping one eye on the road. Some of them were mugshots, others surveillance photos of varying quality, but all with a clear shot of the face. On the ninth one he hit paydirt. "I found him."

The man who had attacked him, whose assault had inadvertently uncovered Geoffrey of Monmouth's hidden grave. "Vincent was right. The Cana family sent a man after me. He must have followed me from New York to Monmouth, then into St. Mary's." The wheels started turning. "Only a handful of people knew I was coming here. I used a false passport." He bit his lip, then swallowed. "Someone told them."

"What does he look like, this man?"

What did that matter? "Taller than me, tan skin, short hair. Diamond studs in his ears. Like an Albanian, I guess. Why?"

Rose almost sounded relieved when she responded. "I thought perhaps I knew him through my work."

Possible, with Rose being one of the city's most successful fences of stolen goods. The Morellos weren't the only gang in town, and it wasn't as though they kept her on retainer. "Do you?" he asked. "I can send you a picture."

"Do that," Rose said. "Though it does not sound like anyone I know."

Harry accelerated into the fast lane. He'd feel better once he was airborne. "Listen, Rose. Don't tell anyone what I found. Vincent and Joey don't even know yet." A nagging voice whispered in his ear that the last thing he and Rose discussed, this trip, had somehow gotten out, though he didn't think Rose was behind it.

"Of course not," she said. "I would never put you in harm's way. Now, would you care to hear my thoughts on the message from Geoffrey?"

"Fire away," Harry said.

"First, this sounds authentic. Verifying provenance is key, and yours is indisputable. Next, the single message from Geoffrey. It is the only one in the book, correct?"

Other than that strange map at the end. He didn't voice this thought. "Correct."

"I agree Theobald failed in his quest, leaving the book behind per Geoffrey's instructions. As to the *forces* conspiring to destroy

Geoffrey's truth, I suspect he again refers to them at the end, this time as the *three forces*. Which tells us how many, but not who."

"Great. I guess I'll watch out for any groups of three in Croatia."

"Particularly those claiming to offer salvation," Rose said. "Though I confess what *savior* Geoffrey references is not clear. A deity, perhaps. Regardless, you have the most important piece. Diocletian's Palace east of Rome, where you must find the Roman leader Artorius. Look for symbols or messages related to females of any kind. Guinevere was a mortal woman in Geoffrey's book, but she can also be viewed as a symbol. The connection need not be literal."

"Makes sense," Harry said. "What about the *cloaked enemy* and *illusory malady*? Whatever he's talking about, Geoffrey wants the world to know. Which makes me ask why he didn't just tell everyone when he was alive. He created one of western civilization's greatest legends. He could have written about this threat to humanity."

"Perhaps he did," Rose said. "And we need only look hard enough to see it." The sound of a lighter flicking, then of tobacco burning. Rose exhaled, long and steady. "Promise me one more thing before you go."

What was she getting at? "Okay," he said warily.

"Trust no one. No matter who it is. Artifacts such as this one bring out the worst in men. Even those you have trusted before could betray you without warning. Better to suspect the worst and be proven wrong than give trust too soon, only to regret it. A lesson your father, rest his soul, never took to heart. I hope you will not make the same mistake."

Harry nearly swerved off the road. "My father? What do you mean?" Rarely had Rose ever mentioned Fred Fox, despite having done business with him since Harry was a little boy. "Tell me, Rose."

"We will talk when you return with the book. For now, do not let emotion cloud your judgment. Remember where you are. Parts of Croatia are less than welcoming for those who look different."

"I'll be sure to hang out around the mosques," Harry said.

"I am serious, Harry."

"I know, I know. I'll be careful, I promise." A sign for the London city limits appeared ahead. "I'll be in touch."

"Please do," Rose said. "Be cautious. I do not want you fighting for your life again."

Chapter Eight

New York City

Vincent Morello had a phone pressed to his ear. Joey severed the connection with Harry, then stood off at a respectable distance, one arm resting on the wooden cabinet holding the better liquor. As the main office door opened, Joey glanced down at the Remington Model 870 TAC-14 short-barreled shotgun hung on the backside of the cabinet. Loaded with 20 gauge. His eyes moved back to the door, then narrowed at the man who walked through. His father hadn't told him who was demanding entry to see him; Joey never would have guessed it was a man he knew well.

"Father Anthony?" The priest who'd baptized most of the neighborhood kids.

Vincent rose to greet the father, a man perhaps half his age, not much older than Joey. "Father, welcome." They embraced, then Vincent offered Anthony a chair. "I am happy to see you, but it is unlike you to arrive unannounced. Is anything wrong?"

"Vincent." Father Anthony sat with his hands folded, Vincent's desk between the two men. He looked to Joey, then back to Vincent. "A disturbing message came to me today. From the highest reaches of our faith. It directed me to deliver this to you."

Father Anthony reached into his pocket and came out with a cell phone. Vincent frowned. "Exactly what were you told?"

"I received a call this morning from the archbishop's office."

The highest-ranking Roman Catholic official in New York, the leader of the city's Catholic faithful. A cardinal appointed by the Holy Father himself. Joey had never met the current archbishop, though his father had spoken with the man in private meetings several times. The archbishop might not want to be seen with Vincent Morello, but he knew what relations should be maintained.

"The archbishop himself came on the line. He made a single request: that I answer a call that would ring through momentarily."

"And this call?" Vincent asked.

"Arrived shortly thereafter," Father Anthony said. "An overseas number, one I didn't recognize. A representative calling from the Holy See in Rome." He smiled when Vincent raised an eyebrow. "It was the chief of staff for the Cardinal Secretary of State."

Even Vincent's eyes went wide. The Secretary of State was the second-most powerful man in Catholicism. The only one above him was the man in white robes. The Pope. And the big man above, of course. "Why did he contact you?" Vincent asked.

"To request a favor."

Joey's body went rigid. He knew more than most what kinds of favors men with power asked for. You didn't want to be on the receiving end of those requests. "What did he want?" Joey asked.

"For me to give you this." Father Anthony held up the cell phone. "It is preprogrammed with a single number. The chief of staff made it clear this is a personal favor. He would like you to call the number at once."

"Whose number is it?" Vincent asked. He sat at the edge of his chair, hands clenched in front of him, offering a brief glimpse into the past, a chance to see the fiery young man he'd once been, a street warrior without equal. "And why could the Vatican possibly be interested in me?" When Father Anthony demurred, Vincent pressed harder. "Father, how long have we been friends? You baptized members of my family. If there is more to this, tell me."

"I wish I could, Vincent. I've never been more surprised. How the Vatican even knows I exist is a mystery. A humble city priest with no ambition beyond serving his flock." He hesitated. "Which is why I suspect they called me."

Joey rubbed his chin. Father Anthony was a bit player, a local man. His reach didn't extend more than a mile from here. *A local man – that's it.* Everything fell into place. "You know our family better than anyone in the church," Joey said. "Only a handful of people in the city can get in here on short notice. You're one. That's why they called you. To send that phone with a messenger we trust."

Father Anthony's head dipped. "I believe that is true."

Vincent still didn't take the phone. "I trust you. And I believe you will tell me the truth about this." He leaned over the desk. "To make this call happen, a man would need the cardinal's ear. Who has that kind of connection?"

"I considered this," the father said. "Two options come to mind. The first is someone with a family or personal connection to the Secretary of State. The chief of staff would never do this without his superior's knowledge, so this request almost certainly came from the Secretary. There are many people or groups the Secretary knows from his position, making this hard to pinpoint. In my opinion, that's less likely than the next possibility."

"Which is?"

Father Anthony bit his lip. "That the request came from a group directly tied to the Pope himself."

Vincent didn't react, didn't ask any other questions. He barely moved. No one budged until Vincent stretched out his hand for the phone. "Time spent considering is time wasted when the answer is at hand."

Father Anthony handed over the phone, then stood. "No need to go," Vincent said, waving at the father to sit back down. "As I said, my family trusts you. I would value your counsel after we learn more."

The father looked less than pleased at this, though he sat.

The phone beeped as Vincent powered it on and navigated to the single stored number. He pushed a button on the underside of his desk, activating the room's recording devices. Vincent put the phone on speaker and dialed.

It barely rang once before a man's voice answered. "Mr. Morello, I presume?"

"You have me at a disadvantage," Vincent said. "It is not often I call a man I do not know. To whom am I speaking?"

"My name is Aaron. Please forgive this unusual manner of introducing myself. I assure you I would not have done so had I any other options."

"We will worry about forgiveness later," Vincent said. "You are a man with friends in the church. The Secretary of State, I imagine. It is nice to have friends. Father Anthony is one of mine, and he deserves better than to be ill-used as your errand boy. However, I understand on occasion circumstances call for action." His voice scarcely rose as he spoke, the words delivered with the same restrained, measured tone Joey had known his whole life. Which was why only a very few people would know this man Aaron played a dangerous game. "Tell me, Aaron. What is so urgent?"

"You have a man in your organization," Aaron said. "He was recently in St. Mary's Priory Church in Monmouth, Wales."

Aaron stopped speaking, though Vincent was far too experienced to fall for that old trick. He had no urge to fill the dead air. Instead, he looked to Joey and raised one bushy eyebrow. Joey gave a half-nod in response. *Yeah, he probably was.*

Aaron continued. "Mr. Fox located a forgotten grave."

Joey started at the use of Harry's name. *They know part of the story. Doesn't sound like they have all of it.* This time Joey shrugged when his father looked over. *Maybe Harry did, maybe he didn't.*

"My patience wears thin, Aaron." Vincent spoke with the ease of a man used to being obeyed. "Your point."

"We believe Harry took something from that grave. Something with information my group requires."

"If the Catholic Church wants something a man who allegedly works for me may have found, why are they having you call me? There are better methods for handling such a situation."

"This situation is delicate." Aaron paused, though this time Joey suspected he was truly thinking, not fishing for information. "Your man doesn't realize what he's done. The man whose grave he uncovered very nearly caused the collapse of society's supporting pillars. My group is attempting to prevent such a disaster from occurring. We need your help, Vincent. I'm asking you as a man of God. Help us. Please."

Vincent's face remained stone-like, a visage reflecting iron will and unforgiving memory. A lifetime of experience kept his true feelings hidden, though Joey wondered if Aaron and his ties to the Vicar of Jesus Christ could leverage his father's faith to get him to bring Harry in from the field. Joey sure hoped not, though he wouldn't disagree with Vincent in front of Father Anthony. There was money to be made in Wales. And Harry Fox could get himself out of this sticky situation if need be.

"Aaron, I believe you speak the truth as you see it. I admire honesty," Vincent said. "Another trait I admire is courage. You have this as well. Above all of these, I admire loyalty. A man is nothing without it." He paused, looking to his son. "I do not know why Harry is in Wales. Perhaps he is on vacation. What I do know is that if you harm him, you will make an enemy of me for life. And no one, Aaron, no one at all, wants me for their enemy."

Vincent ended the call. He stood and handed the phone back to Father Anthony. "Thank you for coming," Vincent said. "Let me walk you out."

As Vincent passed Joey, he turned and spoke so softly Joey had to lean in to hear him. "Tell Harry to watch his back," Vincent said. "Make certain he has everything he needs. They want to threaten us? Show them we will not back down."

Joey watched his father walk away. His hands clenched into fists.

Chapter Nine

New York City

Stefan Rudovic stood outside the Cana family headquarters in Brooklyn, a phone pressed to his ear, when the man approached. A loose-fitting light coat went well past his knees, his pants of the same cream color. The crocheted white cap completed the standard ensemble. Stefan mumbled an apology into the phone and clicked off. *"As-salamu alaykum."* Stefan lowered his head as he spoke.

"Wa 'alaykumu s-salam." The Islamic holy leader smiled. "And peace be upon you, too, Brother Stefan."

"Imam, it is good to see you." Stefan clasped the man's outstretched hand. "What brings you here?"

The imam stroked his neatly trimmed beard, oiled to a rich, obsidian shine. "I wish to speak with Altin. Is he available?"

"He is," Stefan said. "He will be delighted to see you." Their local imam was the leader of Stefan's mosque and the man to whom nearly the entire Cana family entrusted their spiritual well-being. A few decades older than Stefan, he was unflappable, a stoic voice of reason and calm in a world where it seemed Muslims were now blamed for many of the world's ills either by association or appearance, or through ignorance or spite. For nearly two decades now Imam Hussam Shamsi had selflessly supported men and women of all faiths, Muslim or otherwise, often in the face of aggression or outright hatred many non-Muslims couldn't comprehend. The man was a rock. Which was why Stefan asked the question.

"Is everything alright? Forgive me, Imam, but you look troubled."

Hussam Shamsi didn't deny it. "You speak the truth, Brother Stefan. Though I am not here today of my own volition, I trust it is Allah's will which brings me to this place. Only Altin Cana can tell me if this is true."

Stefan frowned. This didn't feel right. It wasn't that he considered the will of Allah to be beyond contestation, though he'd never actually had Allah talk to him directly about his will. "Follow me," Stefan said. "I will take you to him."

Hussam offered greetings to the few men they passed inside, every one of them lowering their head when he and Stefan passed. They found the door to Altin Cana's office open, and were waved in as soon as Altin saw who trailed Stefan.

"Imam, come in," Altin said after he and Hussam exchanged a traditional greeting. "My honored guest." Altin stood and offered a hand that swallowed the imam's own like a hairy bear trap. "Be seated. Will you have tea?" Altin didn't wait for an answer, bellowing out to one of his men to bring some. He motioned for Stefan to sit as well. The imam didn't object as they all sat around a coffee table beside Altin's desk. Altin, of course, sat facing the door. "What brings you here today?"

Hussam opened his mouth, then closed it as tea arrived. Only after the guard who brought it went back outside Altin's office door did he speak. "A strange request," he said, hands crossed on his lap, an inscrutable expression on his face. "From the Grand Mufti of Jerusalem's office."

"The leader of the Al-Aqsa Mosque in Jerusalem?" Stefan asked, and Hussam confirmed it.

Altin rubbed his chin. His eyes narrowed. "Why would one of Islam's most powerful leaders make a request of you?"

"I suspect because of my relationship with you." Hussam reached into his pocket. "I am to give you this." Out came a cell phone, which Altin accepted. "It is the greatest desire of the Grand Mufti that you use this phone to make a call. There is a number programmed in it for this purpose." His hands came up. "Before you ask, I do not know anything further. It is not my place to question instructions from one of our faith's most respected leaders."

Stefan spoke. "He needed a man you trust, Altin. The imam is one of the few who has your full trust."

Hussam shook his head. "I am a humble servant of Allah, grateful for friends such as Altin and yourself. That is all."

The Albanian gangster studied Hussam for several long moments. The imam never flinched. Stefan doubted Altin Cana would ever consider rejecting the request. Part of his unshakable belief that he was meant to succeed in life stemmed from the faith of his homeland, a connection to Allah and the Muslim teachings of men like Hussam. From nothing, he had risen to become one of the most influential men in a lethal trade in the largest city in America. Altin believed Allah and the Islamic faith had helped him do this. He'd be hard-pressed to begrudge them a call.

"For you," Altin said. "And for Allah." He pressed *Send* and a moment later ringing filled the office.

A man answered before the first tone ended. "*As-salamu alaykum.*"

"*Wa 'alaykumu s-salam.* This is Altin Cana. Who are you?"

"I am called Mo. Thank you for speaking with me."

"When Allah calls, I respond. You must have a question. Ask it."

If Mo was perturbed by Altin's direct approach, he didn't show it. "Do you know a man named Gabriel Dushku?"

Stefan's stomach clenched. *Shit.* He hadn't heard from Gabe since he'd followed Harry Fox to Wales. If Gabe had moved on Harry and it had gone bad, this could be ugly. Stefan's guts twisted as Altin turned his way. He shrugged, keeping his face blank.

"Yes," Altin said. "He is known to me."

"He was found unconscious in a Welsh church today. Do you know anything about that?"

"Are you interfering in my business?" Altin asked, turning the tables. "Perhaps you don't understand what I do, Mo. I don't appreciate interference."

"The imam can attest this matter has nothing to do with your business interests in New York. I merely wish, on behalf of the Grand Mufti, to ask a favor. I require information. I hope you will provide it. Altin Cana is a man to be respected, not threatened."

Stefan suppressed a smile. Mo knew what he was doing.

"I appreciate this," Altin said. "For a brother in our faith, I will do what I can."

"Why was Gabriel in Wales?"

"A business trip," Altin said. "I sent him to conduct research on a competitor."

"Will you share the name of this competitor?"

Altin hesitated. A car engine rumbled by outside, faint through the thick glass windows. "Perhaps you will tell me why you are interested."

"Of course," Mo said. "I assume the man who attacked Gabriel was seeking Geoffrey of Monmouth's tomb. Gabriel appeared during this search. A struggle ensued, which resulted in the tomb being discovered. At some point Gabriel was injured, though he won't tell us anything about the incident."

"Are you holding him?" Altin's question came out like a punch. "That would be a mistake."

"We are not," Mo said. "He's in the hospital right now for evaluation. My colleague in Wales took him there before the police arrived. The local priest won't reveal his name to the authorities, I assure you." Mo paused. "That would be the priest he allegedly assaulted."

"In that case, you have my thanks. Please continue."

"There is little else," Mo said. "Geoffrey's tomb was opened. I believe it was looted. However, I suspect Gabriel didn't see this happen as he was unconscious. I need to know what was taken from Geoffrey's tomb."

"Which is why you need the other man's name," Altin said. "This makes sense." He looked to Stefan. "One of my associates is better prepared to speak to this."

Stefan introduced himself. "His name is Harry Fox. Harry works for the Morello family. An antiquities hunter. We heard he was on to something and wanted to see if it was true."

"Harry Fox found more than he could ever realize," Mo said. "Could you describe him?" Stefan did, and Mo didn't speak again until he was finished. "Interesting man to be working for the Italian mob," Mo said.

"He's resourceful," Stefan said. "His luck will run out soon enough, though."

"Soon enough," Mo agreed. "Altin, Stefan, you have our thanks. I ask, as a favor to my group and to our faith, that you tell your man Gabriel to back off. What Harry Fox located poses a danger to millions. He cannot be allowed to share his findings with the world."

Stefan cocked an eye toward Altin. "Sounds valuable."

"No," Mo said. "Not valuable. Incredibly dangerous. We will find Harry, determine what he found, and take the necessary steps to secure this situation. All we ask of you is to have Gabriel come home and forget he ever visited Wales. Will you do that?"

"This request comes from your friends in Jerusalem?"

"It does."

"Then consider it done."

Mo thanked Altin again, and also the imam for connecting the two, before clicking off. As Hussam stood to leave, one thought ran through Stefan's mind over and over. Whatever Harry Fox had found in that tomb was worth a fortune. Stefan couldn't let that walk away, not for any holy man, no matter how powerful. No, he needed to find it, and then make a fortune selling it. Altin would forgive him when he realized how much money it meant for them all.

Now he had to beat Mo at his own game and find Harry Fox first.

Chapter Ten

Split, Croatia

Harry stepped off the Croatia Airlines jet after a direct flight from London to Split. An hour later he fired the engine on his rental car and merged into traffic, following a flow of taxis and rideshare cars heading away from Croatia's second-busiest airport toward the city roughly ten miles distant. Until today he hadn't even known Split existed, let alone had an international airport with direct routes from London.

Distant green peaks rose on one side of the highway, with grasslands stretching all the way to their base. Straight ahead the ice-blue Adriatic Sea ran across the horizon. Harry could just make out the red-roofed town fronting the water's edge, where Diocletian's Palace waited. Despite being here, Harry couldn't shake the feeling he stood close to the edge of an abyss. This feeling had taken root in St. Mary's Priory in Wales, when a man had viciously attacked him for no reason. When he'd identified that man among Vincent's photos of the Cana family operatives, it had deepened.

On the three-hour flight over he had had nothing to do but think. Two things seemed clear. First, there was more at stake here than a first edition of the book that had brought King Arthur's legend into the world. Second, he needed to watch his back like never before. What had Rose said? *Trust no one.* Time he took her advice to heart. Which meant he needed to clear the air with her on several matters.

The seaside town presented itself slowly, first with a few homes grouped together, then with more structures pushing against the road as he approached blue waters. Nearly all sported the burnt-red roofs he'd seen flying in, most with white walls unchanged for centuries. Traffic was surprisingly light for the dinner hour, and Harry made it into the city and within a kilometer of the palace before he made a U-turn and pulled into a street parking spot. If he needed to get out of the city in a hurry, he was already facing the right way. A small measure, but those added up. Before he headed into the palace on foot, he had a call to make.

Ringing filled his car. Rose answered on the second one. "Harry, is it you?"

"Good evening, Rose. Or good morning in New York."

"Where are you now?" she asked. "I have been worried."

He brought her up to speed on his trip. "I'm heading to the palace," he finished. "I have no idea where to start, and finding anything in this place won't be easy."

"The palace covers half the town," Rose said. "All of it enclosed behind thick walls. Over seven acres. It will be a challenge."

"Good thing it really *is* part of the town," Harry said. "It's accessible all day and night. A few thousand people actually live there."

A car passed, one with the brilliant white xenon headlights everybody seemed to have now. Light bounced off his rearview mirror and turned the car's interior a fiery golden hue. Harry instinctively reached for his neck to discover the amulet had slipped out from beneath his shirt. A question formed and escaped his lips before he could stop it. "Rose, did my father ever tell you about the amulet he always wore?"

Silence. Another car passed, this one with a hole in the muffler. Rose didn't reply. Maybe she hadn't heard him.

"Never," Rose finally said. "He wore it everywhere. I assumed it was a family heirloom. It is beautiful. That's all I recall. Why do you ask?"

Rose clearly remembered the piece. According to his father, it was a replica of an Egyptian piece worn by a long-dead pharaoh, the rectangular gold center decorated with faience, a ceramic material prized in ancient Egypt. The opaque blue-green contrasted with the golden center, which featured carvings Harry assumed were hieroglyphs. Once he'd tried to decipher them only to discover the glyphs didn't form a coherent message; they were nonsensical. The only man who could have offered insight into why such a piece meant enough for him to wear it every day wasn't around to give answers, so Harry had ended up with more questions than when he'd started.

"He wore it every day," Harry said. "I assumed it was tied to my mother." His hand formed a fist, which he bounced softly off the steering wheel. "Time ran out before I ever asked him why."

"I am sorry, Harry. Fred never spoke of it to me. The piece must have held a special place in his heart and his mind. You will figure out the story, but I suggest you focus on one hunt at a time."

"Right." He slipped the amulet underneath his shirt again, out of sight.

"Be cautious, Harry. Remember what I said."

"Three forces could be after me – I know. I'll be careful."

"And don't trust anyone." She clicked off before he could respond.

Don't trust anyone. He'd keep that in mind. It was hard to imagine anyone could follow him on his race from Wales through England and on to Croatia. If anything, the quick moves had bought him breathing room to search without having to look over his shoulder. He intended to use the advantage.

His phone vibrated. A familiar number popped on-screen. Harry steeled himself. "Hey, Joey."

"You busy?" Harry said he wasn't. "That guy who came to see my father earlier? It was Father Anthony. Listen to this."

Harry's heartrate slowly increased as Joey detailed the visit from

Father Anthony, a man Harry knew well and whose loyalty to Vincent was beyond question. When Joey recounted how Vincent had told the man on the phone Harry was under his protection and that anyone messing with Harry would face the entire Morello clan, his throat tightened. "Give your father my thanks. I'd be in trouble if he told them where to find me."

Joey paused. "Where are you, anyway?"

Harry paused. Rose's warning buzzed in his ears. "I'm in Croatia."

"You find anything in that tomb?"

It couldn't hurt to tell Joey about the book. The men in Rome must have known something was in Geoffrey's tomb. Why else would they be interested? Whoever *they* were. "I got it. Geoffrey's first copy of *History*. There's a message in it pointing me to Croatia. I have the book with me."

"Good. My father said you'll have anything you need to keep going. Money, information, *items* to protect yourself. Let me know and I'll handle it."

"I'm set for now," Harry said. "Though that could change." He touched the ceramic dusters in his pocket. "Let's hope it doesn't come to that."

Harry was caught off guard when Joey responded. "I know you don't like guns," Joey said. "Hard to blame you. But like I've told you a million times—"

"—don't bring a knife to a gun fight." Harry smiled. Joey used to say that all the time. "I remember."

"Or those ceramic knuckles," Joey said. "They don't stop bullets." He stopped. Harry got the sense he wasn't finished talking. He waited.

"Hey, Harry." Joey coughed. "Stay safe. And keep me in the loop."

It took Harry a moment to find his tongue. "I will. Thanks, Joey. I appreciate that."

Joey clicked off. Harry put the phone down, Geoffrey's book

momentarily forgotten. Joey hadn't said anything that personal to him for months. Actual well-wishes, not just business. It wasn't exactly like the old days before Fred's murder, but maybe now, for whatever reason, it was turning back. Joey had been one of Harry's few friends. Now Harry didn't know what to think.

Two women walking past his car burst out in laughter. Harry shook his head. He'd think more about that later. He looked to the great stone wall surrounding Diocletian's Palace, rising above the homes and offices of ancient Split. The centuries-old leather on Geoffrey's book chilled his fingers as he slipped it into the messenger bag, which went over his shoulder before he opened the door and stepped out, hurrying onto the sidewalk to avoid being clipped by passing traffic. Harry rolled his neck. If Guinevere existed anywhere behind the palace walls, Harry would find her. Only the gods knew what came next.

Across the Atlantic, a few miles from where Joey Morello stood in his father's home, Rose Leroux polished off the last of her martini and immediately set about making a new one. The call with Harry had left her parched, though the ice-cold vodka swirling in her glass wasn't intended only to quench her thirst. Most of it was aimed directly at her conscience. Even after decades in this business, choosing sides never came easily.

"Does anyone else know where he is?"

Rose speared an olive before she looked over to Stefan. "No."

The Albanian gangster nodded. "And you've never heard of any religious groups muscling in on the black-market antiquities trade?" He took a step closer, leaning against the bar across from her. "You know everyone in this game, Rose. Nobody rings a bell?"

Icicles dripped from her reply. "No one. Why an imam would be recruited by one of Islam's most powerful men to find an antiquities hunter from Brooklyn is beyond me. It makes no sense. The book isn't tied to the Muslim faith. It's not even religious. It's a history of

British kings written by a priest, though more than anything it's a story. A fictional one, if you believe the scholars. Why would Islamic powerbrokers care?"

Stefan didn't have an answer. "I'm looking into it," was all he said.

Rose sipped her drink. "It sounds as though you are not abiding by the Grand Mufti's wishes."

"I don't need a self-righteous zealot to make decisions for me. They don't want the book to come out? Fine. They can offer the highest price once I find it. This is a business transaction first, a power move second." He paused when Rose raised an eyebrow. "If I get the book from Harry, I make money selling it. He doesn't. That means the Morellos lose, which means they have less power." Stefan tapped a rapid-fire beat on the bar. "Kicking Vincent Morello down a notch is good for us."

"Courting powerful enemies should not be done lightly," Rose said. She wanted to say more, but instead smothered her concerns under a gulp of ice-cold vodka. Stefan had always been headstrong, ever since he was a little boy. Exactly like his mother, and look what had happened to her.

"Which is why no one knows I'm behind this if it works out," Stefan said. "Except you." His finger stopped tapping. "I know you'd never sell me out. My mother would turn over in her grave."

All the vodka in New York couldn't keep Rose from feeling that one. "Be careful," she said, her words cold. "I cannot protect you from everyone. Especially yourself."

Stefan laughed. "You worry too much." He turned and walked to the door, pausing with his hand on the knob. "My man Gabe in Wales will follow Harry. If this goes south, Gabe takes the fall. If he finds the book, Altin Cana thanks me for kicking the Morellos down. Either way, I win." He turned around to face her. "One more thing. About that amulet of Harry's. Sounds like a nice piece with an even better story."

"You heard everything I know," she said. "It meant something to

Fred Fox. What, I can't tell you."

"Then we'll find out. After I give the Morellos one more thing to worry about." He touched his forelock, then turned and walked out.

Rose counted to five before slamming her empty martini glass on the desk. She loved that boy, same as she'd loved his mother, but this was almost too much. Never had she imagined the quiet, kind child she knew would grow up to give her an impossible choice. Keep her promise to protect him, or protect Fred Fox's son, one of the best men she knew in a terrible world.

Chapter Eleven

Split, Croatia

The Adriatic Sea flashed under a setting sun as though fire raced across it, dancing over a blanket of sparkling diamonds. Harry lowered his eyes against the glare and hurried toward the nearest gate into Diocletian's Palace. Limestone walls over twenty feet high protected his right shoulder, while his left fended off approaching pedestrians, more than a few of them tourists well-lubricated by *slivovitz*, the plum brandy popular in this part of Europe.

Most of the street vendors had packed up and gone home by now, though a few tents remained, their proprietors encouraging anyone who walked by to stop and buy. In no need of patterned blankets or watches of questionable provenance, he forged ahead until a gate materialized in the thick white walls, offering a glimpse of the palace's interior. Dodging a man hawking sunglasses, Harry stepped to one side, his back pressed to the limestone as he took stock of the palace. *Palace* was an understatement. This place was a city unto itself.

A restaurant patio filled with diners was ahead, the modern awnings hanging from colonnaded walls in contrast to the aged stone pillars. Arched columns stretched out in front of him, as though Rome's magnificent aqueducts had been copied in exacting detail. The evening crowd moved at a leisurely pace, allowing Harry to walk behind a vibrant group of French visitors taking in the sights. He passed a standalone column that had likely had a statue atop it at one point, now lost to time.

The walkway narrowed, taking Harry past a shuttered bank before he emerged into another open-air courtyard. This looked more like a town square, with a pair of street guitarists singing in a language Harry didn't recognize. Harry stopped by a white pillar. He'd walked into a maze and gotten himself lost. Thankfully he'd been smart enough to save a map of the palace on his phone in case he couldn't get a Wi-Fi connection. Which, it turned out, he could not.

The map appeared on his screen, and after a few false starts, Harry found not only himself, now a solid blue dot, but also where he needed to go. Artorius had been a vaunted military leader in his day, a man worthy of respect even from his emperor. Diocletian had honored the great general, burying Artorius not far from his own designated tomb, in the cellars beneath the Cathedral of Saint Domnius, built in 305 A.D.

Fifteen minutes later Harry had dodged, pushed, and outright bulled his way past groups of tourists. The next few blocks were quieter, most of the evening's pedestrians drawn toward the palace's nightlife. Harry rounded another corner closer to the center of town, looked up, and kept going. The cathedral towered ahead.

Ground-level floodlights washed over it all, white limestone and marble dazzling against the darkening sky. A bell tower topped the Romanesque structure, semi-circular arches at every level up to the tower roof. The interior flashed briefly into view as visitors pushed through its wooden doors. Harry looked in every direction, forcing himself to take a deep breath. He'd made it this far by being cautious. Mostly. And anything inside had already been there for a millennium, perhaps two. It could wait five more minutes while he surveilled the perimeter.

Slow steps took him around the surrounding courtyard, past each doorway and under every streetlight. No one set off his internal radar, not the couple walking arm in arm, nor the elderly man being pulled by an enthusiastic Corgi. The surrounding buildings appeared to be private residences.

94

The circuit of the cathedral took ten minutes, time he had no desire to waste. Scaffolding spiderwebbed up one side of the entrance, a heavy plastic tarp fluttering on the evening breeze as he stepped up the entrance stairs, past the open iron gate and through the front doors. A low-ceilinged, dark entranceway guided him into the main worshipping area, where bright light painted the floor ahead and gold glittered in the ceiling.

Plaster winged females holding gold cherubic toddler angels proclaimed the heavenly grandeur of this space, with illuminated archways surrounding the scenes of saints and miracles. Harry absorbed it in a flash, his eyes turning to the two tombs flanking the altar. He'd come for the tombs, not the scripture.

Empty pews, a vacant dais behind the altar, no one that he could see in the hallways branching off in multiple directions. The cathedral closed in less than an hour, both good and bad for Harry's purposes. He could come back tomorrow if necessary, but that gave anyone on his tail twelve more hours to find him. Harry approached the tombs and read their inscriptions – two saints, both buried here six hundred years ago.

Where to next? Over time any building became a history map of sorts, telling its story if only you knew how to read it. Structures evolved, changing to match their inhabitants, often growing from simple beginnings to something much grander that would ultimately be unrecognizable to those who had built it. This cathedral certainly didn't come from humble birth, but it was no different than any other place. Its earliest iteration, Harry knew, was as Diocletian's mausoleum. As time passed, new overseers built on top of the already impressive structure, adding a bell tower, expanding sections or adding entirely new ones. To find Artorius he needed to start at the very beginning. You didn't often find burial tombs at ground level. For that, you went deeper.

He looked at the small sign overhead, thankfully translated into English. *Cellars.* That's where he needed to start. His footsteps echoed off the limestone stairs as cooler air snaked down his shirt. Treacherous steps worn smooth spoke of the ages as they led him to the next level. He emerged from beneath a rough archway into a storage vault that at one time had housed wine, food and stores. Now instead of wine and salted meat, the cellar had become what every church needed these days: another source of revenue. It had been converted to a display – a tourist attraction, with offering boxes on every corner.

He tossed a coin into the closest box on the off chance anyone was watching, in this realm or the next. One hand unconsciously went to his amulet as he recalled Geoffrey's message. A vague reference to a *cloaked enemy* and an *illusory malady*. That Geoffrey wanted something to be retrieved was clear, and his initial direction had brought Harry here, to Croatia, where Lucius Artorius Castus was buried. As to *Mordred's seduction*, he would keep an eye out for anything tied to Guinevere.

Like in St. Mary's in Wales, alcoves were carved into the bedrock walls that formed the hallway. Muted lighting was unable to do more than push the shadows back a few feet. One opening held a display of church artifacts, including a ceremonial sword that he couldn't help stopping to admire. The weapon was noted to be nearly five hundred years old and still looked sharp enough to keep invaders at bay if they tried to steal a collection box.

He moved on, surrounded by the soft humming of fans circulating fresh air through the subterranean caves, navigating the cellars beneath curved ceilings that seemed ready to crumble down at any moment. The tombs were located down a short set of steep steps and around one last pillar. Harry kept one hand on the cold stone column as he leaned around, listening for any sound of intrusion. He hadn't seen a single person since coming down here, though he did catch muffled voices coming from a well-lit hallway at one point. The voices had quickly faded, thank goodness.

Darkness waited behind the pillar. Harry frowned, then tugged on the messenger bag strapped across his torso. Artorius's tomb should be right here. He went still as his eyes adjusted to the dark. Then they went wide. He was staring at a construction zone. This was Artorius's final resting place. Renovations were underway.

Or, more accurately, it was an *Area Under Repair*, as the orange sign helpfully explained. "Closed to visitors?" Harry asked the walls. They didn't respond. This was the correct location. He'd found the tombs, though he now had an immediate problem. Namely, the floor-to-ceiling metal fencing blocking him from getting closer. A plastic tarp hung just beyond the fence, preventing him from seeing anything. He walked to where a heavy chain had been looped through the two middle sections. A padlock secured it. Quick checks of either side found the same arrangement, with the thick metal fencing secured by way of chains bolted to the walls. He'd need a jackhammer to get those bolts out.

Harry leaned his weight against the fence, which didn't budge an inch. He pushed an arm through the narrow opening, then ripped off a string of curses when its sharp edge left a gouge in his forearm. Nobody short of Houdini was getting through that opening. Maybe there was a back entrance, another way around to see… *Stop it.* The place was under construction, and a safety hazard. No one could get in.

Harry turned around and leaned against the fence, arms crossed on his chest. *What now?* He could wait until daylight, then come back and try to sneak in when construction crews were working. No doubt they left the gate unlocked during work hours. If he could slip past them, maybe he could hide until they left or went on break.

And then what? Get locked in the tomb at night, or, worse yet, be caught sneaking around? Getting stuck inside for a night wasn't the worst idea, as long as he brought water and a flashlight. Then he'd have all night to poke around and search for any sign of Guinevere. Again, he reminded himself that waiting that long would give anyone tracking him time to catch up. Harry couldn't shake the feeling there was more going on than a rival crime family trying to steal his latest artifact. The uncertainty made him want to do something stupid. He wanted to fight. Which, as his father had told him countless times, should only be a last resort.

"Use your mind, not your muscles." Being unable to think your way out of a problem reflected more on you than anyone else. Fred Fox had disliked violence. Since Harry was a boy, Fred had taught him to avoid physical conflict whenever possible. That's not to say he hadn't trained his son to handle himself if needed. Harry knew his way around the Italian boxing gyms in Brooklyn better than most Italians.

How to follow his dad's philosophy now? *Stay ahead of whoever's chasing you, dummy. Quit wasting time.* Except he wasn't wasting time. A metal fence blocked his way, held together by a padlock. A few good whacks from a sledgehammer might open the lock. This and a half-dozen other options formed in his head as Harry stared back at the pillar he'd rounded earlier. The dim light illuminated the side facing Harry, and he noted a carving in the stone.

His gaze narrowed. It was a *sword.* Like the one on display he'd passed earlier. Harry backtracked at full speed, slowing only while passing connecting hallways, until he came to the sword display. It was mounted on two hooks bolted into the stone wall, with a wide velvet rope put up as a barrier. Up close it looked *deadly.* He ducked under the rope, then reached out with both hands to grasp the weapon. Was it loose? He lifted. The blade stuck.

It couldn't be that easy. What was holding it on? A finger run along the blade's edge confirmed it was somewhat sharp. The sword moved a bit under his grip, so it wasn't soldered to the pegs. He wiggled it again. How was it attached? Harry leaned closer to the wall, so close his forehead brushed the stone. Maybe back here, behind the handle. His hand brushed something, and he squinted. *No way.*

Commercial-quality zip ties. The church had secured the blade to its supporting pegs with a pair of plastic zip ties, looped around the blade. He slid the weapon back and forth, a few inches at a time, using its still-sharp edge against the zip ties, until one end broke free without warning; the other one soon followed suit. He lifted the sword from its display hangings, pleased at the weight. Without any doubt it could smash a small padlock to bits.

His race back to the gate would have been comical had anyone seen him, though Harry didn't find it funny when his foot skidded and he nearly impaled himself on the sword clutched to his chest. Righting himself outside the construction zone, he stood behind the pillar and waited until his breathing slowed. No sign of anyone at all.

Get to it. Harry lifted the sword and held it inches from the lock. One slow-motion practice swing, a slight turn of his head to avoid the worst if it all went wrong, and he hefted the sword. Everything he had went into bringing it back down.

He missed. Metal clashed with a thunderous boom and sparks flew as the sword bashed off the stone floor, rattling Harry's teeth and threatening to dislocate his shoulders. All this before his momentum carried him forward to crash-land into the gates, which still refused to yield.

His face ached where it had hit the fencing, his arms rang with pain, and his head felt like marbles were still bouncing in it. *Forget this.* He hefted the sword and brought it down once more with a vengeance. This time his blow struck true, slicing through the chain and obliterating the lock. His shoulders weren't happy but Harry didn't care. He was in.

He'd slipped halfway through the gate before remembering the sword, and had to go back to grab the weapon and drop it by the fence's bottom links, hidden in shadows. In the murky darkness you'd have to step on it to see it. After looping the chain around to mimic it still being locked, Harry pushed through the hanging tarp where two of the plastic sheets met and ran into a wall of darkness. His phone came out, the flashlight coming on to reveal two rows of ancient tombs.

There were six of them, three on each side, all of them set against the walls. Artorius wasn't the only one buried here. Harry looked back to the thick plastic tarp as he moved, but he couldn't see anything other than a faint glow through the sheets. The room wasn't more than thirty feet deep, though by the time he reached the rear wall the entrance had become little more than an outline in the dark. He found the tomb of Artorius first, then paused. Geoffrey had come through a thousand years after Artorius died. It's possible whatever was here, if anything was at all, wouldn't be in Artorius's tomb. Which wasn't a problem. Harry planned to check every realistic option, Artorius or not. Now, how to get in to these massive stone vaults? A dark shape against the rear wall caught his eye.

Hold on. A massive toolbox was tucked against the rear wall, the kind they called job boxes, which held enough tools for an entire crew. A box that a crew could expect to stay safe behind the padlocked gate.

Harry pulled on one drawer. It opened. He now had every tool he could need. A check of the shorter drawers returned what he wanted most: a headlamp with an elastic band you put around your noggin to leave both hands free. He slid the device on and clicked it to the red light setting to preserve his night vision. It was dim enough that anyone walking past wouldn't be able to see it, while strong enough to illuminate the area he wanted to search.

His cell phone went back into a pocket, and he stowed his bag in a corner before he started his search, arming himself with a crowbar and beginning with a tomb near the front. The tomb reached from the floor nearly to his waist. Carvings ran across the top, hard to make out with the low light. He searched for any markers to tell him whom this tomb contained, and discovered the letters carved across the lid were Latin. Harry was able to translate some of the inscribed words. He traced a finger over the first few letters, then stopped.

Galeria Valeria. Diocletian's daughter. It wasn't a tomb, but a memorial. Geoffrey's message suggested a female influence, and though Galeria was a woman, Harry didn't see any obvious reasons she would tie to Guinevere. However, he could have missed it. Only one way to find out.

Harry forced the crowbar's curved end into the small crack, levering it back and forth to gain purchase. The memorial resisted. *That's how you want to play this? Fine.* So much for silence. Those hanging plastic sheets would dampen the noise of most of his efforts. He flipped the crowbar around and attacked with the flat end. Dust and debris erupted, a fine Martian haze under the red light on his forehead. Harry kept at it, bashing the memorial harder and harder until his tool lodged in too deeply and held tight. He fought back, pulling until it ripped free. Now he had a chance.

Jamming the crowbar's curved side back in, he went to work, leaning on the tool with all his weight, moving one step at a time around the entire stone coffin. It didn't happen until he'd nearly completed an entire circuit. One press down shifted the entire lid, stone and marble grinding as centuries of inertia gave way. The lid scarcely budged, but move it did. Harry stepped back, sweat cold on his forehead in the tomb's dead air. Time for the big guns.

A digging bar emerged from the massive toolbox, four feet of thick, heavy steel. If he couldn't lever the lid off, maybe he could bash it to pieces. Which he desperately didn't want to do. Yes, he hunted artifacts, *repatriated* them for profit, but he didn't want to destroy history. Quite the opposite. Artifact trafficking had occurred for centuries. Harry took care with his buyers. He didn't deal with terrorists no matter what they offered. It wasn't unusual for a seller to contact him with pieces taken from conflict zones, their sale meant to fund groups or organizations whose only promise was carnage. Never once had he knowingly dealt with them. More than that, his refusal to do so encouraged others to decline their offers as well. This either made a sale impossible or drove down the price so far it was hardly worth selling. Of course, that's when less scrupulous buyers swooped in.

Either way, he wouldn't destroy this memorial tonight. Not if he could help it. It took only one stab of the digging bar to gain purchase between the lid and tomb. Harry leaned on the bar, applying steady pressure to try and jar the top loose. Bouncing up and down chanced breaking the stone lid. He put every pound of his entirely average frame on the bar, yet the lid didn't budge. Then he sat on the ground, pushed both feet against the tomb and pulled down on the digging bar until the bar ripped into his fingers.

The lid moved. With a screech and a thud, it slid up and over a few inches. Harry was nearly impaled by the digging bar as it slipped free and crashed to the ground beside him. He jumped up to find the now-open lid revealed a bottomless dark inside the memorial. Nothing but dust and emptiness.

Grabbing the bar and sliding it in vertically, Harry pushed and pulled in alternating heaves until the lid opened enough for him to get a better look. At nothing at all. The memorial was completely empty. No body, no books, no messages.

The next tomb over had a name inscribed on the top. *WENIVER*. Judging from the ornamental decorations, it belonged to a woman. The crowbar worked its magic again, ripping out dirt and debris until Harry could force the digging bar into place. He levered the bar inch by inch until the lid cracked open. Bones gleamed a dull yellow-ivory under his headlamp. Most of the small skeleton had remained intact. Silver bracelets encircled both wrists. A matching necklace dangled between the ribs and rested on her spine.

Harry swallowed, his throat suddenly dry as the tomb. Metal outlasted human remains by far. That jewelry was a good place to check for Geoffrey's message. He reached in, then paused, a nagging thought flickering in his head, a phrase he couldn't let go of. Geoffrey's message said *'The true man behind Arthur's legend points to a sacred message.'*

Initially he had assumed this meant Artorius himself served as a marker, one step on a longer journey. Except writers used their words both directly and indirectly, either to give direction or to hint at the truth hidden between the lines. If Geoffrey had wanted to deliver a message to Theobald or anyone else after his death, would he have chosen obscure words, ripe for misunderstanding? No. He'd have been literal.

Points. That single word grabbed Harry's ear and held tight. Going against every professional instinct in his body, Harry went back over and looked at the tomb of Artorius. Latin inscriptions ran across the top, odes to his military greatness alongside the standard biographical details. However, one item stood out. Or rather, the lack of it.

Artorius had served during Diocletian's rule. As Diocletian had been the last emperor to persecute Christians, Harry wasn't surprised at the lack of Christian religious symbols on Artorius's tomb. In fact, there wasn't a single one. The only etching he found that stood out from the rest looked an awful lot like an arrow. Pointing back to *Weniver's* tomb.

"Weniver," Harry said softly. He said the name out loud again, then paused. He added a terrible French accent to the voice in his head. Now it rhymed with *Revere,* like the American silversmith. *Weniveer.* Which was one step away from something much more familiar.

Guinevere. The very name he needed to locate.

It made sense. "Let's see if I'm right." He used the digging bar to further lever Weniver's lid off. A shiver ran through his torso as her bones fully came to light, not fear or regret, but something in between. Nearly two thousand years ago this skeleton had been a daughter, a sister and a mother. Her impact had been tremendous to those people, to the world itself, and if Harry was right, to generations onward throughout history as Arthur's wife. Now she was a pile of dusty bones.

It'll happen to you one day too. He felt around the tomb's interior, avoiding the bones as he reached gingerly for her silver jewelry. Harry took hold of a bracelet between thumb and forefinger and pulled.

The entire forearm disintegrated. The metal emerged from a hazy cloud, sparkling under his red light. He checked both sides, running his fingernails along the surfaces to be sure. Nothing. No writing, etchings or anything other than filigreed designs along the edges. Same with the bracelet on her other arm, which he managed to get off without it evaporating. That left the necklace, currently tangled in a couple of ribs. This piece of jewelry was made from a sturdy chain with a stone dangling from it, the facets exploding in a cacophony of red light reflecting across the tomb. It had to be a diamond. Then Harry lifted it closer and realized two forces were responsible for the dazzling display. His red headlamp, and the ruby he held. The combination of red light and red-tinted stone painted everything in a ten-foot radius with scarlet brilliance.

His heart sank. Nothing else was in the tomb. No messages, no books, no clue as to what Geoffrey had meant by pointing him here. He'd been so sure. He turned and clumsily banged his arm against the tomb, lost his grip on the bracelets and necklace, and tried to grab them as they fell back into the coffin. He missed the bracelets and his hand sideswiped Weniver's polished skull, sending it up and out of the tomb like a soccer ball.

It settled in the far corner. Harry grimaced. Disturbing the dead wasn't good, mainly because it left evidence someone had been poking around, but also because you never knew what vengeful spirits might be watching. He arranged the bracelets back where he'd found them, laid the necklace aside, then stepped over to the corner and grabbed the skull. Gently, he set it back on the brick of a pillow in Weniver's tomb, angling it to one side so it wouldn't roll. But the block was square and flat, and the skull rolled away each time he tried to position it. This thing was the worst pillow ever. Who in their right mind would use this? The damn thing looked like a cigar box.

His hands went still. A box. What did boxes do? They *opened*.

He gently laid the skull aside. Nobody would have chosen a box for Weniver's eternal pillow unless it served a specific purpose.

Geoffrey had been a senior member of the Catholic church. He could have gained access to the tomb, and once inside, it wouldn't have been impossible to open – Harry had done it.

He took a deep breath, pausing to look over his shoulder. Did he hear anything? What first sounded like whispers turned out to be nothing more than the plastic tarp drifting on air currents. He turned back and reached for the hard little pillow, which turned out to be lighter than expected. He lifted it closer to his headlamp and noted a thin break running lengthwise around the circumference. *It's a lid.* He rattled it like a child holding a present. There was something inside.

A sudden screeching filled the chamber. Harry jumped and the box fell back into the tomb. Twisting, he managed to kick the crowbar away far enough that it banged off Artorius's tomb. The tarp was open. Two men stood in front of him, one holding a sword aloft. A blinding flashlight came on, forcing Harry to cover his eyes and duck down.

"Is that him?"

The words were Arabic. A response came back in the same language. "It is."

The sound of a man spitting. "*Rafida.*"

Harry peered through his fingers, one eye still closed. *Rejector?* A derogatory term Sunni Muslims used for Shia Muslims. Harry wasn't even Arabic. Instinct kicked in, and Harry shouted in English. "What the hell are you talking about? I work here. Turn that light off."

Islam had two main branches, Shia and Sunni. The vast majority of Muslims today practiced Sunni Islam, with violent conflict in certain parts of the world between adherents of the two branches. If this guy thought Harry followed Shia Islam, chances were he was a Sunni with no good intentions.

"It is him," the second man said, the one holding the flashlight. He stood behind the guy with the sword, who was now a dark outline silhouetted against the light.

The sword holder spoke next. *"Allahu Akbar. Almawt lilshiyea!"* *Death to Shia.*

Harry threw himself backwards, scrabbling to move away from a threat he couldn't see. This lunatic thought he was Shia, and he wanted to kill Harry because he didn't follow the right branch of Islam. *Of all the reasons to attack someone raiding a tomb, this idiot tries to decapitate me for being the wrong religion.* Harry hadn't been inside a mosque in ages.

Harry kept one eye closed as he rolled away. A breath later, sparks erupted as the sword slammed down where Harry had been. Harry kept twisting, losing and regaining sight of the madman until he butted up against the tomb of Artorius. Metal clanged as Harry rolled over the crowbar, grabbing for it as he covered his face with one hand to ward off the flashlight's glare. Then the strangest thing happened. The man with the flashlight shouted, "Don't kill him!"

The maniac ignored him, lifted his sword and charged. Harry gripped the crowbar, pulled back and threw it, the metal bar flipping end over end as it buzzed past the swordsman's ear before smacking flashlight man square in the chest. He grunted and fell, the light bouncing wildly away. Harry dove at the swordsman's knees, cutting them out from under him to send him tumbling. Harry went after the flashlight as the swordsman lost his weapon, crashing into Artorius's tomb with a grisly snapping sound.

Harry grabbed the flashlight, leapt up and flicked off his red headlamp. He pointed the flashlight at the other man and everything made sense. It was the assailant from Wales who worked for Altin Cana.

The man flinched under the bright light before he charged. Harry flicked the light off and tossed it, darting to one side as the man barreled past in the darkness, missing him by a foot. Harry had kept one of his eyes mostly closed during the encounter, preserving his night vision. The other man was running blind. Moving on his toes, Harry circled around back of him as the man pulled out a cell phone.

Harry closed in.

The phone's light burst to life. Harry ducked low, crouched like a baseball catcher. The other man spun around, never seeing Harry as he exploded from below with an uppercut at the man's exposed chin.

Harry's knuckles connected with the pain of a direct shot, so pure the man actually lifted off his feet before crash-landing on the stone floor. Harry checked for and found a strong pulse. *Good.* The guy would wake up sore as hell, but he'd survive. Relief turned to angst when he flicked on his head lamp and moved to check on the swordsman, whose collision with Artorius's tomb hadn't sounded good.

The man lay where he'd fallen, head at a grotesque angle against the tomb's base. His eyes shined dull in the red light. Harry stopped. Why was the floor shining? It wasn't water. This place was dry as, well, a tomb. The liquid flowed from beneath the tomb, running under the fallen man's chest – *oh*.

The man's own sword protruded from the middle of his back. He'd been impaled on it when Harry took his legs out and the man had crashed into Artorius's tomb. The metal point sprouted from his back, slick with blood. Harry stepped back to dry ground. He turned to one side, bent over and emptied his stomach.

So much for not leaving evidence behind. Harry ran the back of one hand across his mouth. Death and he weren't the closest of acquaintances. Now, another artifact hunt had produced another body. He hadn't tried to kill this man, of course. But the guy had come at him with a sword even as the Cana man had told him to back off. Harry bent down to study the dead man's face. *Who are you?*

The dead man's clothing and trimmed beard said European, as had his accented Arabic. He could have been hired to shift the odds against Harry, outnumber him two to one. But why had he accused Harry of being a Shiite Muslim? Perhaps the Cana man had hired him here in Croatia and fed him lies about Harry to stoke the hatred that burned in his heart.

In the end, it didn't matter. Harry had killed the man. Until last week he'd never taken another life. Now two men had died by his hands. Harry noted the trembling had already subsided. After the last time, it had been worse. Harry had been forced to find a park bench and sit with his arms huddled around his chest until the shaking eventually passed. The tremors reverberating through his psyche had taken much longer.

He took a deep breath. His immediate concern had to be getting the heck out of here. With the wooden pillow in tow. He stood, circled around Weniver's tomb and leaned over her bones. He gently lifted out the hard pillow-like object. It was smooth to touch, the wood sealed with some sort of paint or oil that had helped preserve it over time. He shook it once more to confirm the soft rattling from inside, then turned the box over to find a small metal hasp. Harry opened the latch, which freed a drawer that he slid open to reveal a single folded sheet of vellum.

Harry grabbed his messenger bag and tucked the vellum sheet into a folder inside it, then replaced the now-empty wooden pillow in Weniver's tomb, wriggling it back and forth until her skull finally rested more or less securely atop it. He paused, looking down on the likely inspiration for King Arthur's true love. Geoffrey of Monmouth, using his first initial in combination with Weniver's surname to craft *Guinevere*. One more way Geoffrey's name would survive the ages.

The Cana family man behind him stirred, groaning softly. Harry had little time to escape. He took a step toward the exit, stopped, then turned back toward Weniver's tomb. *Sorry about this, Weniver.*

The Cana man was heavier than he looked. Harry grabbed him under each arm, the man's heels scraping across the floor as Harry dragged him to Weniver's tomb, taking seconds to slide Weniver's bones to one side before hauling the man up and over the ledge to dump him in a heap. The digging bar helped Harry lever her tomb lid back into place, though he left a crack near the bottom for air. He didn't want the guy to suffocate, just be stuck under the heavy lid until someone found him in the morning. Maybe Arnold Schwarzenegger could push the lid off from inside. This guy couldn't. Harry moved to the hanging tarp, leaning close to the opening and listening before he slipped out and headed for the surface.

A different world waited beyond the dark underground. The church nave seemed an explosion of light and normalcy. Electric candles burned in wall sconces. Two floodlights brought the pair of tombs surrounding the altar to life, while red-carpet runners crossing the room deadened footsteps to silence. A single worshipper sat in one pew, hands crossed and head bowed. Harry kept his head down and glanced down the lone hallway he passed to find a single dark-robed holy man in a priest's collar. He quickened his step through the heavy entrance doors.

The cool night air wrapped him in a welcome embrace, a cleansing tonic for the stuffy tomb. Deep lung-fulls tinged with salt from the Adriatic helped him push the darkness from underneath St. Domnius away. Harry melted into pedestrian traffic as he headed for his car. Now he had a message to decipher.

Chapter Twelve

Split, Croatia

The café on the outskirts of Split was filled with diners, drinkers and couples huddled close together. Harry took a table inside with his back to the wall and a clear view of the door. The ancient vellum sheet sitting in front of him on the table attracted no attention from the waitress as she dropped off Harry's coffee, though he covered it until she walked away. Not that he thought she could read Latin, but Rose Leroux's warning ran through his head at full volume.

Except you couldn't distrust everyone all the time. Especially people he'd known for decades. Rose, for one. Vincent and Joey as well. He could trust the Morellos, even if Joey had a problem with Harry right now. Vincent took the old-world Italian view on things like loyalty, which meant Joey did too. Harry picked up his phone and dialed. It would be early in Brooklyn, though Joey rarely failed to answer calls when men were in the field. The phone beeped three times in his ear before a groggy voice answered. "Harry?"

"Things are happening here."

Joey was instantly on alert. "You run into trouble?"

"Two men. I knew one of them from Wales. The other was new." He recounted his trip to Split, his search of the levels beneath St. Domnius, and the fatal encounter with a Cana family associate and the unknown man. "Chances are the Cana guy is stuck down there until the work crew shows up tomorrow."

"You still have the book?" Joey asked. Harry said he did. "You can't stay in Croatia. Dead bodies attract attention. You should get out of the country – we don't have any friends in Croatia to help if you're arrested."

"It's not just the Cana guy," Harry said. "The priest coming to your father for information makes me worry. Geoffrey's message said *'three forces conspire to end your quest.'* What if the church is one of those three?"

"Normally I'd say you're nuts. Now, I don't know." Joey's voice grew tight. "There's a problem for the family here at home. Word is the Canas are looking to make a move on our territory, take over our card games and video machines. Our two biggest cleaners are close to their neighborhood."

Money laundering was a vital cog in the Morello machine. So-called cleaners took illicit profits from operations such as the gambling machines and card games in Morello-owned bars and social clubs, then ran the cash through legitimate businesses. Dirty money went in the back door, clean money came out the front.

"That part of town has the highest drive-through drug traffic," Joey continued. "Wannabes from the suburbs and bankers from downtown come by to get their fix."

Harry never touched the stuff, stayed as far away as he could, but he knew drugs brought in huge amounts of cash for the Morellos. They were gangsters, after all. With that much cash moving around, someone else inevitably came looking to get in on the action. Someone like Altin Cana, whose territory ran right up against Morello turf. Actual railroad tracks defined the line of demarcation, and encroachment on either side was not tolerated.

"It wouldn't be the first time they blustered about pushing onto your streets." *Your streets.* Not *ours.* Harry wasn't a Morello, no matter how Vincent viewed him.

"This is more than usual," Joey said. "I have the family and our crews on alert. We can't spare a single man right now. We're keeping a strong presence on the street. Maybe that keeps this from getting out of control, unless those Cana punks go too far. If that happens, I'll handle it." Joey yawned. When he continued, his words were softer. "He'd never admit it, but my father is getting too old for this stuff. I've gotta step up this time."

Handling it meant broken bones if things got tense, Harry knew. Corpses in the East River came next. "You'll handle it," Harry said. "Vincent knows that. Need me to come back?" *Please say no.* Geoffrey's trail beckoned.

"Not with you so close to figuring this out," Joey said. "Right now, I can't send anyone to help. A guy coming at you with a sword? That's crazy. And what was that nonsense about your religion? I haven't seen you go near a mosque or a church, well, ever."

That sounded more like the old Joey, the guy Harry had grown up with. "I think that Cana guy found a Sunni extremist over here and hired him. All he needed to say was that I practice Shia Islam. That's enough for a die-hard Sunni to want me dead. I'll tell you all about it when I get back."

"After you find what Geoffrey of Monmouth left behind," Joey said. "What did you find in this coffin?"

Harry described the false headrest in Weniver's tomb. Or *Guinevere*, as he now thought of her. "A message from Geoffrey. Listen to this." He glanced around before he looked down to the vellum sheet. "It's another message from Geoffrey to his servant, Theobald."

"Does it say where to go next?"

"Not directly," Harry said. "It's a story. In Latin. Listen." He spoke softly, almost whispering into the phone.

Theobald, I pray you find this. If so, the genesis of my long sojourn will be clear. What drove me from Wales was a fortunate meeting with an elderly priest passing through Monmouth, venturing to pay homage to the Gallic Roman Dionysus, martyred for his faith. Arthur's tale springs from the priest's recounting of his quest, a journey that would condemn mankind to darkness from the cloaked enemy bringing an illusory malady.

The priest took ill. On his deathbed, he entrusted me to carry on his quest. An evil quest, forged in God's name. I chose to do the reverse. Doing so brought me to Diocletian's estate, though I fear the three forces close behind, determined to finish the priest's effort. I cannot tarry lest I too fall victim.

Know this. Excalibur is real. It will bring the forces to their knees and vanquish the illusion told to us all. Look south from the cone in the Gallic church of Dionysus. Do this, or an unseen darkness will cover men for ages.

Harry fell silent. Joey was breathing on the other end, but he didn't say anything.

"What the hell does that mean?" Joey finally asked. "A sick priest came to Geoffrey's town and told him about Dionysus? Isn't that a god?"

"A Greek one," Harry said.

Joey's words quickened. "Then Geoffrey decides he doesn't like what this priest is up to and takes a different path. What's this priest doing in Monmouth anyway? He must have known Geoffrey."

"That's what jumped out at me first. This priest makes a long journey to Monmouth. He connects with Geoffrey and tells him his story. Why? He *needs* to tell this story."

"Why would he need to?"

"It's possible what he had to say couldn't be shared with just anyone." Harry paused. "The priest was on a pilgrimage of some kind. Maybe for the church. He falls ill or gets hurt, so he decides Geoffrey is the man to take over. Whatever he told Geoffrey frightened him enough that Geoffrey took over the quest to be sure it *failed*."

"Then all of this somehow ties in to Excalibur," Joey said. "I've heard that story before."

"Either King Arthur's sword or the sword of Lucius Artorius Castus. It's hard to say."

"These mysterious forces Geoffrey keeps mentioning," Joey said. "He talks like they're ghosts that can appear out of thin air and kill people."

"The more I read about Geoffrey," Harry said, "the less I think he's a typical religious man. His most famous story isn't about God, at least on the face of it. It's about kings and knights. Arthur battles Saxons and Romans, not Islamic armies. Then a fellow priest dies in his town and entrusts him with a holy journey of some kind. Geoffrey chooses to thwart it instead. Whatever this priest told Geoffrey shook him to his core."

"What do you think the priest told him?"

Harry tapped his fingers on the tabletop. "I'm not sure. Here's what I do know. First, Geoffrey was afraid. The *three forces* coming after him are somehow still a threat. The priest must have known these three groups, or whatever they are. He may even have been part of them."

"The priest viewed them as allies, while Geoffrey saw them as threats."

"Yes," Harry said. "Geoffrey chose to work against the priest, which made these three his enemies. Second, Geoffrey used this story as inspiration for his Arthur legend. It also tells me Geoffrey hadn't written the book yet, but expected to survive long enough to write it. Still, he left this letter for Theobald to find. Why? I think he knew that even if he succeeded on this quest, these forces would still exist. The notes are a backup for Theobald to finish the quest if Geoffrey didn't succeed."

"Hold on," Joey said. "Even if he finds Excalibur? The sword is supposed to vanquish them. Geoffrey said so."

"It could be that finding Excalibur ends the threat, or defeats whatever immediate purpose these three have, though it doesn't end it."

"Makes sense," Joey said. "What's it have to do with the *Gallic Roman Dionysus*?"

The waitress seated a couple beside him. Harry dropped his voice. He'd been waiting for Joey to ask about this part. "I have an idea. I need to take a trip to see if I'm right."

"Where?"

"Listen to my theory first. Tell me if it doesn't make sense." As Harry outlined his theory, it almost felt like old times again, when he and Joey were tight. Joey might have been a gangster's son, but he was nothing like the stereotype in movies. He'd been to most of New York's museums with Harry at one point or another before things changed. He could call out any holes in Harry's theory. "Geoffrey calls out the *Gallic Roman Dionysus*. The thing is, Dionysus is a Greek god, the one in charge of wine, partying, and fertility. Romans basically stole the god and called him Bacchus."

Harry chuckled. "Bacchus, or Dionysus, loved a party. Funny thing, though. The Romans also had a *Saint* Bacchus."

"A man named Bacchus who was martyred? That's usually how it happened."

"I remember reading about him in school. He was a Roman Christian soldier killed by the Roman emperor Galerius. The same Galerius who became emperor after Diocletian abdicated. Not sure if it's related at all, though Galerius and Diocletian persecuted Christians more than almost any other emperors."

"Including killing their own soldiers," Joey said. "But what does it prove? That both of them hated Christians. The name thing could be a coincidence."

"True," Harry said. "Only Saint Bacchus ended up as more than just a forgotten name. Several countries have churches dedicated in his honor."

"Tell me one of them is in Germany."

Joey was sharp. "The most famous one is in Istanbul," Harry said, making him wait. "Or Constantinople, as it was called then. The church is called Little Hagia Sofia, but that's not the only Roman-era church dedicated to St. Bacchus. There's another one." He waited a beat. "It's in Germany."

"I *knew* it. Gallic Roman. Which was a Roman province for a long time."

"Trier Cathedral in Germany. Originally built," here he consulted hastily scribbled notes on a napkin, "around 270 A.D. It stood during Artorius's lifetime. The more important fact? The church honors several Roman gods, including Bacchus."

"I thought Rome turned to Christianity then."

"They did," Harry said. "Rome was nothing if not astute. Part of the reason the empire lasted so long is because they tolerated all religions as long as subjects also honored Roman gods. Having churches built in honor of multiple deities isn't unheard of."

"You're going to Germany to see it."

"The *Gallic church of Dionysus*. Or Bacchus, if you're Roman. I find the cone from Geoffrey's message, look south, and go from there."

"What's the cone?"

Harry watched as a waiter hurried past, drinks balanced precariously on his tray. A fan twirled slowly overhead. "I have no idea."

Joey didn't pick up on his despair. "You'll figure it out." His next words caught Harry off guard like a right hook. "Your old man would have. I bet you do too."

The shadow inside Harry darkened. "I hope so." He fell silent as the memories returned like a movie only he could see. The final time he'd seen his father, Fred Fox was readying to leave Brooklyn for Rome. He had packed lightly as always, everything he needed in a single bag. Harry had walked into their shared apartment to find Fred sitting at his desk reading a letter.

"When are you leaving?" Harry had asked.

"Momentarily." His father's response came from far away, as though whatever he was reading had him entirely transfixed. Fred folded the letter and put it in a lockbox when Harry came over, though not before he caught a glimpse of the writing. Arabic.

"Is everything okay?" Fred asked.

"Yes," Harry said. His father spoke Arabic, a result of his relationship with Harry's mother, the one who provided the quarter-Pakistani part of Harry's makeup. Fred had connections around the globe; some had to speak Arabic. "I'm fine."

Harry recalled every detail of their conversation. Had he known it would be their final one, he would have said more.

He pushed the memory away. "My dad was searching for a lead on something," Harry said to Joey. "Not going to a soccer game. There was no reason for him to be near the stadium."

"He could have been meeting someone. Or just passing by. Chances are we'll never know. The cops never found any leads on the hooligans who attacked him."

That was the worst of it. Not only did Harry have no idea why Fred had gone to Rome, it made zero sense for his father to end up near a soccer stadium during a big match between Italy and Russia, a nation whose fanbase was notorious for hooliganism and violence. Roving bands of Russian fans routinely came looking for trouble, traveling to away matches with one thing in mind: fighting. With anyone they saw. Other teams' fans, people with dark skin – it didn't matter. They wanted to brawl, and a mid-fifties man walking alone had been an easy target.

"They never found anything other than a ripped shirt to identify who did it," Harry said. "The shirt could have belonged to anyone." His father's body had been found on a street, a ripped shirt with Cyrillic writing on it still clenched in one hand. He had been stabbed once in the heart. The case remained unsolved.

"Your father kept things private," Joey said. "His past, that amulet he always wore. My father can be that way too." Joey paused, then continued after a long wait. "Accepting it is hard. For me, you, any of us. I gotta do better at it."

"We're all trying," Harry said. "Your father has our backs, that's what I know."

"Yeah," Joey said. "He does. And I got yours."

Another long wait as Harry felt the world shift back to its normal axis. "Thanks, man."

"No problem," Joey said. "Life's funny. You know my old man never even told me how he met your father? I can't count how many times he said he owes his life to Fred Fox, and that's it. Nothing else. Seems Fred wanted that kept quiet too."

"Vincent Morello doesn't say more than necessary."

"That's the truth. Maybe if you ask he'll tell you, now that Fred is gone. Maybe not. You know us Italians. We take things to the grave."

"I'll ask when I get back," Harry said. "After I make us some more money."

"That book is worth a pile of money. Come home now and forget about this hunt. Excalibur's not real. It's a story, a damn good one. You bring back the original copy of Geoffrey's book and Rose will handle the rest. Then you can ask my father how they met. I'd like to hear the story too."

"That's the smart play." Harry considered it for a second. No longer. "Which I can't make right now. You know what could be at the end of this?"

"No idea."

"Me neither. Which is why I have to keep going. Come on, Joey, admit it. You want to know as badly as I do."

Joey's reply was muted. "Not worth dying over, Harry."

It made sense. This could be nothing more than a dead end, a paranoid priest who was ill and had lost his wits. No matter what Harry hoped, chances were Excalibur wasn't real, and King Arthur sure as hell had never lived. Even in the world of antiquities hunting, this was a long shot.

Except that was what he did. Same as his father. Fred Fox had given his son many things, taught him countless lessons, most of which Harry remembered. One ingrained in Harry from a young age had come directly from Fred: Be curious. The world's a big place filled with mystery. Get out and experience it.

That was what Fred would have done. Harry intended to do the same. Even though Fred's journey had ended in violence. Harry wouldn't let the same thing happen to him.

"I'll be careful," Harry said. "I'll finish this and show you what I find at the end. Over beers, in Brooklyn. You're buying."

Joey grumbled. "Dammit, Harry. I should have known you'd say that." He sighed, a long and drawn-out affair. "You know what I have to do now."

A hollow formed in Harry's stomach. He wouldn't. Joey couldn't tell him to come back, to cancel the trip and get on a plane home. Well, he could, since Harry technically worked for Joey, but Harry was getting closer by the hour. "Don't do this to me, Joey."

"Do what?" Then Joey laughed. "Hold on. You think I'm gonna tell you to come back? As if you'd listen. Come on. You're Fred Fox's son. I'd sooner root for the Red Sox than tell you what to do in the field." Harry couldn't think of a single thing to say. "You wouldn't listen anyway, so I'll do the smart thing. You're getting up to your neck in it. Somebody's gotta watch your back. It should be me, but with the Cana *bastardos* making noise about taking our turf, I can't leave town. I'm sending Dom. He's sharp. You can use a guy like him right now."

Dom Grilli was a good man to have in your corner. Quiet, reserved, he thought before speaking, and was one of the few Morello crew members to treat Harry straight up from day one. None of the 'Hey, Aladdin, where's the genie?' jokes most of them threw out. "You're right, I could."

"He can leave by tomorrow afternoon. I'll make sure he's ready for whatever comes next."

Harry tapped at his phone, checking for the next flight to Germany. "I can get a flight to Germany in the morning, check things out and be ready when he lands." The muted din of conversation had grown during this call, covering Harry's words enough that he didn't worry about anyone overhearing. "You're right about one thing, Joey. This is no joke. I think the Cana man will be stuck in jail when they find him with that corpse, so he's out of the picture."

"Only it's not him you're really worried about," Joey said. "It's whoever comes next."

The three forces. Were they truly still close behind, even a millennium later?

A television behind the bar caught his eye, a *Breaking News* chyron scrolling across the bottom. "Hold on a second," Harry said. His gaze narrowed. Was that…? *Damn.* A female reporter stood inside what looked like Diocletian's Palace. Red and blue lights flashed behind her. Harry didn't need to understand Croatian to know what she said. The body bag a medic carried into what he could now see was St. Domnius said enough.

"Joey, I have to go. I'll be in touch."

Harry threw some bills on the table and stood, heading for the exit. Blaring sirens filled the air as he hurried to his car. He kept his head down as he stepped into the road without looking and was nearly run down by a rumbling full-sized pickup truck. A horn blared as Harry ducked back to safety, warm air lifting his shirt as the pickup barreled past. Of course he'd almost walked out in front of the only damn pickup in Split.

He slipped into his rental car and drove toward the airport as another memory of his father intruded on his thoughts. His final image of a coffin being lowered into the ground as rain beaded on the black metal lid.

Chapter Thirteen

On approach to Split, Croatia

The ground rumbled beneath Aaron Shephard's feet. The flight attendant informed the passengers they were ready for landing in Croatia. Seated along the aisle, he kept his eyes closed, hands folded on his lap. He didn't really hear the voice or feel the vibrations. He was thinking about what came next.

Aaron was on an inbound flight from Greece to Croatia because after his three-man team had learned Geoffrey of Monmouth's tomb had been uncovered in Wales, he'd decided to play a hunch. Aaron had gotten lucky when Hiram had found the surveillance footage from St. Mary's Priory, though whoever had opened Geoffrey's tomb had been cautious, keeping his face hidden, seemingly hyper-alert for security cameras with every step. The few times the unidentified man had passed by one of the cameras at St. Mary's Priory, his head had stayed down, face obscured. All anyone could see was a man of average height, with dark hair and tan skin. He might be Middle Eastern. He might not be. It was hard to say.

Aaron's team had used their connections in the Muslim world to identify the unconscious man found in St. Mary's Priory, the one who had scuffled with the intruder. His name was Gabriel, and he worked for a Brooklyn gangster named Altin Cana who was ethnic Albanian.

"He must be Muslim," Mo had said. "Let me make a few calls."

Phones rang, conversations occurred, and within a day Altin Cana had given a Brooklyn imam a name, a photograph, and the best chance in centuries to finally put a stop to this ancient danger. All Aaron had to do now was find Harry Fox, learn what he'd taken from Geoffrey's grave, and then do whatever it took to be certain that trail vanished.

Harry worked for a rival Brooklyn crime family, this one less willing to cooperate with the spiritual advisor who visited them seeking information. Turns out Vincent Morello had more backbone than Altin Cana. Vincent had made it clear Harry Fox had his protection, and Aaron's team couldn't frighten Vincent Morello into cooperating, leaving Aaron no choice. Find Harry Fox and handle it on his own.

Normally Aaron would take his time, certain Harry Fox couldn't stay hidden forever. But Harry had uncovered a prize that had eluded Aaron's organization for centuries. Aaron had played a hunch and booked a flight to Croatia. He had visited Diocletian's Palace several years ago. Aided by a letter from the Vatican, he had been granted permission to analyze the tomb of the Roman military leader Lucious Artorius Castus.

In the past century, the idea that Artorius had served as the inspiration for Geoffrey's legendary king had gained traction. Armed with the Pope's royal seal, he and a consulting archeologist had spent less than an hour underground obtaining dozens of pictures. The analysis had turned up nothing unexpected. A body, fragments of what used to be clothing, assorted metal objects. None of it stood out.

Yet for some reason Artorius stuck in his head, refusing to give way. Too many unanswered questions and lingering suspicions that Artorius had ties of which only Geoffrey had been aware. Aaron had let it sit, keeping the possibility in the back of his mind. Until now. This could all be a waste of time, but coming here was better than sitting in Athens waiting for Harry Fox to show up on their radar.

Thirty minutes after the Air Croatia flight landed in Split, Aaron hit the gas pedal on his rental car and aimed toward Diocletian's

Palace, acutely aware the vehicle he drove was bigger than anything you'd drive in Athens. A massive American-made pickup truck was the only vehicle available at the small airport and he didn't have time to waste. Aaron gripped the wheel with both hands as he navigated the successively narrower streets leading to the palace, nearly crushing some guy who walked out in front of him near a restaurant. The truck's horn reverberated off the old buildings as the pedestrian jumped for cover between parked cars.

That's when Aaron heard the sirens. He turned the next corner to find blue and red lights swirling outside a palace entrance and two *POLICIJA* cars going through a narrow gate. Aaron swerved into the first parking spot he saw and followed them, heedless of the tourists he jostled and shoved on the way. The cars stopped outside the towering cathedral. Three other police vehicles were parked in front of St. Domnius. His hands tingled, cool and sharp in the night air. *Was Harry Fox inside?*

Aaron faded into a shadow and made a phone call, speaking quietly before clicking off. Minutes later his phone buzzed. The caller spoke a single sentence, his words Italian. "He's waiting for you."

Aaron slipped the phone into his pocket and walked up to the cathedral's main door. A wide-eyed priest stood waiting. "Aaron?"

"Thank you for seeing me, Father." Aaron slipped past the smaller man into the church, noting the gilded decorations above an altar framed by a pair of marble tombs. Exactly as he remembered it from his previous visit. A uniformed police officer approached before he could go any further and lifted a hand.

"Stop."

"He is with the Church," the father said in English. "Please, let him pass." The officer hesitated, then stood back. Only after they were out of earshot did the priest speak again. "This is most unusual. Our Cardinal has never personally called me."

Aaron's call had been to leverage one of his contacts in the Pope's inner circle to place a call to St. Domnius at once, obtaining whatever assistance Aaron needed. He had precious little time to find out what had happened. It could be nothing more than a coincidence. Or, it could be the break he needed to finish their mission.

"What happened here?"

"A man was murdered in our tombs," the father said. "Another was left injured and trapped in a sarcophagus."

Aaron stopped and touched the father's arm. "Which tomb? Is it Artorius?"

"It was not Lucius Artorius Castus. The adjacent tomb was disturbed. No others."

"Take me to it." Aaron looked over his shoulder at the police officer, who was watching them with interest. "We must act before police secure the scene." He looked back down at the priest. "The Vatican will be displeased if I fail."

The man stood taller. "Follow me."

Aaron followed him down a wide set of condemnable stairs, through the damp underground air and around several turns before the priest stopped at an entrance covered by a long stretch of heavy plastic sheeting.

"It is through there," he said, pointing at the hanging sheet. "The tombs are under repair. The crime was discovered after a visitor reported a bloody footprint on the walkway."

That explained the yellow crime scene tape they'd passed. A pair of flashlights moved around inside the room, the beams like fireflies in fog as Aaron watched through the plastic. At that moment a police officer stepped out of a gap in the draped plastic and walked toward them.

"I need to get in there," Aaron whispered. "Distract these guys. I don't care how."

"I'm sorry, Father." The officer removed his hat, holding it in both hands as he approached the priest. Silver glinted between the open top buttons on his uniform. A silver cross. "To think—"

The priest reacted admirably. "Officer." He grabbed the

policeman's wrist. "I think there is trouble upstairs, in the chapel. Please, come quickly."

The officer's face hardened. "More trouble?"

"Shouting. I thought I heard a gunshot." The priest's voice was pained. "I ran here to find you. Please, hurry."

The officer turned and shouted for his partner, who came out at a dead run, one hand on his pistol. The two men disappeared down the hallway, leaving Aaron and the priest alone.

"Shout if you see anyone," Aaron said. "I cannot be disturbed." He didn't give the priest a chance to argue, turning his phone's light on as he slipped through the gap in the plastic and went straight to the open sarcophagus, recalling that Artorius lay in the next tomb down from this one. The lid sat askance, the darkness inside resisting his flashlight's glare. Why this one? What about it had attracted the intruder's attention while Artorius remained undisturbed? He read the faded script. *WENIVER.*

A woman's tomb, based on the decorations. Aaron shone his light along its sides, and his light glinted on a puddle. He shone the light directly at it, and the deadly scene came into full view. Red blood, almost black in the darkness. A man's body was slumped by the tomb with a sword protruding from his back. Who killed men with a *sword*?

He blinked. This dead man didn't matter now. What had the priest said? The unconscious man taken for medical care had been in Weniver's tomb. Sporadic dust motes glinted and then multiplied when Aaron leaned into the open tomb to find dull white bones. He whispered a prayer, asking for forgiveness, then reached in.

The corpse's smaller bones had been crushed into shards now strewn inside the coffin, though most of the larger bones remained intact. Her skull rested near the top, and it moved when Aaron bumped it, rolling off what looked like a pillow or headrest and then stopping. He leaned closer. It wasn't a headrest; it was a brick. What was a brick doing in here?

Aaron picked it up and discovered it was made of wood. It was a support, which the head had likely rested on. Carved wood, not particularly smooth, yet much lighter than it should have been. The priest's voice sounded from across the room.

"They are coming back." Aaron looked up to find the father had poked his head in. "I hear them on the steps."

Whatever had drawn the intruder in here eluded him now, the key to understanding this, to possibly revealing –

The small wooden block fell apart in his hands and half of it clattered to the ground. It took him a second to realize what he was holding now. *It's a drawer.* The block had a recessed drawer in the middle, carved so exquisitely as to be invisible unless you knew it was there. The drawer was *empty.*

Which suggested whoever had killed this man and broken open Weniver's tomb had found the drawer and taken its contents with them.

Aaron collected the drawer pieces and shoved them into his pockets as he ran back into the hall. He made it to the priest's side a half-second before the policemen reappeared, rounding a corner and looking directly at the priest.

The officer who had spoken to them earlier now had a stronger tone. "We found no disturbance. What did you say you heard?"

The priest raised a hand to his lips. "What sounded like a gunshot. I was so certain." He lowered his head. "This night has been so stressful."

The officer's hard gaze melted. "It's no trouble, Father. I cannot blame you after what happened here."

Aaron looped one arm over the smaller man's shoulders. "I will take you to your rooms, Father." Prodding the Father to move more quickly than one might expect, Aaron led him away in silence. Together they ascended the weathered stone stairs to the main floor, where Aaron opened the door to a flurry of activity. A half-dozen cops milled about the chapel, with several more walking through the front door as he watched. No one seemed to notice their presence.

"Where is your office?" Aaron asked.

"This way." They crossed a hallway and moments later turned into a small, spartan office. Aaron shut the door behind them.

Aaron spoke rapidly. "How do I get out of here without drawing attention?"

The priest pointed over his shoulder, to the office's door. "Turn left, go until the hall ends, then turn right. The last door on your left leads out to an alley behind the church."

Aaron turned to leave. He stopped after one step. "The injured man. Who found him?"

"I did. After the bloody footprints were reported. I went to the tombs and heard a voice calling from inside Weniver's tomb. I was able to lever it open and free the man."

Aaron moved closer. The priest stepped back so quickly he bumped against a chair.

"His name. He must have told you or the medical team. What was it?"

"Yes." The father recovered, standing up straight against Aaron's unintentional onslaught. "He was American, and his name is Gabriel."

I knew it. "Look at this picture." Aaron pulled out his phone and furiously tapped at the screen until a photo of the unconscious man from Wales came up. "Is this him?"

"Yes," the priest said. His eyes narrowed. "Why do you have his picture?"

Aaron ignored the question, grabbing a pen and paper from the priest's desk. "Send any surveillance footage you have from the two hours before you found Gabriel to this email address. *Tonight.* Can you do that?"

"Of course," the priest said.

Aaron took the father's hand in his own. "The Holy Father will hear of your excellent work."

Aaron opened the office door, checked that the hallway was

empty, then hurried down to the door the priest had indicated. Once outside, he headed back to the monstrous pickup truck, where he pulled out his phone and called Athens. Mo answered on the first ring.

"Did you find anything?"

"Someone beat us to it," Aaron said. "I'm sure it was the man from Brooklyn."

"The Albanian?"

"No," Aaron said. "Harry Fox. He tossed the injured Albanian in a tomb." Aaron detailed what he'd found in the tombs. "The name on the open tomb was *Weniver*."

"Sounds like another Arthurian character," Mo said.

"Exactly. *Guinevere*. Hard to believe Geoffrey didn't see that tomb and base another character's name on it."

"I call that a connection," Mo said.

"Contact the Cana family. Get their imam on the line as well. They lied about Gabriel not following Geoffrey's trail any longer. We'll give them one chance to make up for it."

Chapter Fourteen

Brooklyn

The cell phone on Stefan's nightstand vibrated. It didn't rouse the slumbering man the first call. Or the second. He finally stirred on the third one.

Twisting in bed, he fumbled for the phone and succeeded in knocking it to the floor. It went silent for a moment, then started buzzing once more. He finally managed to lift it and see who was calling.

Stefan sat straight up. His throat constricted as he checked the screen again. *Altin Cana.*

Stefan cleared his throat. "This is Stefan."

"Be at my office in fifteen minutes," Altin said. He clicked off without another word.

Stefan could only stare at the phone for several beats, as though it had transformed from an everyday device into a hand grenade with the pin pulled. Altin Cana didn't sleep much, but Stefan could count on one hand the number of times he'd called Stefan this early in the morning. Trouble brewed early today.

Stefan threw on clothes and jogged the five blocks from his apartment to Cana headquarters. He found a single window aglow – Altin's office. Stefan paused at the top step, then knocked on the front door. It opened at once to reveal one of the household guards.

"Mr. Cana is in his office."

Stefan knew the guard well, and the look on his face was puzzling. The guy didn't seem afraid. Not at all.

Stefan spoke in low tones. "Any idea what's going on?"

The guard shrugged. "I would ask you the same thing. All I know is the imam arrived twenty minutes ago. Then Altin said to expect you. That is it."

The imam? Twice in a week now – *damn*. Stefan's heart sank. *It has to be Gabriel.*

"They are waiting for you," the guard said.

"Thanks." Stefan felt the guard's eyes on him as he passed. He found Altin's office door ajar, light falling onto the hallway runner. He lifted a hand to knock.

"Come in." Altin spoke before Stefan made a sound. He must have been following him on the monitors that provided a live feed from all around the facility, including outside Altin's office.

Altin sat behind his desk. The imam was already seated in front of it. Altin waved at the open chair beside the imam. "Sit." He settled into the chair as Altin studied him. "There is a problem."

Stefan fought to keep his voice level. "What kind of problem?"

"You told the imam we were not interested in the Monmouth book. You would not lie to him." Altin put his hands on his knees and leaned forward, never taking his eyes off Stefan's. "The imam just told a distressing story. Gabriel was found inside a Roman tomb in Croatia. A man was found dead nearby. Stabbed." Stefan controlled his reaction until Altin continued. "Gabriel is in jail. The imam believes this is tied to the Monmouth book. How is this possible if we were no longer interested in that artifact?"

The implication was clear. Altin thought Stefan had gone behind his back, sending Gabriel hunting even after he'd promised it was done. Stefan had two choices. He didn't hesitate.

"I told Gabriel to stop searching," Stefan said. "He went there without telling me. I suspect he was trying to prove himself, to make money for you." Yes, he was throwing Gabriel to the wolves. The least he could do was try and help him survive the subsequent mauling.

"Is Gabriel the type to disobey orders?" Altin asked.

Stefan shook his head. "I didn't think so. Even if he only wanted to prove himself to you, it's still not right." Stefan turned to the imam. "I am deeply sorry. I had no idea Gabriel would keep searching."

The imam spoke as he always did, in a cool and collected manner. Nothing seemed to upset the man, though his mouth had a hard cast. "It is not I who am displeased. My associates in Europe are disappointed directions were not followed. They requested Gabriel stop searching to give them room to work, to stop this pursuit from threatening their interests." He didn't elaborate on what those interests might be. "However, the situation has worsened."

"I will do anything I can to make this right."

Now the imam's face softened. "Do not punish Gabriel further. I am sure he will be properly chastened after the Croatian courts are through with him." Stefan nodded his understanding, and Altin did as well. "My associates hope you will help end this charade before it worsens." The imam now mirrored Altin's pose, leaning closer to Stefan. "They believe a Morello family associate was there."

Stefan practically spat the name out. "Harry Fox."

"Yes. He likely took an artifact from one of the tombs. No one has been able to locate him. Can you locate him?"

"Who would know where to find Harry Fox?" Altin asked. "A girlfriend? Or a boyfriend, maybe? There must be at least one person we can approach."

Stefan knew well what Altin's approach could be like. He frowned. "The man doesn't have friends outside the Morello crew." Harry Fox had focused on being his father's sidekick until Fred Fox died in Italy.

But Stefan avoided the topic of Fred Fox at all costs. "I do know one person Harry Fox speaks with. Rose Leroux."

"Talk to Rose," Altin said. "See if she knows where Harry is."

"Who is Rose Leroux?" the imam asked.

"A buyer and seller of goods," Altin said. "No one crosses Rose. Not me, not Vincent Morello. No one."

The imam paused at those words. "I am merely a messenger, asking for a favor. I want no further part in this."

"Stefan will talk to Rose," Altin said. "Won't you?" Stefan said he would. "We will be in touch."

The imam thanked them and hurried out, clearly eager to leave. Stefan stood to go, but stopped when Altin raised a hand. "A moment, Stefan. I need the truth." A chill coursed through Stefan's body when Altin's hard, dark eyes locked on him. "Reassure me. You did not send Gabriel to Croatia. You told him to stop this search. He chose to continue on his own. Is that right?"

It took Stefan a moment to find his voice. "Yes, Mr. Cana. I knew nothing."

Altin tilted his head a fraction. "Good. Don't ever lie to me, Stefan. It will not go easy for you if you do." He stood and indicated the door. "Now go to Rose and see what she knows. We have other matters to handle beyond this item the imam's associates seek."

The guard let Stefan out, and he waited until he was nearly home before stopping, leaning against an apartment building and putting his head in both hands. How could Gabriel have been so stupid? Getting stuck in a *tomb*, and with a dead man close by? Stefan would deal with him later, after he figured out how to make this up to the imam's associates. Whoever the hell they were.

To do that, he simply had to get information from one of the city's toughest and most private people. The biggest fence in the city, a woman no one crossed.

A woman who had once saved his life.

Chapter Fifteen

Luxembourg

The floor rattled as Harry woke with a start, thrashing in his seat and sitting bolt upright. He blinked once before he remembered. *Luxembourg. I'm in a plane.* The passenger beside him was leaning as far away as possible. Harry cleared his throat. "Sorry," he said. "Don't like landings."

Once the plane had taxied to the gate, Harry bolted off with his single bag in tow and headed directly for the car rental counters to secure the most German car they had. Chilly morning air sweeping south from the North Sea washed the last vestiges of sleep away, helped by a steaming cup of strong coffee. It took him a few tries, but he finally found the correct Volkswagen sedan, hidden in a long row of nearly identical vehicles.

The car hummed as he made the crossing from Luxembourg into Germany in under twenty minutes. Dom Grilli was following the same path en route from Brooklyn, though Harry didn't expect him until much later in the day. By then he hoped to confirm that Geoffrey of Monmouth's clues did point to Trier, Germany. He knew where to look. Trier Cathedral, the oldest church in Germany, built during Diocletian's reign in honor of several Roman gods, including Bacchus.

Uncovering the secret headrest in *Weniver's* tomb had confirmed Geoffrey had indeed come this far and left a marker for Theobald. But his servant had never found it. Harry had. Now to find the *cone* in

Trier Cathedral. Would it lead to a mythical sword? Geoffrey had thought so, though how it tied to Lucius Artorius Castus was a mystery. Harry would worry about that after locating a marker he could recognize as a cone in a building that had been under construction for over a thousand years – including expansions, renovations and demolition.

Snow-capped mountains marked the horizon as Harry accelerated around slower traffic. He bit his lip. *Stop worrying.* Whatever waited, he'd handle it, just like his father had taught him. Fred had never doubted himself, not ever.

Harry touched the amulet around his neck. *Don't worry, Dad. I got this.* First step, find the cone. A pinecone, if his hunch proved correct. Many Roman religious structures had been dedicated to more than one god, in part because Rome had allowed conquered peoples to continue worshipping their traditional gods as long as they also paid homage to Roman gods. It was tactically brilliant, giving new subjects a chance to maintain a shred of dignity through the impression of continued normalcy despite having just been defeated by the Romans.

Roman gods were often thinly veiled adaptations of Greek gods. Why? It made things easier. Steal a fully formed god, slap a different name on it, and voila, a new *Roman* god. The Greek god Dionysus had become Rome's Bacchus, from his love of wine and song down to the staff he carried. A staff topped with a *pinecone.* Geoffrey's reference to the *Gallic church of Dionysus* was even more clear to Harry. Prior to their defeat by Rome, Gaul had been a land of Celtic tribes situated in modern-day Germany. One church in Germany that dated to Roman times was dedicated to Bacchus: the High Cathedral of Saint Peter in Trier.

The sun was a beacon chasing him across the sky when Harry spotted a pointed tower in the distance. The road turned to follow the Moselle River as it wound through a valley, bringing Harry to the doorstep of Trier via a bridge that could have been original in

Geoffrey's time, all dark stone and craggy mortar. He held his breath going over, emerging unscathed. Wooded hills stretched away from the city in a landscape punctuated by the rich, brown earth of vineyards. Harry didn't need his GPS to tell him where the cathedral waited. It punctuated the town, the pointed tip of a pointed roof calling to all for miles around that this was a house of God, a place of refuge for the faithful.

In Geoffrey's time the roads would have been stone at best, more likely packed dirt. Homes or shacks would have dotted the central road, with rough thatched roofs and shuttered windows. Harry parked the Volkswagen at the crest of a hill and got out. The cathedral glistened in the sunlight, a beacon impossible to miss. Four towers of Romanesque architecture, white stone topped with dark roofs standing guard around two square towers.

Harry kept stealing glances as he walked toward the cathedral, catching glimpses of it between buildings as he approached. A ringing bell grabbed his ear an instant before three speeding bicyclists whizzed past, the lead one nearly clipping Harry, who twisted and stumbled toward the far sidewalk, cursing himself even as he fell for not looking both ways. Arms pinwheeling, he managed to get his feet beneath him as he pitched forward. That all stopped when he crashed into a wall and bounced off, finally catching his balance. Then he looked up. He hadn't run into a wall. He'd hit a man. A big, bald man, who was now staring daggers down at Harry.

"*Du Bastard.*"

Harry noted it all in a flash. The man's ruddy cheeks, his shaved head, the tattoos covering his forearms. The pub beside them was filled to capacity, patrons spilling out onto the sidewalk. Two other men without hair turned at his word and took a step toward Harry.

"Sorry about that," Harry said. "I tripped."

He ducked his head and tried to pass the man. A meaty arm shot out and blocked his path.

"*Auslander.*" The bald man practically spat the word, then switched to English. "Look where you are going." The other two appeared beside the bald man, and their arrival seemed to fuel his xenophobic rant. "Go back to where you came from, *schmutz*. Germany is not for you."

Harry lifted one hand, his palm toward the man. His other hand slipped into a pocket and felt for the knuckle dusters. "I don't want any trouble."

Two of the three men had several inches in height on Harry, while the only one who was his height had been built of bricks. If they came at him, he'd deck the bald one and run for it. No shame in living to fight another day.

The acrid smell of beer flowed off their ringleader. "This is not a place for you. It is a man's tavern. Go clean the toilets."

His friends seemed to enjoy that. Harry stepped back as his fingers slipped into the duster. If he had to punch, he'd swing first and hard. Another step back as they kept coming, now taunting him in German, and Harry tensed his arm. *The middle guy. He's getting it. A knee to the junk, then an uppercut.*

He readied. The center man took another step. A torrent of German stopped them all in their tracks.

Someone shouldered past Harry, shoving him aside as they went right at the three men, shouting all the while. Harry reached to grab the person, to pull them away, only his arm froze halfway. It was a woman, and she kept going until she smacked her hand into the center man's chest.

No one tried to stop the woman's onslaught as the three aggressors quickly tucked tail and left. The woman turned to face him. "Are you alright?" she asked in flawless English. "They were just looking for trouble."

It took him a second to find his voice. "Yes, I'm fine. Thank you, but you didn't have to do that."

"What was your plan, kick all their asses?" She frowned. "You have to stand up to people like that. Catch them by surprise, show them strength. They won't know what to do."

That's when he noticed her caramel skin. Not so unlike his own. "I had a plan," he said, rallying. She blew air through her nose in a stream. "I did," he continued. It sounded lame even to him. "But thank you."

"I've dealt with punks like that all my life," she said. "Egyptian heritage isn't always popular in Germany. Or most countries, for that matter." She tilted her head. "You're not Egyptian."

"American," he said. "My mother was Pakistani." The woman didn't respond. Harry stuck his hand out. "Harry Fox."

She took his hand. "Sara Hamed. I'm on my way to kickboxing class. Where are you headed?"

Harry answered carefully. "To the cathedral. I've heard it's beautiful."

"Yes, it is." Her gaze fell to his neck. Harry reached up to find his amulet was in plain sight. "That's an interesting piece," she said.

"It was my father's." He started to tuck it back in, hesitated, then left it out. She'd just had his back against a trio of racist skinheads. The least he could do was talk to her. "He was a collector. It was his favorite artifact."

Her eyebrows rose. "Artifact? It looks genuine."

"Honestly, I don't really know a lot about it."

Sara leaned closer, then abruptly turned away. "Follow me. We need better light." They crossed an intersection before she stopped where sunlight colored the sidewalk, turning on a heel and grabbing his shoulder. "Turn into the light so I can see. That's better."

Harry fought the urge to pull away. "My father never told me what it was. All I know is it meant a lot to him." A thought occurred to him, one that made his stomach tense. "Have you seen this before?"

She didn't answer. Her fingers were warm on his bare skin as she held the piece, seemingly unaware of the concept of personal space. Or unconcerned. Sara turned the amulet over, having the effect of pulling Harry even closer to her. A hint of lavender floated from her scalp. Harry couldn't recall being this uncomfortable in quite some time.

"You really shouldn't have this around your neck." Sara took a step back, then poked him in the chest. "I'd need a lab to confirm it, but that piece is an Egyptian artifact made of faience and solid gold. Faience was popular in ancient Egypt, and that brilliant blue is fantastic."

All unease vanished. Along with his vocabulary. "What?"

"It's real," she said quickly. "Tell me about it."

"How do you know this is real? And I told you what I know. It was my father's and it meant a lot to him. He got it while my mother was still alive."

"Oh." Sara's eyes went to the ground for a moment. "I'm sorry."

Harry gave the same response he always did. "It's fine."

"It's extremely old." She cleared her throat. "Those symbols on the front. Any idea what they are?"

"Hieroglyphics."

"Yes." Sara said, rolling her eyes. "But do you know what they mean?" Harry shook his head. "Neither do I. I do recognize part of it." She didn't ask before touching the amulet again. "Do you see here, what looks like a knife, a string with a knot, and this bird?"

Harry knew exactly what she meant. A short string of images was etched into the faience face of the amulet, a ceramic material Harry knew Egyptians appreciated for the sapphire-like blue shade. "I've tried to translate them," he said. "They don't make any sense."

"Unless you know the secret," Sara said.

Harry laughed. "You read Egyptian hieroglyphics?"

"I'm Egyptian," she deadpanned. Harry's jaw dropped, then she grinned. "A joke. I am Egyptian, but not all of us can read hieroglyphics. No more than you could read Old English. I'm an Egyptology professor at the University of Trier. I can read the piece, and it's incomplete."

Before his father died, Harry had never given the amulet's meaning much thought, other than the fact that it was eye-catching and a potent reminder of his father.

"How do you know?" Harry turned the amulet around and stared at its face.

"Look at the final symbol."

"You mean the sideways V and the half-circle below it? It's unlike any Egyptian writing I've ever seen."

"It's not Egyptian, and it's not writing." A cool breeze ruffled the loose hair at Sara's neck; a shiny braid extended halfway down her back. "This is a symbol. A *Roman* symbol for a person."

"Hold on. I asked people I work with about this. People who know quite a lot about Egyptian history. None of them had ever seen it before."

Her gaze narrowed. "What do you do for a living, Mr. Harry?"

Harry found the sidewalk suddenly interesting. "I work in antiquities. Buying and selling. For collectors, mostly." He looked up to find her eyes on his.

She held his gaze. "I see," she finally said. "It sounds like your colleagues are qualified. However, not many people would recognize this person."

"What person?"

She tapped his amulet. "The man referenced in this passage. Or rather, the *couple* it references. Look." Sarah pointed to the leftmost carving. "The images are a knife, a primitive fishing line, a rectangle and a bird. Then, the sideways V and half-circle, as you described them." She stifled a laugh.

"That's what it looks like," Harry protested.

"An accurate description." She patted his arm. "I'm only teasing. 'I' is a Roman symbol for a man. But not just any man."

"Who?"

"Patience. The other symbols first." She tapped the first four. "Taken as a whole, these are part of how Egyptians wrote the name of a leader. The reason no one could read it is that it's incomplete. It would be like you seeing a few letters from the middle of someone's full name. For instance, without any context, you'd never know *R-A-H-A* was part of *Abraham Lincoln*." Now she tapped his chest with one finger. "Context is what this Roman symbol gives us."

"Okay, you have my attention. Who are we talking about?"

"Cleopatra and Mark Antony."

Harry struggled to find his voice, and failed. *Cleopatra?* The final ruler of Egypt before it fell to Rome. And this piece somehow tied her to Mark Antony, Roman dictator and Julius Caesar's top general? Too many questions flooded his mind.

"You had no idea," Sara said when she read his face.

"How do you know?" Harry asked. "No one else I showed this to ever did."

"I saw this exact line during my research. On a two-thousand-year-old scarab medallion. Given to honored guests by Mark Antony and Cleopatra to mark their successful invasion of Armenia."

"They gave out *scarabs* to celebrate?"

"Egyptians saw them as a symbol of rebirth, or regeneration. Antony and Cleopatra awarded golden scarab amulets to their military leaders during the celebration in Alexandria." She pointed to his neck. "I'd bet a lot of money that inscription is tied to those scarab amulets."

Now Harry was truly at a loss. "Why?"

Sara shrugged. "Beats me. I'm an Egyptologist, not a fortune teller." She turned and started walking, forcing him to catch up. At the end of the block, she stopped so quickly he nearly ran her over. "This is my kickboxing class. It was nice meeting you." She put a hand out, and before he shook it Harry noted the business card. "If you're ever interested in learning more about that piece, call me. And be careful with it, will you? It's more valuable than you realize."

He couldn't muster up a response as she opened a tinted door and vanished.

"Thanks," he finally managed. Too late. The door closed behind her. Harry stood for a full minute. What the hell had just happened? He'd nearly gotten his ass kicked by a group of skinhead thugs, only to have an Egyptian woman six inches shorter than him jump in, then decipher the single biggest mystery in his world.

He could only shake his head and look at her card.

Sara Hamed, PhD
Professor of Egyptology

"I'll be in touch, Dr. Hamed." He looked up. The cathedral waited two blocks away. "As soon as I find a pinecone." Harry lowered his head, heading for a cathedral solid enough to stand for two thousand years. Or in his mind, a fortress hiding the key to Geoffrey's path. The cathedral's shadow fell over him long before he walked up the front steps and went inside.

A towering nave stretching well over a hundred feet skyward stopped him in his tracks. Mixed stonework defined the interior, muted silver granite and ivory sandstone mixed with original Roman brickwork. Harry backed up against a wall, pressed his palm to it, and breathed deeply. The familiar chill ran up his back. He loved places like this, a building from the ages reminding him his existence was brief, that so many had come this way before him and were now gone. The thought was both terrifying and freeing.

Seconds passed. A pair of tourists came in, pointing and talking in hushed tones as Harry headed for the closest set of ragged brickwork. Thank goodness the Romans had built walls to last. Their specifications hadn't always included aesthetics, however. Portions of the walls dating from Roman times were readily identified by the uneven stones, often of mixed colors or consistency. Certain sections were built so the brickwork formed symbols or designs. Crosses dominated these efforts, along with nods to the Roman gods through crescent moons, circles with dots in the middle to represent the sun, and the modern symbol for male, a circle with an arrow pointing out of it.

The nave and surrounding antechambers were massive. He moved slowly along the walls, checking every decorative carving or symbol. Dozens of options presented themselves. Not a single pinecone. Harry crossed in front of the altar as the first seed of doubt formed. Could he be wrong? He actually shook his head. No. Geoffrey's message tied the Gallic church of Dionysus to the cone. The Romans had stolen Dionysus from the Gauls and Greeks before them, changing his identity to Bacchus while keeping the pinecone imagery. It all fit. Now he had to find this cone, look south, and the answer would be revealed. The answer was here, waiting for him, as it had been for a millennium.

Harry worked his way around the interior and back to the front entrance. No luck. *Fine. It's not inside. Check the exterior walls.*

Cylindrical towers, darkened doorways and false pillars underwent his scrutiny as he walked around the entire cathedral, finding precious few decorative carvings or inscriptions. He came back around to the front entrance, having succeeded only in eliminating the few possible places where Bacchus's lost pinecone might have been hidden. If the damn thing even existed.

He stood still. *The cone wasn't here.* He ran a hand across his face. He must have missed something. Even as he walked back inside to start another circuit, Harry knew he was lying to himself. He'd checked every inch of the structure that had existed during Geoffrey's time. Should he check the newer areas? No, that didn't make sense. Geoffrey had died around 1155. Any portion of the cathedral built after that couldn't hold the pinecone. If it was here, the cone was in part of the church built before his death.

In desperation Harry pulled out his phone and typed assorted phrases into the search engine. No luck. The collective online wisdom of humanity couldn't confirm the existence of any sort of cone in the cathedral. Five minutes of fruitless research later, Harry turned to the nearest wall and leaned against it, hands on his head. Three hours spent searching this place and nothing. Keyword searches wouldn't change that. What now?

The cathedral had grown steadily busier as he searched. On his journey around the various perimeters, he'd seen a handful of cathedral staff, none of whom gave him more than a kind look or word before going on their way. He sensed a presence close to him, felt rather than seen, and turned to find a nun standing no more than a foot away.

"Hallo. Wie geht es dir?"

"Hi," Harry said. "I don't speak German."

"How are you?" she repeated, switching smoothly to English. "Are you unwell?"

What could he say to that? *I can't find a thousand-year-old carving that will help me locate Excalibur. Yes, that Excalibur. Any ideas?* Even as it ran through his head, Harry laughed. "I'm fine," he said.

Decades of wisdom lined her face. She knew he was lying. Instead of calling him on it, she lightly touched his elbow.

Which caught him completely off guard. He looked down, then at her face. The kind eyes crinkled at the edges. Harry bit his lip. *What the hell.*

"Actually, I could use your help," he said. She raised her eyebrows. "I'm looking for an engraving on the wall. A symbol of a cone. A pinecone. Like the one on the staff Bacchus carried." He flinched as soon as the words left his mouth. *Nice move, throwing out Roman gods to a Catholic nun.*

Her expression never changed. "I see." A pause. "Perhaps I can help."

"Really?"

"Is this important to you?"

"Very."

"I noticed you walking for some time. Were you studying our walls?"

"Yes. Didn't have any luck." He found himself warming to her offer, though he'd already been through the entire place. "I didn't find cones of any kind. I know it would be on the part of the church built before 1155."

The nun didn't ask why. "That is useful."

Then she waited. Harry was out of steam.

She tapped his elbow. "I do not have the answer, though I may know a person who does. Follow me."

The nun turned and moved off at a smooth pace, leaving Harry to follow as she headed toward the altar. They passed in front of it, the marble pulpit towering over them as she took him past a row of unlit candles. She led him to a doorway tucked between two columns; it opened to well-lit halls with tall glass windows throwing copious sunlight on the floors. Offices lined either side. An exterior wall was to his right, and through the windows above the office doors Harry spotted several familiar towers he'd passed during his circumnavigation of the cathedral.

The nun stopped in front of an open door, knocking softly. "*Hallo?*" A man's voice replied in German, and a rapid conversation ensued. In short order the nun turned to him and spoke in English. "This is our records room. Timo is our historian. I believe he has documents that may interest you."

Harry didn't realize she was leaving until she'd already passed him and headed back to the main area. "Thank you. What's your name?"

"Sister Nina."

"Thank you, Sister. You don't know how much this means to me."

She acknowledged his thanks, then turned and walked out of sight. Only after she was gone did Harry turn and walk into the records room, which turned out to be much more than a room. The interior extended at least fifty feet to a wall made mostly of tinted glass, beyond which he could see nothing. He hadn't passed any exterior glass walls, so this room had to be only part of the records area. A singularly tall man stood in front of a desk, and he reached out to offer his hand.

"Hello." The man's arm finally stopped extending, and Harry took his hand. "My name is Timo."

"Nice to meet you, Brother Timo."

"I am merely Timo," he said. "I work for the cathedral. My job is archival record-keeping."

Harry looked behind the man, eyeing shelves that extended back to the smoked glass. "You have that many records in this place?"

Timo chuckled. "More than you see here. We have vaults on lower levels, as well as additional digitized images and documents."

"I'm actually looking for a very specific record. Or picture." He gave Timo an abbreviated version of his search for the cone symbol tied to Bacchus. Timo didn't question when Harry offered a vague "personal" search as the reason for his hunt.

"Sections of the original Roman walls have been lost over time," Timo said. "Fortunately, cathedral staff preserved a range of documents tied to the building, including photos and other mediums."

Other mediums? "How old are the photographs?"

"Many date to over a century ago."

Harry's shoulders drooped. What were the chances an old photo had captured part of the Roman walls that no longer existed? Maybe he was lucky and one did, but he'd have to be lucky twice. First, the photo still had to be around. Second, it needed to show the cone in enough detail for him to figure out what Geoffrey wanted to say. A blurred or distant image wouldn't do any good. "That could take a lot of searching."

"Through the snapshots, yes. Which is why I recommend starting with the sketches."

Harry perked up. "Sketches?"

"Hand-drawn by monks and nuns over the years. Many servants of God copied different images to share with Christ's followers near and far. For centuries most Germans lived in small villages, not traveling any great distance their entire lives. Making and sharing copies of the artwork on our walls was a way for monks and nuns to offer the faithful a way to connect with this magnificent cathedral from afar."

Harry moved closer, now staring almost straight up at Timo. "How many of these images exist?"

"Thousands. Even after photography became available the priests and nuns continued their work. Some continue today, bringing the drawings or rubbings to the sick to lift their spirits."

"May I see them?"

Timo gestured to a door behind him. "Follow me."

The door opened to reveal a staircase descending to one of the lower levels Timo had mentioned. Far from the dungeon-like rooms Harry expected, these stairs led to a bright room of concrete walls, long tables, and steel filing cabinets. Lots and lots of filing cabinets. Timo flicked a switch and bright light filled the room. Cool, dry air circulated, sneaking down the front of Harry's shirt.

Timo pointed to the closest cabinet. "These are files I have not yet digitized. The area I suggest you check is this way."

Down a long aisle formed by the shoulder-height cabinets, then a sharp turn and Timo stopped. "Is this it?"

"This row," Timo said. "The imagery captured in the form of personal drawings or similar mediums is stored here." He waved, indicating a row of at least fifteen cabinets. Three drawers in each meant forty-five to check. "Both sides," Timo finished.

Make that ninety. "May I look through them?" Harry asked.

"These are open to the public. All I ask is that you wear gloves when handling the materials." He indicated a box of surgical gloves on a table. "You may stay for as long as you like. I will be in my office."

Timo smiled, turned around and departed, leaving a somewhat stunned Harry in his wake. These Germans were really going to let him poke around their archives without supervision? What if there was something valuable down here? He chuckled to himself. It was obvious. They were letting him look because there *wasn't* anything worth stealing down here. Who wanted these faded pictures and drawings? Well, maybe Harry Fox did. Dropping his messenger bag on the table, he donned a pair of gloves and opened the first drawer.

A stale, brittle odor crept to his nose. Heavy file folders were packed inside, stuffed with more types of paper than Harry had seen in a long while. Thick paper. Translucent sheets he didn't want to disturb in case they crumbled under his touch. Rough, scratchy sheets more like burlap than pulp. Faded photographs on heavy stock. All this and more, in just the first drawer. Then he spotted a label on the first folder, listing two dates. *1812 – 1814.*

Two different hands had written the years. "They must start a new drawer when the old one fills up," he thought. Sure enough, he opened the drawer beneath to find it marked *1814 – 1815.* Harry sighed. Might as well start with this one. He removed several folders from the first drawer and took them to his borrowed desk, getting to work.

An hour passed as Harry searched through every folder in turn, finding primarily drawings, though several grainy photos were mixed in. He even pulled out a few daguerreotypes on silver-plated copper sheets, the precursor to more modern photographic methods. Not-Brother Timo had been right. All manner of drawings were in these files, including many images that Harry recognized from his search of the cathedral, though some were new. Through it all, though, no cones. Of any kind. Harry had just started into *1858* when Timo reappeared in the doorway.

"Having any luck, Mr. Fox?"

"Not yet."

Timo lifted a finger, dotting the air as he spoke. "Have faith. I am sure you will succeed. Miracles happen every day."

"Send up a prayer for me if you can," Harry said, which got a smile out of the gangly archivist.

"I will. Is there anything I can get you? There is an espresso machine in my office. I'd be happy to make you a cup."

"You know, that would be great. If you don't mind."

"Not at all."

Timo turned and went back upstairs, leaving Harry to his work. As he flipped through this latest folder of imagery, Harry's mind began to wander. Here he was, a perfect stranger, and everyone in this cathedral went out of their way to help him with what must have sounded like ridiculous requests. They'd set him up with a desk, provided access to their records, and offered espresso to boot. They didn't even seem to care *why* he wanted to find this pinecone image. His request was taking them away from their duties, of which they certainly had enough, but instead of grumbling, these total strangers were doing everything in their power to help him. Harry didn't look like them. He didn't worship the same God – not that he worshipped any gods in particular, though he wasn't above throwing out an occasional prayer to whoever happened to be listening. They had no connection to him, no reason to let him in here, yet they did, happily. All because Sister Nina and not-Brother Timo chose kindness.

His thoughts turned to the altercation earlier, which was such a sharp contrast to what he was experiencing here in the cathedral. Those Germans had also seen a man who didn't resemble them, but deemed him the kind of person they didn't want in "their" town. They'd decided to pick a fight, to have some fun with the foreign-looking guy. The incident could have taken a much darker turn, Harry knew, if Dr. Hamed had taken another route to her kickboxing class today. Harry had been ready to hit first and hope for survival, a situation he'd dealt with dozens of times before, all around the world. That was his reality.

Timo's footsteps sounded on the stairs. Harry blinked, realized he'd been turning pages without looking, lost in his thoughts. He looked down at the page in his hands. A pinecone stared back.

"I brought cream and sugar in case you—"

"This is it." Harry stood so fast his chair fell over. "I found it."

Timo was at his side in three long strides. "My goodness." Timo leaned over Harry's shoulder, setting the espresso tray down. "Yes, that is a pinecone at the top. Is it what you are searching for?"

Harry held an etching, one that had been created by someone holding the crinkled sheet of paper against a wall and rubbing a pencil on it. The original carvings had been on a single large stone, as there weren't any brick lines on the sheet. A single pinecone stood front and center. This had to be what Geoffrey had referenced in his message. Harry's gaze moved down the page to the script beneath the drawing. "It's in Latin." He frowned.

"Yes," Timo said. "*Quaerite autem abbatia de Josepho memorantur in Britanniam.* An odd phrase. It says—"

"*Seek the abbey of Joseph in Britain.*" Harry translated. "Does that mean anything to you?"

Harry turned to see Timo looking down at him with his head tilted to one side. "You speak Latin."

"Not often," Harry said. "My father insisted I learn it."

"How interesting," Timo said. "Not many outside the faith speak it any longer."

"It can be useful," Harry said. "This phrase." He pointed to the sheet. "I assume it's talking about Joseph of Arimathea, who buried Jesus after he was crucified."

"Yes, Mr. Fox. I agree. It seems Joseph's abbey held an interest for our Roman builders."

Harry stood from his chair. "Do you know any abbeys in Britain dedicated to Joseph? I'd guess there are dozens of them."

"One abbey comes to mind, though it cannot be correct. This Roman engraving dates to the fourth century, or perhaps the fifth, when this cathedral was originally constructed. As you said, the pinecone would be found on a Roman portion of our walls."

Harry didn't think that was necessarily the case. Geoffrey could have made this inscription on a newer part of the walls. He also saw no reason to tell Timo this. "Still, this is interesting. Which abbey are you thinking of?"

Timo didn't seem bothered by the discrepancy. "Glastonbury Abbey. Legends say the first holy structures on that land were founded by Joseph of Arimathea. An interesting story that is likely only that. A story."

Harry wasn't listening any longer. Glastonbury Abbey had another legend associated with it, one far closer to Harry's search. He'd read about it in his research on Lucius Artorius and the Arthurian tales. Part of the legend suggested inhabitants of what was now Britain had another name for the lands now called Glastonbury. In ancient times the place had supposedly been an island, and that island was called the Isle of Avalon.

"May I take a picture of this etching?" Harry asked.

"Of course." Timo waited while Harry took several, then helped him return the files to their cabinets. "I hope this proves useful."

"It will," Harry said. The big man waited, though Harry declined to fill the silence with an explanation. "I can't thank you enough for your hospitality. You and Sister Nina have been incredibly welcoming."

"Should you ever find yourself in Trier again, please say hello. Perhaps then you can share the next steps in your journey."

"I will," Harry said. He grabbed the espresso cup and drained it in one gulp. "I have to go."

"Let me walk you out."

Timo led Harry to the front door. Harry spotted an offering box beside the entrance and stopped, digging into the messenger bag over his shoulder. "Here, Timo. Would you make sure this goes to good use?"

The man's eyes went wide. Harry was giving him a thousand euros. "This is not necessary, Mr. Fox."

"Trust me, I should give you more." He looked over both

shoulders. "And if anyone comes around asking about a guy who looks like me, I'd appreciate it if you didn't mention my being here."

Timo held his gaze. "I trust you have noble motives for this request. I will honor it." The bills disappeared into the offering box. "Safe travels, my friend."

Harry took his outstretched hand. "Thank you, Timo."

He left Timo inside the front door as he turned and hurried off, phone in hand. Glastonbury was just under nine hours by car, which included crossing the English Channel. Flying time was closer to six, though with time spent waiting at the airports it was a wash. Not to mention Dom Grilli should be getting to Trier soon and he didn't have a false passport. The *three forces* trailing him had proven more than capable of latching on to loose ends no matter how far removed from Harry. No, airports didn't make sense. A car ride offered more flexibility if any obstacles came up.

As he headed back to his car, Harry started to take a detour to avoid the troublesome bar from earlier, then reconsidered. Missing the bar also meant missing Sara Hamed's kickboxing studio. Chances were she was gone by now, though she might still be around. Why pass up a chance to run a few questions past the person who had identified his father's amulet? He'd pushed that potential breakthrough to the back of his head, where it now waited for his full attention. Harry rubbed his fingers together. No telling when he'd be back in Trier. Might as well give it a shot.

Harry slipped his hand into the knuckle duster and headed for trouble of several kinds. Past the kickboxing studio, he slowed his pace to a near crawl, checking every window and alleyway for Sara, so focused on her that he jumped when his phone buzzed. Dom Grilli was five minutes outside of town. Harry sent him an intersection near where he'd parked and told Dom to have his hired car drop him there. He resumed walking, keeping watch as he moved, first for Sara, then for the skinheads when he passed the bar. His luck held level, for he didn't spot them before his car came into sight. But he hadn't spotted Sara either. Should he go back, give it one more pass? He stopped, turned, and then caution won out.

He had Sara's number. She'd helped him enough for one day, cracking the amulet's mysterious language and giving him a lead to unravel the truth behind it. Another few days wouldn't matter. Harry approached his car and saw that Dom had not yet arrived, so he climbed in, settled behind the wheel and pulled out his phone, unable to let the amulet's tantalizing possibilities go all at once.

Rose answered on the first ring. "It's Harry. Is this a good time?"

"Harry, my dear. Are you safe?" He assured her he was. "Any luck on your search for truth behind the myth?"

"Yes, but that's not what I'm calling about." He plunged on, not wanting Dom to hear any of this. "I need your help."

"You have it," Rose said.

"My father's amulet. I haven't been able to learn much about it. Until today. A friend told me what the hieroglyphs mean." He paused, letting his heart slow. "They reference Mark Antony and Cleopatra." Rose drew in a sharp breath. "The only other place this specific message exists is on scarab medallions they handed out as gifts after winning a battle. Ever heard of an artifact like that?"

"No," Rose said. "Would you like me to see what I can learn?"

"Quietly," Harry said. "I don't even know if it's correct. Plus, the last thing I need is someone asking questions about my father's amulet. I have enough going on."

"Where are you?"

"Germany. A city called Trier. I'm actually leaving in a few minutes and driving to Glastonbury."

"I trust you will be cautious, and I cannot say this enough. Be careful. Trust no one."

"I didn't forget," Harry said. "And I won't. You'll call if you find anything?"

"Of course. Let me know when you are safe. I worry about you."

Harry laughed. "I'll keep my head down, I promise." He clicked off, forcing thoughts of his father's amulet aside when he looked up to find Dom Grilli standing on the street corner, watching the roads. Harry flicked his lights and waved Dom over, flicking the locks open to let him sling his bag in the back and climb in beside him. He brought Dom up to speed as they headed out of Trier and Harry pointed the car west, toward England.

As Trier's downtown gave way to open roads, Harry couldn't have known that his call to Rose had been overheard. Every word of their discussion had been listened to by a man who had betrayed the trust of them all to save his own skin, and to learn the truth behind what Harry Fox was doing in Germany. And more importantly, where Harry could be found next.

Chapter Sixteen

Brooklyn

Altin Cana's solid gold lighter sparked to life, the flame throwing shadows across his face as the Albanian mob boss lit a cigar, puffing until the end burned a fiery red and white smoke curled toward the ceiling. From Stefan Rudovic's viewpoint across Altin's desk, it was like curtains parting when Altin waved a hand through the haze. His expression hadn't changed.

"How did you learn Harry Fox's plans?"

Stefan never considered lying to Altin. He'd done that once. Even crazy men didn't risk it twice. "I bugged Rose Leroux's home. If Harry Fox was going to tell anyone his plans, it was her." He made no mention that she claimed to have no knowledge of Harry's plans. Rose had told him she knew nothing of Harry's whereabouts, and even Stefan's warning that the imam's associates might end up killing Harry because of Gabriel's continued involvement – which Stefan had orchestrated against Altin's wishes – had failed to move her. Only after listening to Rose's phone calls was he able to confirm she was telling the truth.

Altin lifted an eyebrow. "Rose would not be pleased if she knew."

"I did it for the family. For you." Stefan paused, exactly like he'd rehearsed. "I don't know who the imam's friends are. Even so, I don't want to bring shame on the Cana family. Giving them the information on Harry Fox's movements will make sure they view us as friends, not enemies."

The cigar's end glowed. Altin blew out a storm cloud, then leaned through it as his elbows found the desk, a deadly mirage coming into terrible clarity. His face betrayed nothing.

Altin pointed the cigar at Stefan. "To care about my family's name is important. You took a risk. It paid off. I agree, this will show the imam and his associates Gabriel went to Croatia on his own."

Stefan nearly sank through the chair. *Thank the stars.* He had had no idea how Altin would react.

Altin aimed the cigar at him like it was loaded. "You are sure Rose has no idea?"

"I left the device during a visit earlier today. She is many things. Suspicious of me is not one of them. Also, the battery only lasts for a week. After it dies, there is no way to trace it to me."

"Then we will call Hussam Shamsi right now. Good news should not wait." Altin dialed, ringing filled his office, and the imam picked up moments later. After the men exchanged greetings, Altin's heavy-lidded eyes lifted to study Stefan. "Stefan wishes to speak with you. It is about the question your friends asked."

Stefan paid his respects before saying, "Imam, I worry we left your friends with a poor view of the Cana operation."

"I cannot say," Hussam Shamsi replied. "I only served as the messenger."

"Are you able to contact them again?"

"Yes."

Stefan leaned closer to the phone. "Harry Fox will be in Glastonbury within eight hours. They should look for him at Glastonbury Abbey."

"That is valuable information," the imam said. "I suspect my associates will be grateful to you and the entire Cana family."

"Please remind them that when Gabriel kept searching for the lost path, he did so on his own," Altin said. "We are pleased to be of service to such a just cause."

Imam Hussam Shamsi assured Altin he would relay the message, then rang off. Altin puffed his cigar for some time after the line went dead. Smoke hung below the ceiling for only a moment before the humming air purifier whisked it away, all while Stefan kept still through a supreme act of will. He could not afford to alienate Altin Cana over something as stupid as an old book. There were thousands of other relics waiting to be found. The only way Stefan would become the Cana man searching for them was if Altin said so.

What Altin finally said caught Stefan off guard. "I sense you are concerned." Stefan didn't respond. "You should not be," Altin continued. "Your ambition brought reward. It was a risk. Given my reputation is recovered, a worthy risk." Altin's jowls perked up, his face, now weathered to pure grit, regaining what had once perhaps been a boyish charm. "You will go far, Stefan. Already you are one of my lieutenants, coming from nothing at all." The cigar waved around them, taking in the room. "The same as I did."

Stefan sensed there was more to come. Altin's dark eyes latched on to Stefan's. "Allah has not blessed me with children. My wife will never have the son I wanted, and it is her greatest sorrow. Who are we to question Allah's will? He has given me much. When I am gone, others will need to build on what I started. Perhaps you will be one of those men who lead this family in the next generation."

Stefan nearly fell from his chair. Altin considered *he* could take charge one day? Stefan Rudovic, an Albanian born with nothing who had come to this country as a boy, he and his family ferried across the border in the back of a smuggler's truck. Yet now he had the ear of one of the most powerful crime bosses in New York. A man was lucky if he got one chance like this in his life.

"Mr. Cana, I am honored to be part of what you have built."

"Stay focused, Stefan. Forget this book and the Morello man who chases it. I suspect he will soon find more trouble at his door." Embers sparked as Altin stubbed out his cigar. "We have plans to carry out closer to home. Brooklyn is too small for the Morello and Cana families to exist together. We require room to grow. The road ahead will be dangerous. Are you the man to help me see it through?"

Stefan leaned closer, on the edge of his chair. All thoughts of Geoffrey's book vanished. "I am."

Chapter Seventeen

Glastonbury Abbey

Cars rumbled down cobblestone streets on routes laid out centuries ago when the quiet town had been a bustling center of commerce. Harry Fox snapped awake when Dom slowed and pulled the car into a parking spot, yawned, then tried and failed to stretch his none-too-long limbs in the European sedan. "I'd kill for a coffee right now. What time is it?" Dom told him it was early afternoon. "That drive took forever."

"English roads are slow," Dom said. "They need more highways. I think I found coffee." Dom pointed to a café down the street, and Harry obligingly stepped out to do the honors. Dodging between people walking in and out of the electronics goods store next door, Harry made his way into the shop, ordered two wonderfully caffeinated drinks, and ferried them back to the car. Dom pulled back out into traffic and continued motoring them onward. Their coffees hadn't cooled enough to drink before Glastonbury's best-known abbey, or what was left of it, appeared in their windshield.

Dom frowned. "This place is a mess."

"They're ruins," Harry said. "Easier to search these than a church people still use." The truth, but that did little to ease his concern that they would find nothing. Most of Glastonbury Abbey had been repurposed for building materials in the sixteenth century to support Henry VIII's military campaigns. What had once been Britain's second-wealthiest abbey behind Westminster was now a site of fallen, roofless buildings with only the pillars and sturdiest exterior walls remaining. Still, several of the partial structures stretched nearly a hundred feet high and held the outlines of intricate stained-glass windows and grand doors.

Harry had no idea what they'd find or even where to start. The one place he knew to avoid was actually the most enticing: a purported tomb beneath where the abbey's high altar used to stand, said to contain the remains of King Arthur and Queen Guinevere. Unfortunately, it was a ploy dreamed up by poor abbey leaders after fire had destroyed much of the abbey in 1184. Pilgrims had flocked to the supposed tomb, bringing with them riches to rebuild. This would be the worst possible place to hide Arthur's sword, and since Geoffrey had died in 1155, the timing didn't fit.

"Where do we start?" Dom asked.

"It's thirty-six acres," Harry said. "Lots of places to hide things. We focus on the standing structures first, anything that was around when Geoffrey might have been here in the early twelfth century. That would be the great church and what they call the Lady Chapel. The chapel still has subterranean rooms."

Dom followed Harry towards the main entrance; they passed a handful of tourists on their way. Manicured lawns stretched out around them. Numerous trees stood where once there had been grand stone buildings. Paved walkways guided visitors around the extensive grounds. Harry kept moving as they passed a standing structure.

"What about that place?" Dom asked. "It's the only one with a roof on it."

"That's the Abbey House. Built in 1829. But good thought," he said quickly. "Don't keep any ideas to yourself."

A row of trimmed hedges nudged them onto a paved walkway shaded by leafy limbs swaying in the afternoon breeze. Harry pointed to the closest set of ruins. "That was the main church, the abbey. We'll start there, then move to the Lady Chapel." The chapel sat beyond what used to be the abbey's main entrance, a pair of towering columns that would have held massive wooden doors and a soaring archway. Time had claimed all but the pillars.

Harry stopped beside one of the side walls. The great church had been rectangular, with the longer side walls scarcely half as tall as the front and rear ones, though the massive window openings, built in the shape of upturned arrowheads, would have turned the interior into a palette of colors when the sun hit them. Harry paused, considering. Dom waited quietly.

"You take that side," Harry finally said. "I'll start here. Look for anything remotely tied to Rome or Joseph of Arimathea."

Dom went off without a word. Harry watched him go, then looked to the blue skies and took a deep breath. *You're not helpless. Stay focused and figure it out.* Somewhat to his surprise, the self-pep talk actually boosted his spirits. Geoffrey seemed to have left nothing behind, yet Harry was certain Geoffrey meant for his servant to come to Glastonbury.

An hour later he met Dom by the massive front pillars. Both had checked the great church's interior and exterior walls without result.

"No worries," Harry said with confidence he didn't feel. "It must be in the Lady Chapel."

"There's more to that place than this one," Dom agreed. "Gives us more places to check. More chances to find what we need."

"I like the way you think," Harry said. Walking side by side, they crossed an open area flat enough to be a soccer field. "Thanks for coming from Brooklyn. Having someone I can trust is huge."

A few steps later, Dom surprised Harry. "You know, some of the guys wouldn't want to come here."

Harry knew why. "Because it's me."

"Yeah." Several steps passed in silence. "Dumb. Those guys have a thing about you being, you know, not like them."

"Not Italian." Harry knew. He was no fool. Their distaste for him was obvious. "It's dumb, like you said, but I can't blame them."

He looked sidelong at Dom. Half of what he'd said was true. Yes, it was dumb. No, he couldn't blame the men for feeling that way, but he did. Harry hadn't done anything to them. He'd come into their world with his father. It's not like he'd *wanted* to be part of an Italian gangster's crew. It would have been hard for anyone to insert themselves into the gang, let alone a Pakistani-American whose father had had the unswerving loyalty of their boss. Harry hadn't asked for the breaks he'd been given. If these Italians wanted to hate him for it, that was their problem. Not that they'd ever say anything within earshot of Vincent Morello.

"You should," Dom said. "They're *cretinos*, fools. You work harder than any of them and make Vincent rich. Most of them are jealous. I'm not." He looked up from the grass. "You're alright."

That was more than Dom had ever said to Harry in one go. He was quieter than most of the Morello associates, one major reason Harry had been glad Joey had chosen him to aid in the search. Dom and Harry also shared another trait. They'd both grown up without their mothers, though at least Harry's father had been around. Dom had come to Vincent Morello's team from a foster home, doing anything Vincent needed to convince Vincent to keep him around. Nearly a decade later Dom had become one of Vincent's trusted foot soldiers, and a guy Harry could now call his friend.

"Thanks." Harry opened his mouth to follow up on the lame response. It stayed open, though nothing came out. The view behind Dom grabbed his attention.

"You okay?" Dom said after a few moments. He turned to look behind him. "Something wrong?"

"The great church," Harry said. "The pillars." He trailed off into silence. The *pillars*. Ten of them on the long sides. Along the front he counted three pillars on each side of what used to be a massive door. Along the back, nothing except an unbroken foundation line. What would have been the rear wall. *Ten and ten, with two sides of three. A single line at the back.*

Harry ignored Dom's questioning look as he dug in his messenger bag, pulling out the book from Geoffrey's tomb in Wales. Hardly two days ago, yet it seemed so much longer. All that had happened had brought Harry to this English holy ground, a place of myth and legend. And perhaps more truth than anyone realized.

"In Geoffrey's original book?" Dom asked. "You didn't say anything about a clue in there."

"I didn't realize until now." He flipped pages as quickly as caution allowed. "Here, on the last page. Look at this." He turned the book around to show Dom the hand-drawn rectangle. "Ten dots on each side. Three at the top, unconnected, and a solid line at the other end."

"What's this plus sign in the middle?"

"It's a cross, and I think it represents an altar."

Dom looked up, saw Harry staring past him, then turned. Back to the book, then back around again. "Ten circles," Dom said. "Ten, and three at the top. You think this drawing is the large church." It wasn't a question.

"The pillars match," Harry said. "They're not connected because there would be a huge door between them."

"The solid line on the other end was a wall," Dom said. "There's a solid foundation at the back but no pillared columns."

"It matches. Even the cross."

"Good thing those monks made up finding Arthur and Guinevere's grave under the altar." Dom pointed to a sign indicating where legend said the pair had been buried. A ruse by church officials in need of funds for repairs, it had grown far beyond the original fundraising goal and spawned a massive following of people who associated Glastonbury Abbey with Avalon. Even today people still came. What was the biggest reason for this association with Arthur and Guinevere? Geoffrey's book, published only a few decades before their grave was 'discovered'.

Dom continued to study the drawing. "What's this?" He pointed to the two letters beside a circle, the lone one of which had been filled in. "*EX.*"

"I think it's a marker," Harry said. "See how the pillar beside it is filled in? Geoffrey wanted Theobald to find this specific pillar. *EX* may tell us exactly where to look."

Dom shielded his eyes against the sun. "I hope it's not near the top. That pillar is at least thirty feet high."

"Worry about that after we find the letters."

It took a little time to confirm there was no writing visible on the pillar. *EX* was nowhere to be found, at least not at ground level.

Harry frowned. "There are too many people around to try climbing." He considered the pillar, as though staring at it would make the chiseled stone sprout handholds. A helicopter buzzed overhead. Inspiration struck. "We don't need to climb it," he said. "We need to fly to the top."

Dom raised an eyebrow. "What?"

"There's an electronics store back in town," Harry said as he started walking briskly back to the car. "We're going to buy a drone."

An hour later Harry and Dom returned to the same spot, the new owners of an exorbitantly priced drone that came with a high-resolution camera, a half hour of guaranteed flight time, and a charged battery. Now all they had to do was fly the thing close enough to spot any writing on the higher portions of the pillar. Harry took the controls. "Stand back," he said. "These blades are sharp."

The sun had fallen low on the horizon. Most visitors were leaving before dusk, the site's official closing time. The drone had a small light attached in case it got too dark, but it wouldn't pay to be noticed by anyone official. Harry didn't even know if they were allowed to fly a drone here. He looked around, found no one watching, and shrugged. "Here goes."

Blades whirred, and they had liftoff. It took off like a bullet, so fast Harry let off the gas and it came tumbling back to earth. He smashed the accelerator and sent it careening off at a crazy angle, buzzing Dom's head as his partner hit the deck. This machine would make one hell of a weapon.

"Watch it!" Dom stayed down, hands covering his head.

"Sorry." Harry had it airborne again, practicing basic maneuvers well away from Dom's head until his confidence grew enough to aim it at the pillar. "Can you see the video feed?" Harry asked. "Mine's good."

Harry's remote control had a screen displaying a live feed from the drone's camera. Dom held a larger monitor showing the same. "Same here."

"If I crash this into the pillar you'll have to climb," Harry deadpanned.

"I'll be right behind you."

Harry smirked as he worked the controls, gradually bringing the drone closer to the targeted pillar. By now the grounds were empty. Harry squinted in the fading sunlight as the drone now buzzed within feet of the pillared wall. He nudged the controls. *Just a little closer.*

The drone took off like a shot, headed straight for the stone. Harry panicked, then got it high enough to clear the wall. Almost. Stone chips fell as their drone clipped the pillar before disappearing from view. Harry pulled back, realized he was actually aiming down, then reversed course as the ground rushed up at him on the screen. An instant before impact he let go of everything. The screen did not go blank. Instead, he took a deep breath and walked around to the far side. The drone was hovering in place, a foot off the ground.

Dom's voice rang out. "That is the most piss-poor flying display I've ever seen."

Harry couldn't help but laugh. "I think I've got it now." Operating with a lighter touch, he got the drone to within two feet of the pillar this time, close enough for their camera to make out weathered scrapes in the rock and individual pebbles on top of it. "You see anything?" he called out to Dom.

"Nothing. Check every side, and the stones above those window frames. It looks like there used to be a walkway or floor up there. Geoffrey could have gotten a lot higher than we can today."

Harry spotted the line of different-colored stones. Yes, it could have been another floor or a rotunda. *Great.* Now he had to get close enough to read all around the top of the pillar without smashing his drone. Thank goodness it wasn't windy today. As the sun's lower lip touched the horizon, he moved in closer, checking his side of the wall first.

The drone revealed a few jagged edges, more smooth ones rounded by weather, and a close-up of a pockmarked surface. The machine descended closer to the window arches, each one wide at the bottom and rising to a sharp point. Decorative molding surrounded each arch, smoother masonry than the uneven stones on the main wall. Harry hovered around the first window frame, then followed it back up to the top. Nothing.

Now half the sun had disappeared from view. Shadows stretched from one end of the open park to the other, pushing away the daylight, and with it any chance of deciphering Geoffrey's next clue tonight. It would be no problem coming back tomorrow, but that meant an extra day for the Cana family to follow their trail, or for the three unidentified forces to pursue him. They could already be here.

His heartrate picked up. Harry took his eyes off the screen and checked the grounds. One couple still in sight, far down near the Lady Chapel. If anyone was on the other side of this wall, Harry wouldn't know. They could come up from behind Dom and he'd never see them.

"Go back," Dom called out from the wall's opposite side.

"Did you see something?" Harry asked.

"Maybe. On the window frame. Could be a half-circle on the decorative part."

Harry reversed the drone, drifting back the way he'd come. "This far?"

"Keep going. Another foot or—*there.*"

Harry's throat caught. *Writing.* High up on the wall, right outside the window frame. Not on the front where churchgoers could see it. This was outside the stone arch, facing the rear wall. A wall without windows to allow light inside. In a shadowy Dark Age abbey, the writing would have been impossible to see. "It's a word," Harry said. The drone hovered as he squinted. No, not a word. *Two letters.*

"*EX.*" Dom called out as Harry read them. "You see it too?"

Harry blinked. Every part of his body tingled. *I was right.* He tilted his head and leaned closer to the screen. "Dom, come here." The Italian appeared moments later. "You see the cracks?" Harry asked. "Around the letters?"

Dom studied his screen, then Harry's. "Those look man-made. They're straight." He turned from the screen to the pillar. "Or it could be an old repair. If a piece cracked off, they could have cut a new one and dropped it in."

"That would be a heck of a tight cut," Harry said. Dom shrugged. The sun was now only a slice of fire above the distant hills. "We're the last ones here," Harry said. "I don't want to wait another day. We need to check it now."

Dom shook his head. "It'll be completely dark soon. How are you going to get up there?"

Harry knew the basics of rock climbing. Keep your hands and feet on the wall and your ass in the air. He swallowed, hard. The very basics. "I'll do it."

Dom stared at him. Harry stared at the pillar. "You're serious," Dom said. "Wow." This time Dom looked in every direction. "There's no one here. There are trees all around us. No one can see us here unless they walk toward us." He turned back to Harry. "I still think it's crazy."

"When would be better?" Harry asked. "I can't climb up there during the day. I'm not waiting."

"The Canas could show up, but they'd be sorry."

"It's not just them. You read Geoffrey's letter. We aren't the first to follow this trail."

Dom shrugged. "Fine. Tell me how to help."

Purple now tinged the sky; darkness would soon follow. How to climb a thirty-foot pillar in the dark? "Keep an eye open for anyone," Harry said. "The outside wall has more spaces in the stonework for handholds. I'll go up that side, get to the top, then come around. It's easier to shimmy down the molding than climb it."

Dom clearly thought Harry had one oar in the water with that plan. "Hold on. I can't catch you if you fall from way up there."

"Get out of the way if I do," Harry said. "I don't need you injured too. Who will carry me to the hospital?" Dom didn't laugh.

Harry checked his screen once more. He and Dom went to the outside wall and, after landing the drone at their feet, Harry set down his remote control. The framed window area was smooth, with only a few blocks of carved stone set atop each other to form the window area. The uneven, rough rocks offered solid handholds – if the centuries-old mortar held.

Only one way to find out. Harry stood at the wall and reached for the window frame. "Boost me up." Dom put his hands together for Harry to stand on. He lifted Harry and when the frame was within reach Harry pulled himself up to sit on it. A moment to catch his breath, then he vaulted up to stand inside the window frame. Now anyone looking toward the window would be able to see him, backlit against the darkened sky. He felt for a handhold in the irregular rock face, finding one and pulling hard on it. The stone held. He tried again with his other hand and had the same result, then took a breath and stepped up off the ledge, his feet finding larger stones that stuck out from the wall.

Hard earth waited if the stones broke. Harry concentrated on the rock inches from his face. Three points of contact at all times, and take it slow. He ascended one stone at a time, finding solid holds in the irregular masonry as he moved, never thinking about anything other than the next move until he was reaching for the pillar's top and hauling himself up to sit on it. He looked at Dom. It was a long way down.

"You good?" Dom asked.

Harry flashed a thumbs up, then lay flat across the top of the wall, getting low to stay out of sight. He peered over the top at his target, about ten feet down. The hard part would be keeping hold of the wall while he inspected the letters and the lines around them. If *EX* marked the location Geoffrey had indicated, Harry had to figure out what came next while clinging to a sheer wall twenty feet in the air.

No reason to sit here worrying about it. Harry took his time finding a solid foothold for both feet before descending. As his father had always told him, most climbers didn't have accidents on the way up. It was the way down that killed you.

He gritted his teeth as the rough stonework cut into his hands. The jagged edges were smaller on this side and harder to grip. A few feet lower and he'd be able to see the letters. His shoulders burned. Boxing and lifting weights didn't work climbing muscles. The wall, inches from his face, blocked out what little light remained, forcing him to climb as much by feel as by sight, using the window frame as a marker. He was getting close. Another step down, and he reached for the thick molding. It should be right about...*here.*

His fingers brushed over the letters. *EX.* An image of his father flashed through his mind, from their first expedition, when Harry had been a boy – a journey to Norway where they had located a Viking runestone based on Harry's research. That's when Harry had realized he wanted to be like his father. An explorer.

His foot slipped. Harry twisted as he fell, swinging and sending his other foot flying loose. He dangled by one hand, twenty feet in the air. He fought a losing battle, fingers slipping as he scrambled to lodge a foot in the wall, trying and missing twice. The wall would carve gouges in him as he fell, scraping into his flesh like a cheese grater – *Got it.* A last, desperate kick caught, giving him a toehold.

"You okay?" Dom called out.

Harry opened his mouth to respond as his foothold vanished, the stone cracking under his weight. A garbled shout escaped his throat, loud as a roar in the quiet night air. Dom yelled a response, though Harry didn't catch any of it. He was too busy grabbing for anything to hold on to as he lost his grip one finger at a time. Holding on with three fingers, he looked down towards the ground, which was now almost swallowed by darkness.

Harry kicked away from the window frame, then swung hard back toward it. His free hand reached out, scrabbling for purchase as both shoes scraped uselessly at the wall; panic gave his frantic kicks extra strength as he swung. *Too far.* He went beyond his reach, three fingers sliding off the stone as he floated weightless for an instant, careening toward the window molding.

Gravity took hold and Harry fell, kicked one last desperate foot out, and reached for the dark wall. His hand found purchase. So did his foot. The fall stopped as fast as it had started, leaving him hanging with his face pressed to the wall, never more grateful to have rocks cutting into his forehead. He found another foothold as Dom's voice floated from the darkness below.

"Still good?"

Harry took a deep breath, his eyes closed. "I'm good." He opened his eyes to the window molding. The letters were right there. "The letters are up here. And I can see the lines around them." He leaned closer, moving with the utmost care as he pulled out his phone and turned the flashlight on. "These are definitely man-made." The lines surrounding the two letters ran down the molding until the darkness hid them. "It could be a repair."

Hanging from the wall with one hand while holding his phone with the other left him no way to thoroughly check the cracks. Every time his hand moved the light went with it. "This will have to work," he muttered, then clenched the phone with his teeth. He cocked his head and angled the light on the molding, showing the carved line as a thin shadow running along one side. Perhaps it really had been a repair, a slice of stone carved to match the original after some damage, then mortared into place. One way to find out. He grabbed the molding and tried to break it away. If this was a repair, it was solid. Harry sighed, sending a little shower of dust billowing from the rocks in front of his face. *What now?*

His right hand burned, tired from being latched in place with a death grip while he tried to break down the molding with his left. Light invaded the crevices between stones as he clung to the wall, shifting his weight when his leg shouted for relief. He pulled himself up a level, so that now he was looking down on the molding and the jagged stones beside it. He couldn't see anything between the stones, and his shifting weight now forced him to move one level higher. Harry blinked, then stopped breathing.

Letters were carved into another stone now in front of him. *EX.*

Seconds passed. Dom called up, a note of urgency in his voice. "Harry? Someone will see your light if they look over here."

Harry didn't respond. The same two letters, carved into a stone only inches from the other letters. Why two sets? Someone had carved the letters twice, both sets near an odd repair mark on the molding. He shook his head. No, not just someone. The people whom Geoffrey had been following had done this. *This* was what Geoffrey had been after, what the dying priest had told him about in Monmouth. This was what the *three forces* in Geoffrey's letter were searching for. Now all Harry had to do was figure out what it all meant.

He reached out and grabbed the stone. Maybe that line wasn't a repair after all. His fingers pressed on the carved letters as he pushed down, leaning into it. Nothing. He pushed again with all he had.

Without warning a crack filled the air as the stone gave way. But rather than falling free, it simply moved at an angle, so that Harry's hand slipped off. He gave a yelp as he lost his balance and pitched sideways. The only thing he could do was kick against the wall as he fell so the stones didn't shred his face on the way down. His stomach went to his throat as he twisted toward the ground and braced himself. It was dark, so dark he couldn't find the ground and it was coming up right—

The ground found him, *giving* when he landed, cushioning his blow before he bounced, as though he were caught in a net. A net with muscles.

"Got you." Dom grunted, falling to the ground, tossing Harry aside before they both collapsed. "Damn."

Harry stopped rolling. Dom had caught him, breaking his fall before he crash-landed. Slowly, the world righted itself, and Harry sat up. Dom sat a few feet away, rubbing his knee.

"You okay?" Dom asked.

Fingers flexed and legs moved. Everything seemed to work. "I think so. You?"

Dom stood, grimacing as he took a step. "Twisted my knee."

Harry's heart sank. "Sorry, Dom." He got carefully to his feet. "I think you saved my life." Dom waved off his thanks, still rubbing his knee. Harry looked back up at the spot he'd fallen from. *The rock.* "I found a second set of letters up there," Harry said. "By the molding." The words tumbled out. "The same letters, *EX.* I tried moving the stone to see if it was a lever of some kind. The molding repairs were too good, too smooth, and it moved when I touched it. But why would someone put two sets of letters up there? It doesn't make sense."

Dom pointed to the ground, below where Harry had lost his grip. "You ripped a chunk of wall off when you fell."

Harry jogged over – then went sprawling into the grass again as his foot caught on something heavy. *This is not your night.* He got to his knees and shone his phone light back to try and see what he'd tripped over, turning the grass a dazzling hunter green. A long, narrow stone glinted in the beam.

Harry stood and moved closer. Stone didn't reflect light that way. There was a metal ball attached to the broken stonework. He crouched down, reached for the rectangular section and discovered it was hollow, with something dark underneath. Leather, it looked like. Someone had carved out a spot in the molding and put a release lever beside it. Now he grasped below the ball and pulled again. Every nerve in his body tingled as he kept pulling to reveal what had been hidden inside.

At last, it slid open. Harry gasped, reached in, and then held their prize up so the moonlight caught it. "It's a sword," he said, his voice barely a whisper.

White light danced on the blade as Harry held it aloft, turning it back and forth. The thing was *solid*, stretching three feet from tip to handle.

"It's a Roman sword," Harry said, turning toward Dom. "You can tell by the handle. This is what Roman infantry carried."

"Hold on," Dom said, hobbling closer. "I thought Geoffrey lived in the Dark Ages. Why would he hide an old Roman sword?" His face lit up. "It must be valuable. And why hide it in here?"

"I don't think he did," Harry said. "But I think I know who this belonged to." He turned the weapon upside down. "I *knew* it. Look here, on the bottom of the handle. This is who owned it. *Castus.*"

"The military leader from Croatia," Dom said. "Where you found the map and Guinevere's tomb."

"It makes sense he'd have a sword like this, long enough to use on horseback. Look at the blade, where it's nicked and been repaired. This wasn't a show piece. This was a warrior's sword." Harry studied the pommel, frowning. "The balance is wrong."

The blade swished in the air as he sliced it up and down, testing the weight. It felt off, unbalanced. The very last thing a Roman soldier's primary weapon would be. "Here, try it." He handed the sword to Dom, who mimicked Harry's cuts. "Do you feel it too?"

"You're right," Dom said. "It's—"

Something cracked on the wall behind them. Harry spun around as a small shower of rock dust tumbled to the ground.

"Harry Fox."

The strange voice stopped him in his tracks. Harry turned toward it, aiming his light into the blackness, and suddenly a burst of white light blinded him, an almost physical force he had to throw an arm up against. He twisted away, trying to peer through his fingers while fear's icy hand grabbed him by the throat and squeezed. *He knows my name.*

The voice, a man's, spoke again. "Don't move." Now the light flicked over to Dom, back to Harry, then to Dom again. Harry glanced over to see Dom in much the same position, one hand shielding his eyes, the other behind his back. The sword had vanished.

The man spoke sharply now. "Put your hands up." As he spoke, he continued to flip his light between the two of them as though he were looking for something – or someone.

He doesn't know which one is me. Harry didn't have to make it easy on him. He waited for the flashlight to flick back over to Dom, then he shut off his phone light and sprinted toward the wall, angling for the far end so he could go around and put solid stone between himself and whoever had shown up without an invitation. He made it halfway before the first sparks burst to life, a firework blooming on the stone wall. Then another muffled *pop* and more sparks.

Gunshots. Harry hit the deck. Another shot smacked the wall a good ten feet over his head. Warning shots. Harry buried his face in the grass, becoming one with the ground. *Don't make a sound.* The beam of light played over him, washing past him in a blur as it went toward the wall, scanning and coming back just as quickly.

"Stop!" the man shouted as the light vanished. Another muffled shot, and Harry got up, looking back to see the man intent on where Dom had been moments ago. There was no sign of Dom. Harry went straight for the wall, aiming toward the stone window opening. Five steps. One chance or he'd be a hanging target, good as dead. The wall in front of him suddenly blazed white again as Harry leapt for the windowsill. His arms stretched to catch the lower lip as his feet scrabbled on the rough stone to propel him over the edge, never slowing until he scampered through and over to the other side. A shower of sparks trailed him down as bullets pinged the stone beside him. Sharp stones peppered his arms.

He crash-landed, mind swirling as he bounced up, then crouched low by a pillar in case the guy ran around the far end. The muffled sound of the shots told Harry he had a suppressed pistol. Guns were hard to come by in England. Suppressors even more so. And out here, he could shoot with little risk of being discovered, as the closest occupied buildings were several hundred yards distant at best.

The man's voice rang out again. "Hands up. Now."

In an instant, Harry realized the man wasn't speaking to him. He sprinted to the next window opening and poked his head up. The man had his flashlight on Dom, who was kneeling in the grass, his body angled away from the man, one arm shielding his eyes. The other stayed hidden. *Dom has the sword.*

Harry ducked back down. He needed to get closer and distract the intruder so Dom could get away. Dom was fast. He'd hang on to the sword, vanish into the night, and then they could rendezvous later. Harry dropped to his knees, flicking on his phone light and shielding it with a hand so only a faint beam escaped. Something like… *There it is.*

The man was still shouting at Dom to stand up when Harry powered on the drone. The blessedly quiet motors whirred as it lifted into the sky. Harry kept it below the windows, hovering in front of him as he ran to the wall's far end, which brought him behind the intruder. He could see Dom captured in the flashlight beam, one arm still behind his back as the gunman shouted and aimed at Dom's chest. Harry crept toward them, keeping one shoulder close to the stone wall as he moved. The drone mirrored his pace, buzzing softly in the night.

Harry moved forward, his footsteps silent on the lush grass. He got a look at the guy, a stranger, and definitely not one of the Cana men in his file.

"Okay." Dom finally responded. He raised one hand, keeping his other hidden. He stayed in a half-crouch. "You shot me. I can't move my other arm."

Harry's chest clenched. He'd gotten Dom shot. The gunman hesitated. He was backlit by the clear night sky, giving Harry a direct view of his rear. Harry knelt down, set the drone on a collision path and hit the gas. The device took off like a hornet.

Steady red lights were the only sign of a drone hurtling on a collision course with the gunman's head. The man never turned as it closed in. Harry opened his mouth, preparing to shout for all he was worth once he'd knocked the gunman down and give Dom a chance to run for cover.

The drone accelerated. Seconds from impact the gunman sensed something, or maybe heard the buzzing, but as the drone bore down, he turned and looked right at Harry. He tried to bring his gun around as the drone crashed into his face, a direct hit. Down he went.

"Run, Dom!" Harry bellowed. "Go go go!"

But Dom stayed frozen in place. *What the hell is he doing?* "Go!" Harry shouted again, and to his relief, Dom started to move. His relief was short-lived, though: instead of turning and heading for cover, Dom took a step *toward* the gunman, then another, and on the third one he started screaming and hefted the Roman sword over his head.

He was halfway there before the gunman sat up, his arms flailing around in the dark grass. *He dropped his gun.* Dom's suicide run might just work, Harry thought, if Dom could knock this bastard on the head and disarm him. Dom's eyes were two crazed white orbs in the darkness as he started to swing. One final step and it would be over.

Dom screamed as his knee gave out mere feet away, sending him sprawling to the grass. The knee he'd injured catching Harry. Dom staggered to his feet again, roaring with pain and rage, as the gunman found his weapon and ripped off two shots at point-blank range. Dom went down and didn't move.

The gunman whirled toward Harry now, searching in the dark for his target. Harry's fingers moved of their own accord, flicking a switch to turn the drone light on while mashing the gas. The drone leapt back into the air at once, spinning silently to face Dom's killer. Its powerful little light seared his vision and sent him stumbling back, covering his eyes with one arm and firing aimlessly into the night. Harry turned the drone's nose down and aimed it into the man's chest. The gunman leapt to one side and the machine whizzed harmlessly past, inches from his neck. Then, foolishly, the shooter turned and followed it, blasting away. Harry jammed the controls into his pocket and sprinted noiselessly over the grass after him. The man gave a grunt of surprise as Harry rammed his shoulder full force into the man's back and sent him tumbling.

There was no time to waste. Harry spun and ran back to Dom's fallen body, grabbed the sword from Dom's hand, and dashed back to the gunman, who was gasping and struggling to his feet. Harry grasped the handle of the sword in both hands, and tried to smash the flat of his blade on the gunman's head. Only the gunman stopped running. Harry's timing was off as he ran, the blade coming down too fast before it vanished, lost in the gunman's shirt. Harry's momentum carried him ahead as he smacked into the shooter before finally stopping. Harry went still. *I stabbed him.*

The shooter looked down at his chest, at the metal shaft sticking out of it, then looked up at Harry with shock in his eyes. He dropped the gun. Harry let go of the sword's handle and kicked the gun out of reach. The gunman found Harry's gaze again.

"I didn't mean to kill him," he rasped. A dark stain was spreading across his shirt. He reached an arm out and shakily touched the sword's hilt. "Is this it? What Geoffrey's message told you to find?" Harry struggled to find his voice, then said it was. "Where?" the man asked, speaking with difficulty now.

"In the window." Harry pointed. "A hidden drawer."

The man's fingers brushed over the blade. "You must destroy this." Fire blazed suddenly in his eyes, the hot intensity wildly out of place against his deathly pallor. "This will ruin us all, Mr. Fox. Throw it in the ocean and forget this ever happened."

Harry buried the ice-cold shock in his gut. The shooter was lying. Harry wasn't buying it. He pushed aside the fact this was a dead man talking. "Why did you come after us? What's so special about this old sword?"

"This sword will rock the planet to its core. Billions of lives upturned. We have sought it for two thousand years to stop that from happening."

Harry frowned. "*We?* Are you one of the three forces Geoffrey mentioned?" He looked left and right, finding nothing but darkness.

"Yes. I am one of those three. Sworn to secure this knowledge, to save man from himself. Our faith separates man from beast. It makes us who we are. You must understand that." He pled with Harry even as his eye lids fluttered. "Don't keep searching. You must stop now."

"Where are the other two?" He reached for the man's outstretched hand, then stopped. "Who are you guys? What *forces* are you talking about?"

"I am Aaron. My brothers will follow. Stop this now." Those words came out as a whisper. Harry leaned in to catch a final breath exhaled into the night. Aaron's body went limp.

Harry turned and walked over to his fallen friend. He suddenly felt exhausted, empty. He sank to his knees beside his friend's body and dropped his head into his hands.

He couldn't say how much time passed before he heard the sound of traffic in the distance.

Get it together. Harry gained his feet and stepped back over to Aaron's body. The sword had to come. He tugged on it and eventually levered the blade out of the man's chest, cleaning it on the grass. *Grab the drone,* empty Aaron's pockets, *leave the gun.* A simple cross necklace around Aaron's neck stayed as well. That done, he knelt beside Dom for several long beats, thinking about how this good man had died because of him. If Harry hadn't fallen from the wall, Dom wouldn't have caught him. His knee would be fine and right now they'd be on their way out of Glastonbury, prize in hand.

Instead, Harry stood and bit his lip, steeling himself against the tide of emotions threatening to overwhelm him. Not here, not now. Later. All of it could come later. Harry took a direct route for his car, heedless of being spotted. If the gunshots hadn't alerted people to their presence, his footsteps sure wouldn't. He made it to the car and dropped everything except the sword in the trunk before heading as fast as caution allowed for the city limits.

He could run from the Glastonbury carnage, but the questions burned, Aaron's dying pleas circling in his mind. Brothers, billions of lives upturned, men and gods. Two other forces were coming. But who were they, and what did it mean? He'd figure it out, avenge Dom, and find what Geoffrey had hidden.

The Volkswagen's engine screamed as Harry merged onto a highway. He knew where to find these answers. His eyes flitted to the footwell, where he'd laid the sword of Lucious Artorius Castus. Whatever lay ahead centered around that piece of forged metal, an ancient relic now soaked in fresh blood.

Chapter Eighteen

Outside of Glastonbury

An anonymous room in a forgettable hotel provided Harry the perfect refuge. An hour earlier the only person he trusted for thousands of miles had been shot by a man Harry had then stabbed to death with a Roman sword. Now Harry, clad in a hotel bathrobe, huddled behind a locked hotel door, the deadbolt shot. His entire body ached. Harry wanted nothing more than to collapse onto his bed and sleep. If it weren't for the sword lying nearby, he might have done it.

He drummed his fingers across the table. Dom was gone. Harry had killed a man named Aaron who was somehow tied to three forces who were searching for the sword he now had in his possession. What did it mean? Practically, it meant at least two other people were out there hunting him. How had Aaron located Harry and Dom when there was no way in the world he should have been able to?

Harry kneaded his forehead. *He found us. Start there.* How? Easiest answer: someone had told Aaron where to look. Harry traveled under a false passport with the name Daniel Connery. Dom had flown directly into Germany and driven with Harry to Glastonbury. So there was no way Aaron could have used Dom to track Harry. Which meant Aaron had found Harry another way. Only Vincent, Joey and

Rose Leroux knew he was in Glastonbury. None of them would sell him out.

The chair creaked as Harry jerked upright. Unless, of course, one of them had. He rubbed his eyes until white lights flashed on the backs of his eyelids. No, they wouldn't do that. There was the possibility Aaron had somehow stumbled across their path during his own search. Regardless of how Aaron had found them, however, Harry was aware that a third option would likely come into play now: once the two other forces realized Aaron was dead, they would come after Harry to finish what Aaron had tried to do.

The room's heating system kicked on, forcing hot air through the vents to warm Harry's bare feet. The clothes he'd been wearing, socks included, were caked with blood and dirt. They were now in a garbage bag ready for the first dumpster he saw tomorrow. After that, he was getting as far from here as possible. But where? The only way he could see to stay ahead of the other forces was to follow Geoffrey's trail and uncover the truth behind this web of cryptic statements and hidden messages. *Two brothers. Billions of lives. Messages hidden in graves.* All tied to one of the most enduring legends of the last millennium.

Harry checked the deadbolt again. Still locked. Having the sword in the room with him made him nervous. The weapon was three feet long and surprisingly lightweight, yet it seemed to fill the room with its presence, carrying the weight of centuries and untold secrets. One of which Harry was about to uncover. Harry had noticed when he first picked it up in Glastonbury that the weight seemed off. Dom had noticed too; it was the kind of thing a Roman soldier would never tolerate.

A silver ball at the hilt's bottom was worn to a high sheen through decades of use, smooth even after two thousand years. He tapped it and was rewarded with a satisfying *thunk*. It sounded solid. His eyes and fingers moved to the handle, where you gripped the weapon, and which at one point had been wrapped in smooth leather, now reduced to dry shreds. Harry tapped a bare spot with his fingernail. His nerves tingled. No *thunk* this time. In fact, this part sounded hollow.

Harry grabbed the sword blade firmly and twisted. He nearly sliced off a couple of fingers, put the sword down and grabbed a blanket to hold the blade before going at it again. The metal ball on the bottom refused to budge. Redoubling his efforts, he twisted until his arms ached before picking it up with the blanket and smashing the handle on the ground, over and over, as he cursed the rust that had to be holding it shut. When he stopped flailing around, he'd managed to cut a long hole in the blanket while doing nothing to dislodge the handle.

Harry sat down on the room's single chair and slumped back, the sword resting on his lap. The wall light in front of him caught his eye, an electric bulb set in what resembled a candle sconce. Harry sat up. *Candle sconce.* He bolted from the chair, checked that his robe was tied securely, grabbed his room key and stepped out into the hall, locking the door behind him. At the front desk, the young female attendant smiled at him from behind glasses thick enough to stop bullets.

"May I help you?"

"Do you have any matches?"

"Of course, sir."

She reached under the desk and handed him a box of matches before turning back to her work. Harry thanked her, turned and headed back towards the stairs, leaning stealthily to one side as he went and scooping a decorative candle from a lobby table. He then made a beeline for his room, where he bolted the door behind him once more. He grabbed the sword, went into the bathroom and turned the exhaust vent on.

If he was right and the ball at the base of this sword handle unscrewed, the thing had likely rusted tight. He needed some sort of lubricant. Too bad he wasn't near a garage, where a shot of WD-40 or a torch would do the trick. Instead, he planned to melt candle wax to act as lubricant, then use the matches to heat the metal hilt. As the hot metal expanded, the melted wax would seep in to lubricate the threads. Not the best plan, but he had no other options. He stepped into the bathtub, laid the blade across his knees so it balanced and struck a match.

The candle wick caught fire and wax began to drip. Harry sparked another match and began warming the hilt, the flame going back and forth, holding each precious match until his fingers burned then quickly firing another to keep heating the metal. When he was nearly out of matches, Harry tipped the burning candle until wax almost covered the hilt. Finally, he blew the candle out, wrapped his hand in the towel and paused.

The hot metal was uncomfortably warm under the towel as Harry tucked the blade under his shoulder and twisted the hilt with both hands. No luck. He tried again, then leaned out and bashed the hilt on the floor to loosen it. Teeth gritted, arms straining, and in no small danger of stabbing himself, he twisted. Hard, until his back and neck screamed for relief. He gulped air, cursed, and tried again.

The hilt broke off. One second it was stuck tight; the next, Harry lost his balance and stumbled forward, dropping the sword onto the tile floor. He flailed and grabbed at the bathroom vanity lest he fall and impale himself. The broken hilt rattled around on the tiles like a ball on a roulette wheel. Harry kept both eyes on the sword as he stepped out of the tub. On the first try he burned a finger grabbing the scalding hilt, then used the towel to pick it up and lay it on the vanity beside the sink. The stark white bathroom light showed a dinged, scratched ball of metal that had grooves cut into the middle, allowing it to latch on to the handle.

Harry bent down and grabbed the blade so he could look at the handle where the hilt had separated. As he turned it, something fell out of the handle and landed in the toilet.

Splashing and cursing, he pulled whatever it was out and hurriedly found another towel to lay it on. It was a narrow leather bag. Cinched at the top, the bag was longer than his closed fist, and it resisted any attempt by the water to penetrate it. Harry gulped. This was what Geoffrey had been after and what Aaron had been willing to kill for in Glastonbury.

Harry went back out into the bedroom and grabbed his phone. He snapped several photos of the bag, then gingerly pulled at the dry leather string holding it shut. It scraped his fingers as he pulled, finally loosening its hold on the top of the satchel until he could see inside. *It's a scroll.*

He tipped the bag over and a tightly rolled sheaf of rough material slid out onto the vanity. *Papyrus.* A common writing material in Roman times. He dried his hands before touching the rolled papyrus, unrolling it with excruciating care, fighting centuries of stiffness as he flattened the paper against its will. Handwritten letters covered the surface in a tight script, the dark ink clear to his eye. *Latin.*

Harry took more photos from different angles, fighting the urge to translate as he went. Only after he was certain the text had been captured did he start to translate. The message began without preamble.

Diocletian denounced the Christian faith. All troops must sacrifice to the Roman gods and reject the Christian God or lose rank, and with it the life we know. Every man must obey. I hide my faith to save the life I built.

The true Word must survive, for as emperors change often, the Savior's message is strong and unyielding. These records remain hidden from the Roman gods, for I hold the messages of a mightier god. This proves to me the faith I possess is the one true path. I must protect it.

The Christian who receives this sword must retrieve the recorded truth. It will be found in the Flavian Amphitheater arch by following the XX on my sword. Look beyond, to the VII, to find his Word.

L.A.C.

The only sound was Harry's breathing. He read the missive again, ending on the three initials that confirmed all Geoffrey had said. Lucius Artorius Castus, whose sword he held and whose missive he now translated. Artorius, one of Rome's most powerful leaders, had practiced his Christian faith in secret. He had risked his life to keep those truths from his emperor. Diocletian had declared war on the Christian faith, never realizing his trusted commander would undermine those efforts to preserve that faith.

Ordered to abandon his faith, Artorius, a devout Christian, had chosen to keep it hidden until he'd been forced to protect a *recorded truth*. Whatever that *truth* was, exactly, it was tied to his faith and had been hidden from Roman rulers since the time of Jesus, two hundred years earlier. The final sentence caught Harry's attention with a vise-like grip: the Flavian Amphitheatre made a second appearance in this quest, first as a reference point and now as a destination. Harry chewed his lip. The Colosseum was big. Where to start? And how would Harry know if what Artorius referred to still existed?

Only one way to find out. He booked the next flight from London to Rome, then called the front desk and requested help mailing a package to the United States. How large? About three feet long and a foot wide. The desk assured him they had plenty of packaging materials to secure anything of that size, and they'd be happy to send it for him. Yes, add it to his bill. He could pick up the box and padding in a few minutes.

It wasn't as though you could take a sword on a plane. His safest bet was to mail it to Vincent and Joey. They could always work with Rose to sell it if for some reason Harry couldn't come home. He didn't consider why that might be. With the logistical details handled, he made one final call.

"I wondered when you were going to check in," Joey Morello said. "How are you and Dom?"

"Dom's dead."

Silence met his words. Joey's response was so low Harry had to strain to catch it. "My father is here. Tell him. Then tell us how."

Joey put the call on speaker. Vincent Morello's voice came through. "Harry, what is wrong?"

Harry repeated the news, then recounted what had transpired, starting at the beginning. "After we left Glastonbury, Dom and I drove to—"

Vincent cut him off. "Stop. Do not tell us where you are. Tell me how anyone could have found you."

"I'm not sure. This wasn't the Canas."

"Are you certain?" Joey asked.

Harry said he was. "There's more than one person after us. I – I just know. Trust me." His conversation with a dying man named Aaron had nearly slipped out. "At least two more people knew where we were tonight."

"Any chance there's a leak?" Joey asked. "Either on our end or yours?"

"You think someone would sell us out?"

Vincent spoke. "It is not always intentional. Your whereabouts may have been compromised on our end without us ever knowing. That is why you should not tell us where you are. Assume everything we discuss is being overheard."

Vincent and Rose Leroux were more alike than either of them realized, Harry mused. He could do worse than take their advice. "I suspect the people who found me aren't from our part of town." He paused. "They've been involved with this project for far longer than I have."

"Say no more," Vincent said. "Will you be returning home?"

"You'll get a package from me," Harry said. "I hope to be back shortly after. There's one more stop to make."

"Do not stay longer than necessary," Vincent said. "That is tempting fate."

Harry assured them he wouldn't. "If for some reason I don't come back, talk to Rose about what—"

"Stop. You will return," Vincent interrupted. "Focus on that alone. You cannot afford distractions."

"Thanks, Mr. Morello. I appreciate it."

"It is Vincent," he replied. "One item before you go, to hearten you on this journey. I know your father's death weighs on your shoulders."

"Yes," Harry said. "It does." He couldn't think of anything else to say. *Vincent brings this up now?* Odd, to say the least. "I'd like to ask him a few questions, that's for sure."

"Fred Fox was one of the most wonderful men I ever knew," Vincent said. "Direct and complex at the same time. You are wondering why I say this." Harry was indeed. "Today I spoke with a man who knew your father. An Islamic cleric."

Harry drew in a sharp breath. *Cleric?*

"This cleric knew your father for many years. He also knew your mother."

Dani Fox had died when her son was a little boy, leaving him with precious few memories. One was of him and her together outside their house, Dani pushing him on a swing as the wind blew her hair. Another was of him seated in her lap, the two of them reading a book together. There was a dim image of walking hand in hand with her on a sidewalk. Beyond that, he didn't have much.

"I did not realize Fred had kept in touch with anyone connected to Dani after she died," Vincent began. "For all those years afterwards, Fred took an interest in your mother's faith, more so than when she was alive. A private part of his life, one that I think you should know about."

"Why do you say that?" Harry asked.

"The cleric knows of you. He asked if Fred's son held an interest in his mother's religion. Your Pakistani heritage ties you to the Islamic faith forever, Harry. If you wish to learn more about it, or about your mother, this cleric will speak with you."

A disdain for organized religion had taken root inside Harry over the years, in part from working with his father. Many of Fred's projects had been tied directly to various religious artifacts, and it seemed every time religion had come up during their searches, it had revealed man's darker nature. Harry had no love for any of it now.

But maybe he was wrong. He had just learned that faith had kept Dani Fox alive in her husband's mind after she was gone. He shook his head in surprise. His father, an academic who had previously eschewed all forms of religion, using it to keep his deceased wife's spirit alive? Harry touched the amulet around his neck. *Maybe you have more to learn about a lot of things.*

"I'd like to meet him," Harry said.

"I will arrange it. A man's past should not be forgotten." Vincent coughed. "You must be tired. Stay vigilant, Harry."

He assured them he would and clicked off. His mother's face stayed in his thoughts as he packed what little he had, then retrieved a shipping box and materials from the front desk and readied the sword for shipping. Harry set the weapon on a sheet of foam padding, then snapped a photo of one specific spot: the row of engraved Roman numerals that ran across the blade, right above the handle. He'd looked past them when he'd first found the scroll. Not any longer. *Tricky, Artorius. I like it.*

With that done, he put the leather pouch and letter back inside the handle, sealed the box and addressed it to Vincent. If he didn't make it back to New York, that letter would sell for far more than an anonymous Roman sword. He dropped the package at the front desk, then locked his door, lay down and turned out the lights to catch a few hours' sleep. His flight to Rome left in the morning. The Colosseum was a massive place to search, but Harry wasn't concerned. Artorius had already told him where to look.

Chapter Nineteen

Athens, Greece

A local news station broke the story first.

Hiram had started checking for any reports of incidents in Glastonbury when Aaron failed to check in on time. Aaron had last spoken with both Hiram and Mo as he stood outside of Glastonbury Abbey. Hiram had convinced him to check the parking areas first, and Aaron had found only a few cars still there. Only one had foreign tags on it. Aaron had sent the information to Hiram so he could check for any connection to Harry Fox, though so far they'd struck out. Fox was likely traveling under an alias, but maybe they'd get lucky and find a passport with a photo. Fox could change his name, but he still had to use his real picture.

"Mo, get over here." Hiram pulled up the news station's social media feed. "This was just posted. Police activity at Glastonbury Abbey. Locals reported possible gunfire. Wait, here's an update." Hiram's stomach sank. "The coroner just showed up."

Bad news, yes. If it was Aaron, there was nothing he could do for him now. "He'll call us if he can," Hiram said. "I'll check this foreign car tag." He didn't have to explain to Mo why.

Hiram quickly discovered that the foreign-registered tag Aaron had sent him came from Luxembourg. "What's the car doing in England?" he asked no one. "It's a long way from home."

The principal strength of their organization was the three men who staffed it, the current seekers of the knowledge lost several thousand years ago. However resourceful they might be, the three men still had limitations. Which is why they had leveraged connections with worldwide faith communities to do more than should have been possible. Hiram put in a call to one of his contacts in Germany, a rabbi whose brother worked for the *Bundespolizei*, the German federal police force. It was after midnight in Germany, but the rabbi answered at once, and after Hiram explained his concern, promised to get information on the car rental within the hour.

Hiram clicked off. He looked up to see Mo standing behind his desk, a cell phone pressed to his ear. Mo's face had gone white. Hiram waited for Mo to hang up. "What is it?"

"I think Aaron's dead." Mo fell into his chair. "That was a guy I know who listens to UK police radio. They found two corpses in Glastonbury. Both Caucasian males."

Hiram jumped from his chair. "Two white men?" Then he frowned. "Harry Fox is Pakistani-American."

Mo nodded gravely. "He's not dead."

"Harry could have had other men with him." Hiram sat back down, his knuckles turning white as his hands clenched into fists.

"Harry Fox may already have the information," Mo said. "Glastonbury may have been the last stop."

"We simply don't know." Hiram pushed his anger aside, tamped down the urge to strike back at Harry Fox with everything they had. That wouldn't get them any closer to holding what had been lost so long ago. "I may have a lead on him with the car tags Aaron sent us. The car's registered in Luxembourg."

"Why would Fox drive from Luxembourg to England?" Mo asked.

"If he wanted to get into England without anyone being able to track him. Border crossings don't have flight plans. If I wanted to get from Germany into England, I'd rent a car and drive too."

"Fox could have made another stop before Glastonbury," Mo said. "Aaron only picked up his trail in England."

"We can't know about that," Hiram said. "Harry Fox went to Glastonbury Abbey to follow Geoffrey's trail. Aaron tried to stop him. It looks like he failed. Now we have to hope there's more to this hunt than Glastonbury, or else Harry Fox is in the wind with information we need."

Neither man had to say what could happen if they lost Harry Fox. If he really had found the trail's end, what he now possessed could change the face of humanity forever. Their entire existence would be a failure.

Hiram's phone rang. The country prefix for Germany flashed on-screen. "Yes?" he said. "Good. Send it to me. Thank you, my friend. *Leitraot.*" He clicked off and checked his email. "The rental paperwork from Luxembourg is coming to us now. Along with the passport photo for the man who rented it."

"No chance the name is Harry Fox?"

Hiram shook his head. "No." His screen flashed. "Here we go." Hiram opened a file and a dense rental contract appeared. He scrolled to the bottom. A scanned copy of the renter's passport was attached. Hiram smacked the desk. "Got you."

Harry Fox stared back at them.

"That's his face," Hiram said. "The passport says Daniel Connery."

"I doubt it's hard for him to get false documents," Mo said. "Either way, Harry Fox drove across Europe and the English Channel to Glastonbury. He was there tonight and it seems he wasn't alone. The other body at the abbey may be someone who was with Fox."

"At least Aaron stopped one of them." Hiram caught himself. "He could be alive but injured, or have lost his phone, or a dozen other things." Although he voiced his thoughts, that didn't mean he believed them.

Mo knew it too. "Let's hope you're right," he said sadly. "For now, we track Harry Fox. Call your friends in Tel Aviv, see if Daniel

Connery had any airline bookings, car rental agreements, anything tied to a passport. It's a long shot, but if Harry Fox is headed somewhere else, we could get lucky."

"If he found what Geoffrey of Monmouth sent him to find, then Glastonbury Abbey was the final stop." Hiram glowered at the desk. A low growl sounded in his throat. "I'll call my Mossad contacts."

For now, Hiram and Mo busied themselves trying to reach Aaron and obtain information on the bodies in Glastonbury. Neither had any luck. Several hours after his initial call to the Mossad, Hiram's phone rang.

"It's Tel Aviv," he said to Mo, then connected the call. "Yes? I see." He scribbled on a note pad. "Got it. *Leitraot.*" He looked up to Mo. "Daniel Connery is booked on a morning flight from London to Rome. He lands at nine."

Mo ran over to his desk and typed furiously on his laptop. "I can get us there at eight."

Hiram lifted his phone. "I'll call Rome. They need to know that Aaron is probably dead, and we need weapons. They'll give us backup and any hardware we need."

Mo looked up. "And a place to get rid of a body."

Chapter Twenty

Rome

Daniel Connery boarded his morning flight from London to Rome, taking his seat in first class before leafing through pages of handwritten notes, the dense script impenetrable to anyone without a knowledge of Latin and a healthy understanding of Roman and Christian history. He had plenty of time to study them, as the plane was delayed and they didn't land in Rome until well past noon.

He raced off and pushed through the terminal, bobbing and weaving through the crush of passengers clogging Rome–Fiumicino International Airport to find a taxi, which promptly got stuck in horrendous traffic. Road construction, accidents – you name it, Daniel Connery ran into it before finally getting to his hotel as the afternoon sun broiled Rome.

The man traveling as Daniel Connery made it to his hotel room, shut the door, and then Harry Fox let loose a heartfelt stream of invective fit to peel paint from the walls. Over half the day wasted. He fell onto the bed, rubbing his palms over both eyes. He had made it to Rome, was in a hotel room barely a mile from the Colosseum. That was good.

Harry sat up. First, a shower. Then, food. After that, on to the Colosseum. If he was right, Harry needed to find a good place to hide inside it. Either that or break into the Colosseum after dark.

Showered and fed, Harry slipped a single page of notes into his back pocket and walked out of the nearby café into Rome's evening embrace. Warm air carrying dust and diesel fumes tickled his nose. Crowds lined the Via dei Fori Imperiali, forcing him to make detours around stopped groups or those with small children. Harry passed kiosks of vendors hawking maps and replicas of the Colosseum, restaurants with outdoor tables packed together close enough to induce panic, and a dazzling marble-fronted basilica dedicated to martyred Christian brothers. The pavement stretched straight ahead of him, terminating at one of the most recognizable structures ever built. The Flavian Amphitheatre. The Colosseum. What Harry hoped was the final stop on this path laid out two thousand years ago.

Pedestrian traffic thinned a bit closer to the Colosseum. The dry air parched his throat to the point Harry bought water from a street vendor and drained it in one go, change rattling in his pocket as he kept walking. The Colosseum closed in a little over an hour, so Harry encountered few people as he stood outside with his neck craned to take in the uppermost stones. He had precious little time to search. It wasn't like they'd turn on the lights for him to keep looking. Even now, long shadows fell from the circular amphitheater, stretching hundreds of feet back toward the city. Harry patted the small flashlight in his pocket he'd picked up from a street vendor. It would come in handy if he ran out of time and was forced to somehow stay inside past closing.

Harry approached an entrance gate and produced his ticket, dodging among people streaming out and back toward the city. This was his third visit to the Colosseum. The first two times, he'd come with his father. Harry stepped from light into shadow, the hair on his arms rising as the ancient stones cast shade over him. He squinted in the suddenly dim light. Electricity ran through his entire body. Fred Fox was gone, so it wasn't quite the same feeling he'd got before. Still, the weight of centuries pressed down on him and made Harry forget, for an instant, why he'd come.

Gladiators. Roaring crowds. Christians and criminals executed on these grounds in horrific fashion, some eaten alive by starved lions while fifty thousand spectators roared their approval. Harry shivered in the shadows.

All of it had been chronicled, studied and shared exhaustively. However, for Harry the Colosseum had at least one more secret, if only he knew where to look. He turned to look back the way he'd come, at the interior side of the gate. At the arch above it, to be exact, searching for something that wasn't there today, but had been two thousand years ago. Gate numbers.

Roman builders had chiseled numerals above each gate. All seventy-six of them. The numerals had faded, yet were still there if you knew to look. Harry squinted and could just make out the *LXV* above the gate he had entered. Gate sixty-five. That meant he had a long walk to find the gate number Artorius had carved into his sword. Harry set off, the already sparse crowds thinning even more as he moved down the rounded walkway, keeping close to the exterior curved wall. Past another gate and the hairs on his neck rose for no apparent reason. A sheet of newspaper skipped past his feet.

He spun on a heel. A man walked some distance behind him, holding one of the selfie sticks for sale on seemingly every corner. A cell phone was tethered to the end as the man recorded his visit. Harry slowed and waited for him to pass, moving on only after the yarmulke atop his head disappeared from view around a corner. The guy never even looked his way, the trim mustache on his upper lip flapping as he kept up a running commentary on the Colosseum. No one else was around. No one could know he was here, not even Vincent Morello. He'd be fine as long as he avoided attention.

Harry passed gate forty-nine, moving deeper into the Colosseum, while a few more stragglers walked the other way. A sliver of doubt nagged at him: assuming Artorius had left something to be found, could it possibly still be here undisturbed? And if it was that well-hidden, how would he recognize it?

Gate thirty-seven. Almost there. Two more people walked past him on their way out, though Harry spotted the yarmulke guy still up ahead, heading on a loop around the walkway and still using that awful selfie stick. Gate thirty-three passed. Harry flashed back to the numerals engraved on Artorius's sword, the *XX* along one half of the blade. On the other half, *VII*. As Artorius had said, he had to *look beyond* – in this case, from the first side of the blade to the second. Put those two points together and he had a destination. Gate twenty-seven.

Which was where he now stood. Harry licked his lips, dry from gritty dust floating on the breeze. This was the spot. He looked up to the *XXVII* carved above the gate. He moved closer, ignoring the question demanding an answer in his head. No, he didn't know what to do now. This was it. He'd figure it out right now, or hide somewhere in this massive place and wait for nightfall to keep searching.

He lifted his arms. His fingers didn't come within fifteen feet of the arch's lowest point. This could be a problem. Artorius would have left the *recorded truth* in a secure space. Could it be inside the walls, hidden behind or near the gate number? Harry had thought so, at least until now. There was no way to get up there to check without a ladder and a whole lot of privacy. Two things Artorius likely didn't have. Which meant Artorius was pointing him either someplace lower or somewhere more accessible. The stones to his left were weathered, clean and utterly unhelpful. He looked to his right. *What's that?*

An engraving at eye level in one of the stones to his right. He stepped over and the object became clear: it looked like a large pin or spike, with wings attached at the top. A pair of twisting serpents circled the spike until they faced each other at the top, below the pair of wings. He knew that symbol. It was a caduceus, and it had symbolized healing and medicine for millennia. Yet there was more detail to this carving. Two small crosses on either side of the serpents, both with ovals attached at the bottom. Beneath that, what looked like water dripping from the ovals. He didn't recognize them, yet for some reason they seemed familiar. Why?

Harry's gaze unfocused. An image struggled to take shape in his mind's eye. He closed his eyes. *Where did I see that before?* His eyes flew open as he remembered. "On the church. The one I just passed right down the street." He smacked the wall with an open palm. "That's it."

He'd seen those crosses *not an hour ago*. On his walk to the Colosseum, inscribed across a brilliant white stone archway above the basilica's front door, a quarter mile distant. The *Basilica Sancti Cosma e Damiano*, or the *Basilica of Saints Cosmas and Damian*. It was set back from Via dei Fori Imperiali, the road running directly from the central Piazza Venezia to the Colosseum. Many of the buildings in this area had existed since the time of Christ, including this basilica dedicated to the two well-known saints. Arab twin brothers, both were physicians who had been murdered for their Christian faith, dying under the persecution of Diocletian. The same Roman emperor involved with nearly every aspect of this lengthy search.

Cosmas and Damian had been immortalized right down the street. Artorius wanted Harry to go back there. The doubling back, the hidden codes left in plain sight, the steps leading across Europe – it was logical if you thought about it from the perspective of Artorius, who had focused on staying alive and hiding his faith while in active service to the empire. Discovery meant losing everything, including his *recorded truth*.

The Colosseum was not the end point. Artorius hadn't chosen to hide anything here. No, he'd looked somewhere else. A less public but also a secure location. Like a nearby basilica.

Conversation sounded behind Harry. He spun to find the mustached man with the selfie stick had returned, now headed back to the entrance, one hand pressed to his ear while the other kept waving that awful stick around. Harry kept an eye on the man, who never looked Harry's way as he carried on a one-sided conversation in English. Harry turned back to the engraving, checking above and below for other clues as to what Artorius had intended to say. He found only smooth stone.

Selfie-stick man was now almost directly behind him. Close enough for Harry to make out what he said. "…it's amazing here, really it is. I'm heading around the walkway near gate twenty-seven, and it's empty this late at night. Well, there's one person here. Look at that, it's my friend Daniel Connery. He's right here."

Harry's brain caught up with his ears. *Daniel Connery.* The name on his false passport. He spun around and came face-to-blade with a knife.

"Don't move." The selfie stick clattered to the ground as yarmulke man grabbed the front of Harry's shirt. The knife gleamed inches from Harry's chin. "I just want to talk."

"Then why the knife?" Harry didn't move as he spoke, though his eyes darted in every direction. Nobody in sight. "No need for that."

"I know what happened to Aaron," the man said. "You're tougher than you look."

Harry felt a burst of indignation as he lied. "I don't know anyone named Aaron."

"You killed him in Glastonbury. We only wanted to talk." The man must have seen Harry flinch. "Now," he said, and moved the blade a fraction closer while pulling Harry toward him. The metal was warm on Harry's chin. "Tell me what you found in Glastonbury. What sent you here?"

We? The three forces. The man at Glastonbury, Aaron, had come alone, but he wasn't a solo operation. This man was with him. Which left one more. Even as Harry did the math, footsteps sounded from down the curved walkway and another man appeared, stopping yards back from where Harry stood. Any hope of salvation was dashed when he pulled a gun from inside his pocket, the barrel sporting a suppressor that he aimed at Harry.

"I won't ask again." The blade scraped Harry's stubble. "What did you take from Glastonbury?"

"A sword. That's all."

Yarmulke man frowned. "What sword?"

"A Roman one."

The man inhaled sharply. "*Artorius*. His sword." The grip on Harry's shirt loosened. "That's why you went to his tomb in Croatia. Geoffrey of Monmouth was following the path of Artorius."

The new man closed in on them. "What does he have?"

"He found a sword in Glastonbury," yarmulke man said.

The new guy waved his gun. "Where is it?"

"On its way to America," Harry said.

"You're lying."

The gunman stepped closer, only to be stopped when yarmulke man let go of Harry's shirt to hold him back. "No. He's telling the truth. He couldn't transport a weapon from England to America himself. We can worry about it later." He turned back to Harry, who stepped back a fraction to get some breathing room. "You said the sword sent you here. Why?"

Time to delay. "You're the three forces Geoffrey wrote about. How are you still pursuing this a thousand years later?"

Yarmulke frowned. "Three forces?" Then something Harry might call understanding dawned in his eyes. "I see. Yes, three. We are here, as we have been since Rome ruled the world."

"You killed Aaron." The gunman stepped toward Harry, close enough to poke him with the suppressor. His teeth flashed when Harry winced. "I know Aaron didn't go down without a fight. Now I'll finish it for him."

Yarmulke barked at him. "Put that down." The man glared at yarmulke, but did as he was told. "Daniel Connery still has much to tell us. Starting with why he is in the Colosseum."

Harry's mind raced. All he could do was buy time. He had no idea what these guys already knew. An obvious lie and that nut with the gun might shoot him. "The sword. There was writing on it."

Yarmulke frowned. "I'm listening."

"The Roman numeral twenty was inscribed on one side." That was true. "The name *Flavian* and *A-M-P* were on the other. I remembered this place had gate numbers, so I played a hunch and came here. Artorius was saying to go to gate twenty."

"If he was pointing to gate twenty, why are you standing at gate twenty-seven?"

"The other side had Roman numeral twenty-seven on it," Harry lied. "That's Artorius's legion number," he said quickly when yarmulke scowled. "The same number was also written on his tomb in Croatia."

Yarmulke grunted and turned to the gunman. "Check the wall where he was looking. There's something there."

The sun had fallen below the horizon to leave them in twilight and shadows. The gunman stood in front of the gate, leaning close to the engravings Harry had studied a minute ago. Yarmulke man never took his eyes off Harry. "What did you find?" he asked.

"A picture that makes no sense." If he could mix truth with lies enough to keep these two men off balance, maybe he'd have a chance. "I recognize part of it. The drawing of a staff with wings and two serpents is the caduceus, the Greek symbol for medicine."

"It made a strong impression on you. Don't lie. I watched." Yarmulke's face hardened. "Why?"

"Because there's more to it – a couple of crosses I've never seen before, and I know a lot about the past. If you know what they mean, I'm all ears."

Yarmulke man blinked. "What do you see?" he finally asked the other man, calling over Harry's shoulder. "Recognize anything?"

"Looks like some kind of medical symbol," the gunman said.

"What else?" Now yarmulke wasn't actually looking at Harry but over Harry's shoulder toward the arch. Harry took a half-step back, repositioning his feet, sliding one in front of the other and crouching ever so slightly, weight on his toes like a boxer. He tensed. Yarmulke didn't react.

"Two crosses," the gunman said. "With circles at the bottom."

Yarmulke looked further over Harry's shoulder. The knife edged away, giving Harry breathing room. Harry's fingers quivered. Wait for it. Wait... *Now.*

Yarmulke's eyes were on his associate, not Harry. He didn't notice as Harry reached up with two open palms, one going for the inside of yarmulke's wrist, the other striking hard on the back of his knife hand, forcing it open and sending the knife flying. Harry darted in low, punched yarmulke in the nether regions and then grabbed him behind the neck before flipping the larger man up onto his shoulder. Harry pivoted, using his legs to hurl yarmulke man directly at the gunman. A muffled gunshot sounded, no louder than a cap gun.

Harry ducked, reaching into his pocket and coming out with the handful of coins. His change from the water vendor. The heavy metal discs turned into shrapnel when he whipped them at the gunman's face. The man lifted both hands to protect his eyes. Harry leapt over yarmulke and smashed an elbow into the gunman's jaw, knocking him back but not quite going down. The man snarled and brought his pistol to bear as Harry bunched a fist around his knuckle dusters and socked him in the stomach. The gunman folded with an *oomph*, his forehead coming down at incredible speed and smacking Harry between the eyes. Stars burst and filled Harry's vision as he stepped back, tripped on the prone body of yarmulke man and crashed to the ground.

The gunman kept his feet, stumbling as Harry tried to right himself, getting only one foot under himself before the shooter threw a wild punch and knocked him off balance again. The pistol came up. Harry lashed a foot at the other man's knee. It connected, the knee twisting with a sickening sound like something wet snapping. The gunman howled as he fell toward Harry, who could only twist away as the man's entire weight crashed down on him, pinning him between yarmulke man below and the shooter above. Another suppressed shot popped off. Harry spun, rolling and turning until he slipped free and rose to one knee. His body seemed weightless, so amped with the fight-or-flight response he could have run through a wall. Harry patted his chest, arms, legs, searching for but not finding any holes.

The shooter lay on his stomach. A red circle bloomed on his back. Harry jumped over, ready to pummel him if he moved. The shooter didn't budge as Harry felt for a pulse. Nothing. He didn't see the gun, couldn't see much of anything in the shadowy dark, so when a deep groan filled the air he jumped up and took cover behind a pillar. The moaning continued for a long beat. It wasn't the shooter; it was yarmulke man, groaning and struggling to get out from under his partner's corpse.

Harry bent over the man, keeping one fist cocked. Yarmulke man's eyes opened as Harry leaned over him.

"Get him off me."

Harry didn't respond, instead digging for the gun. *Which hand did the guy shoot with?* His right. He pulled the man's arm out from under him to find the pistol still in it, the man's finger caught in the trigger guard. Harry stopped pulling.

"You shot me." Yarmulke man stopped groaning to curse at Harry. "Bastard." He offered several more epithets before Harry realized they were aimed at the dead gunman, not him.

"You're hit?" Harry extricated and unloaded the weapon, tossing the bullets and magazine into a darkened archway across from them, and the unloaded pistol the other direction, far down the corridor. He grabbed the knife and tossed it out of reach. "Hey." Harry smacked yarmulke man's chest. "Where are you hit?"

"On my *side*," he said through gritted teeth.

The guy was keeping pressure on it, though he didn't resist when Harry pulled at his hands to get a better look. Yeah, that was a bullet wound, all right. Not that Harry knew much about gunshot wounds, but it looked like the bullet had clipped his stomach and sliced a chunk of flesh out. Blood stained the man's shirt.

"Stop moving." Harry looked in every direction. No one in sight. The suppressed shots hadn't attracted attention. So far. "I'm going to move him." Harry met the man's eyes. "Don't do anything stupid now. I'm trying to help you."

The man nodded. He must have been in more pain than Harry realized. He grunted hard when Harry dragged the shooter's corpse away, and then Harry lifted the injured man by both shoulders, pulling him as gently as he could to the nearest column. He set him in a semi-seated position against the marble, picked up the man's hand and clamped it tight over where the bullet had scored his flesh. "Hold your hand there and keep applying pressure," he instructed.

The man did as instructed, and Harry stepped back. "Don't try to move," he told him. "I'll go and fetch help." Yarmulke man didn't blink. "I will," Harry said. "Whatever's at the end of all this isn't worth dying for." His father's face came to mind. "Trust me," Harry finished.

"You really don't know, do you?" the man asked. "What you seek could upend the world."

Harry squinted at him. "What is it that's so dangerous? *Upend the world?* You say these terrible things, like I'll unleash a plague. What the hell are you talking about?"

The man grimaced. "I can't say."

"Can't or won't?"

"Can't. Geoffrey of Monmouth and others before him prevented our brotherhood from uncovering what was left behind."

He expected Harry to buy that line? "Two thousand years chasing after whatever Artorius had, and you tell me none of you even know what it is? That's bogus." His jaw grew tight. "You know what's out there. If it's worth spending so many lifetimes searching for, then I know one thing." He leaned closer to the man. "I'm going to find it. Once I do, you find me. Maybe I'll sell it to you for the right price."

Harry stood back. The Colosseum must have night staff, people to check every section after closing time. He hadn't come this far for a security guard to catch him. He left yarmulke man slumped against the pillar and headed for the basilica of *Santi Cosma e Damiano*. He didn't pass another person until the exit was in sight, an elderly man tottering along with a cane to hold him up. Only after Harry made it through the arched entranceway did the Colosseum's cold, stony embrace release him. At least out here he could run if the cops showed up.

The city's lights had come on in full force, hiding all but the brightest stars overhead. After he cleared the Colosseum grounds he turned around, looking back under the light of a half-moon to find no one following him. He'd left one man wounded, his partner dead. Even if yarmulke man pursued him, the red herring of gate twenty should slow him enough for Harry to get to the basilica and uncover what Artorius left behind.

A new purpose filled his steps. The two other forces from this brotherhood had managed to find him in the Colosseum, which meant he needed to be careful. It also suggested he was getting close. Close enough to have brought the only two men left to stop him out of their lair in order to find what had been missing for so many years. He reached for the amulet. *I wish you were here, Dad. This should have been our journey, our find. Together.*

Harry sighed. What he wouldn't give for Fred to be with him again. He shook his head, pushing the thought away. What would Fred say? *Stay focused. Stay alert.* Harry laughed to himself. *Don't worry, Dad. I hear you.*

Harry moved toward white stone gleaming in the moonlight ahead. He could see a pair of spoons with crosses on their handles etched across the top, homage to two Arab brothers, physicians martyred for their faith in the time of Lucius Artorius Castus. And he moved toward Artorius, the hidden Christian who had laid out this path. The marker calling Harry Fox to a small, quiet basilica to uncover the *forgotten truth* behind this ancient mystery.

Chapter Twenty-One

Basilica of Saints Cosmas and Damian

Light foot traffic moved on either side of the Via dei Fori Imperiali; couples walking hand in hand in the moonlight, adventurous tourists hoping to capture images of the Roman Forum in a new light, or clergy moving purposefully from one building to another. Within this slow trickle of people one man darted to the side, hurrying up the sloped walkway to the twenty-foot doors.

The man's progress slowed as he closed in on the church. Almost as though he hadn't seen the scaffolding set up in front of the tall doors, metal poles crisscrossing them in a latticework pattern, blocking any path forward. The man leaned over to inspect the sign indicating renovations were underway, with the basilica now closed. A thoroughly non-religious string of words filled the air.

Harry skirted the scaffolding and stepped deeper into the shadows. He'd taken in the metal framework on his way past earlier, but he hadn't truly *seen* it, not with the Colosseum demanding his attention. Now that the finish line was potentially in sight, he couldn't get inside this place for at least a week. More than enough time for anything left of the *three forces* to regroup and hunt him down. Harry slipped between the scaffolding, turning sideways to squeeze through and reach the front door. He pulled the handle. It didn't budge.

Buildings stretched to either side in an unbroken row. He could go around, though the Roman Forum stretched out behind these buildings and was certainly patrolled by police. Scratch that. He couldn't go in the front, couldn't risk going around the back. No convenient cellar doors offered a chance to slip in below ground level. That left one option. He craned his neck and looked up. The scaffolding looked sturdy.

Wooden boards ran horizontally across the vertical metal frame, allowing workers to move from left to right, though moving horizontally required climbing up the exterior portion while taking care not to mistake a board for a solid foothold. Do that and hopefully you were still close to the ground. If not, it was a long way down, and the cement ground promised a hard landing. Harry set a foot on the closest metal pipe and started climbing. He nearly smacked his head on a metal hasp, part of the fall protection required for such dangerous operations.

This place must have upper windows, or if it came to it, a chimney. With the building to his back, Harry climbed, one hand at a time, up the solid structure. Halfway up he looked down and immediately regretted it. A fall from here entailed spinning around as he bounced off scaffolding, likely hitting the building a few feet behind him. He'd be lucky if he didn't break his neck. Not to mention the steady foot traffic along the Via dei Fori Imperiali meant he could be spotted at any moment. Construction workers would not be out at this time of night. One wrong move and the cops would show up with questions he couldn't answer.

Harry kept his eyes facing ahead, climbing until he turned to see roof tiles below him. A pair of boards traversed the gap between the scaffolding and the roof, a sturdy, unprotected bridge thirty feet in the air. One wrong step and whatever Artorius had left inside would have to wait for someone else. Harry looked straight ahead as he crossed. Two long steps later his feet found the roof tiles. Harry stopped. Why didn't they have more scaffolding up here? The tiles rose at a sharp pitch to the peak in front of him, not far at all but requiring him to scale up a forty-five-degree slope to the top. What waited beyond, he had no idea. The breeze had become unpleasantly brisk at this height, enough so that he latched on to each tile like the lifeline it was as he ascended to the peak, where he stopped, blinking down at what now spread out beneath him.

An open courtyard. Water trickling from a stone fountain, green foliage overhanging the walkways on all four sides, each with a half-dozen curved archways disappearing into the interior. Windows dotted the upper two levels. A quaint oasis hidden in one of Europe's busiest cities. White blinds blocked him from seeing into the rooms, but not a single light glowed behind any of them. Soft yellow light slid out from the interior walkways, giving shape to the courtyard's shadows. Moonlight painted the upper half of each wall.

A drainpipe connected the roof to the courtyard below. He leaned forward, reached under the overhang to grab hold of the iron tube. Several U-bolts anchored it to the wall. He could shimmy down, though if the pipe didn't hold all Harry could do was try to grab the decorative masonry that ran around each window, hope to catch it with his fingertips and somehow clamber down like Spider-Man. He gave the pipe a serious shake. It seemed to hold.

One foot went over the edge as Harry scooted back until his entire lower body hung free. The drainpipe angled in toward the wall, away from him, so he slid until only his fingertips looped over the gutter. Harry clenched the drainpipe between his knees before one hand flashed to the pipe. He held on tight, repeated the process, then did his best fireman impersonation and slid down in a poorly controlled freefall. All went well until he went beyond the moon's reach and into darkness, descending at speed toward a ground level he could no longer see.

He locked up. Arms, knees, everything clenched. The pipe squealed, his hands burned, and the ground smacked him without mercy. Sky and ground flipped in a terrifying whirl until he thumped off something solid and the world spun no more. Groans filled the air. His own, Harry realized, and he quickly shut up. He stretched out one arm and flexed each finger. All seemed in order. Same with the other arm. He stood. Both legs seemed to work as well, though one knee barked in displeasure. All in all, not too bad. He'd made it.

Getting in was the easy part. Now he had to figure out what in this basilica tied back to Artorius. *Use your head.*

Harry had everything he needed to figure this out. Fred had taken him on many journeys, first by telling young Harry the stories of his adventures, then by bringing Harry along with him. Fred had had a process, and it worked. First step, look for patterns. A man had laid this path out, a man with his life on the line, yes, but a man all the same. People followed patterns.

In Monmouth Harry had found the first edition of Geoffrey's *Historia Regum Brittaniae*, which had sent him to Diocletian's Palace in Croatia and the graves of Artorius and Guinevere. In her grave Artorius had left a message pointing to the church of St. Bacchus in Trier, Germany. From there, on to Glastonbury Abbey, where the letters *EX* on a ruined wall tied back to a map added to Geoffrey's book.

As for Roman clues, he had a letter, two symbols, and an abbreviation, followed by the most improbable piece so far: Excalibur, the sword with one missive secreted in the handle and another etched on the blade, taking Harry to the Colosseum and an engraving honoring two Arab physicians.

The clues ran through his head again, then once more – and then the ground seemed to quake as suddenly it clicked. What tied every clue together, the single common thread running across each? They all had remained hidden while *existing in plain sight*. Each was somehow tied to a Roman world. To Artorius, it had been unthinkable Rome could ever cease to exist. The world's greatest empire had dominated Artorius's every moment. This Roman military leader who had secretly worshipped an outlawed god would have hidden each piece of knowledge in the open so it didn't stand out *to a Roman*.

What did Romans love more than war? Symbols. Of power, of gods, of themselves. So Harry was looking for an image no Roman or religious leader would think twice about even if they saw it every day, one tied to the path he'd taken. It could be associated with St. Bacchus, but that didn't fit. Plenty of churches in this city had ties to Bacchus. This one did not. No, he suspected the answer lay with one of two images. Either the caduceus, or the two crosses with spoon-like ends. He'd already seen the crosses far over the basilica's front door. Now he had to hope those two weren't the only ones around here.

Harry made a fist. *Thanks, Dad. Right again.*

His back was to the entrance, so he turned and walked that way. There had to be signs around here, something to help visitors to find their way. Once he passed out of the courtyard's walkways and into the actual basilica, Harry flicked on the penlight from his pocket and crept forward, keeping close to the stucco walls. The place was empty, and the weak electric sconces did little to combat the gloom. Artwork dotted the walls, saints and angels from centuries ago, none related to the Arab brothers or to ancient symbols of medicine. He passed a window as a cloud scudded across the moon.

It took longer than he hoped to find his way through the interior maze of passages and hallways, eating up precious time. The three forces may have been waylaid, the last of them left for dead in the Colosseum, but that didn't mean he could afford to spend another night in Rome.

His light flashed across a sign as he finally neared the front door. Arrows pointed in every direction, offering help in Italian and English. Two locations caught his eye. *Crypt* and the *Temple of Romulus*. Of these, one spoke to him, demanding his attention. He'd learned long ago to trust his gut at times like this.

On to the crypt. Artorius and his mysterious *truth* had tracked closely with graves and bodies so far, from Geoffrey's grave in Monmouth to the crypts beneath Diocletian's Palace. It could be coincidence, yet he'd be foolish to ignore this obvious connection with the dead. He wasn't surprised when the hallway led to a descending staircase.

Harry kept one ear open for company before he made it to the bottom step and found a sign attached to the wall. *CRYPT.*

Underground, the place was even darker, shadows taking over every corner and chasing the scraps of muted lighting away. He followed the rounded hallway to a double set of wood doors with iron bars laid across them. Harry tried the handle on one of them. Unlocked.

He pushed it open. Metal shrieked in protest. A quick inspection showed a foot bolt at the bottom hadn't been lifted before he pushed, scoring a gash across the marble floor and making a serious noise. He kicked the lock open and pushed again, and the door swung back silently to reveal a crypt that looked for all the world as though it had once been a chapel, down to the black-and-white stone altar. Memorials lined the walls, a continuous circle of tombs. He closed the door and flipped a wall switch, bringing frustratingly weak lights to life.

A painting behind the stone altar depicted Mary holding baby Jesus as she looked down on two men who sat below her doing not much of anything. Cosmas and Damian? Hard to say. A decorative piece above the painting showed two arms intersecting in front of a cross. He turned his penlight on. Were those arms and the cross the same as the ones he'd seen in the Colosseum? There was a small wooden chair by the door; Harry hauled it over and jumped up on it for a better look. The crosses were two detached arms, shaped like an *X* over a very traditional Christian cross.

The chair creaked as he hopped off and turned to the altar. Placed in the center, the altar had an open bible atop it, along with two unlit candles and a metal cross. *Think like Artorius.* Where would he put something if it had to *stay* hidden? Harry's penlight beam dropped to the altar block, white stone with black veins running through it. He touched the surface, smoothed by untold elbows resting on it during prayer over nearly two thousand years. His fingers dipped under the lip of the altar's top level and hit a rough spot. *What was that?* Harry leaned over and shone his light. A cross engraved in the stone. Next to it, another symbol, what today was called the sign of the fish. Or, as Harry knew it, an *ichthys*.

He circled the altar. More symbols and carvings, two on the next side, and two more on the front, facing the congregants. None matched what he was looking for, but there was a grate covering an opening carved into the altar's base. Above the grate?

Two crosses with spoons on their ends, with liquid dripping from each.

Harry dropped to his knees and grabbed the decorative copper grate. It was bolted to the ground at the bottom, with the other three sides free. A glass plate behind the grate reflected his light, and by shielding it he could see through the glass. Two oversized metal-and-glass vials stood side by side. The center part of each vial was entirely glass, offering a view of small, ivory-colored sticks. Not sticks. Bones.

Of course. They were relics, the finger or toe bones believed to be from a venerated saint. They could even be remains of Cosmas and Damian. Would Artorius have left his message inside one? No, these relics were clearly valued, cared for and guarded within the basilica. Hardly the ideal choice for hiding anything else. He angled his light to see around the vials. While the relic containers weren't likely hiding spots, the open area inside the altar had more promise.

Harry's light couldn't reach beyond the vials. With the copper grate in front, Harry couldn't get a good angle to see much else. He sat back. *Only one way to solve this problem.* The grate was bolted to the ground, but the copper didn't hold up well under the pressure he put on it, levering the grate back and forth until it gave way. Harry offered a silent apology to anyone listening, and after pushing the shards and vials aside, he leaned in.

First thing he noticed was how *clean* it was under there. No rodent droppings, no dust balls or spiders, not even any fingerprints on the vials. If they kept this opening so clean, anything down here would have been found long ago. He moved the vials aside. The opening extended another few feet into the altar, and despite lying on his stomach and sliding in until he could touch the back wall, Harry found nothing. He repositioned the vials, wiping them with his sleeve to remove fingerprints, then slid out and leaned the broken grate against the altar.

Strike one. He still had the Temple of Romulus to inspect, and if that didn't pan out, the rest of the basilica. Yes, the place was big, but his father had done more with less to go on. Harry would do the same.

Back upstairs, this time turning deeper into the basilica, Harry skirted around the open courtyard and through the sanctuary. Frescoes covered the walls and ceiling. Harry's light washed over the main altar and apse beyond it, the curved ceiling an explosion of golden light. Thousands and thousands of tiles came to life, magnificent skies with white lambs beneath saints and Jesus himself, all looking out over the congregation. Latin inscriptions ran beneath the lambs. He couldn't make out the words from where he stood. His light ran across the sanctuary, which was filled with artwork, engravings and sculpture displays. After the temple, he still had plenty of other places to look.

He moved with a quickened step toward the temple. Strangely, the directional arrows told him to walk straight toward a wall. A glass wall, situated at the far back, well beyond the last row of pews. A rope held between two stanchions stood in front of the glass. Where was the door? This wasn't how you got to the temple, he realized with dismay. It was how you *saw* it. The temple was at least fifteen feet below floor level, with no apparent way to get to it. The basilica and temple were attached in name only. Through the glass he noted the temple's front doors, which opened out into the Roman Forum. The double doors were latched tight, with only a thin streak of white light showing through the crack between them.

Harry pressed his penlight against the glass, finding frescoes on the stone walls below, with partially broken statues taking place of honor in the middle, all of them roped off and standing tall on pedestals. Parts of several horses and a pair of male torsos were also on display. No sign of Saints Cosmas or Domnius, and no medical symbols. Harry straightened his back. No matter. He still had—

"*Non muoverti!*"

The voice boomed beside him. Harry spun around, directly into the path of a blinding beam. He covered his eyes, looking down and stepping back into the rope behind him. The poles holding it up crashed to the ground in a thunder of clanging metal.

"*Mi scusi, mi scusi.*" It was the only Italian Harry could muster at the moment.

The light came closer. "*Cosa stai facendo qui?*"

"*Non parli italiano,*" he managed.

The voice responded at once. "Who are you? What are you doing here?"

Harry noted the accent. One he knew well. *African.*

"I'm lost," Harry said. He still had one hand shielding his eyes. "Can you help me? I took a wrong turn and can't get out."

He sensed hesitation. "How did you get in here?" The voice had less aggression in it now, more question. A man's voice.

"I'm not armed," Harry said. He lifted his hands, still squinting against the light. "Can you put that light down?" The light lowered, though the man holding it stepped back. Harry flicked off his own light. "Thanks," he said. "Can you tell me how to get out of here?"

The man stepped back into a strip of moonlight. Clean-shaven, with dark hair, the man couldn't have been much older than Harry. His teeth glowed white in sharp contrast with the dark face around them. "You are not supposed to be here."

"I took a wrong turn outside." Harry lowered his voice. "I'm really sorry, I didn't mean to come in and cause any trouble."

"The doors are locked. How did you come inside?"

Harry couldn't answer the guy's question. He stalled. "Over there," he said and pointed toward the front. "The side door."

"Side door?" the man said. He shook his head, and then muttered barely loud enough for Harry to catch it. "*'ant majnun.*"

Harry went still. The man had said he was crazy, in Arabic. Harry responded in kind. "*'ana last majnunaan.*"

Now it was the other man's turn to gawk. "You speak Arabic?" he asked in the same language.

"I do," Harry replied in kind, then continued in his mother's native language. "I'm sorry." He didn't have many choices at the moment, so he took a leap of faith. "I lied to you. I broke in here and I need your help."

The man's mouth dropped. "You want my help?"

"I'm in trouble," Harry said. "There are men after me. They'll kill me if they find me."

The man's eyebrows furrowed. "What men? You are alone."

"They're chasing me," Harry said. "I just ran in here from the Colosseum. They had me cornered, but I escaped."

"Why do these men want to harm you?"

"They think I have something they want," Harry said. "Only I don't. If I can find it before they do, I'll be safe. That's why I'm here. I think what I'm trying to find is in this basilica."

"In *here?*" The man spread his arms wide. "This is a place of worship. What could be in here?"

Harry tried a different strategy. "What's your name? Mine's Harry. I'm American, and I'm way out of my depth here." Most of that was true.

The man hesitated. His lips pursed, he frowned, then he shook his head. "You are a strange man, Harry. I hope you are not here to hurt me."

Harry leaned back. "Hurt you? No, I'm trying to save my own skin, not hurt anyone. Besides, aren't you a guard? You could call for backup."

"I am not a guard. I am studying to become a brother in this basilica." A true smile spread across the man's face. "My name is Ibra."

"You're not Italian, Ibra. How'd you end up here?"

"I am from Sudan. My family was killed in the civil war. The church took me in, and I will soon be a brother here." His movements became animated as he shined the flashlight around. "While the construction is happening, I stand watch. It is my honor."

Harry's ears perked up. "Been here long?"

"More than one year," Ibra said. "It is now my home, thank God in heaven."

"You know the basilica pretty well, then." Ibra nodded. "These men chasing me, they think I can find something they want. Only I don't know where to look." He stepped closer, keeping his movements slow. "Can you can help me?"

"I will call the police to help you." Ibra pointed behind him. "We have a phone in there."

Harry raised his hands. "No, no police. I—" His mind raced. "I don't trust them. The men chasing me have important friends. I'm worried the police may be working with them."

Ibra's face fell. "How do I know you are not the criminal?"

"I don't know if I'd believe me either. But hear me out. I'll tell you what I'm after, and if you still think I'm a bad guy, call the cops." He had no intention of letting Ibra call anyone. However, he needed the man's knowledge about this place. If he could get Ibra to believe him and help in the search, this could end tonight.

A distant siren blared. Ibra studied Harry. "I will listen," he finally said. "Tell me what you wish to know. Then I will either call the police, or I will help you."

"Good man." He turned so Ibra couldn't see his right hand as it

214

slipped into the dusters. A last resort in case Ibra left him no choice. "Have you ever seen medicinal crosses in the basilica?" He had no idea if that's what they were actually called as he described the spoon-like lower ends with medicine or some liquid dripping from them.

Ibra's face remained steady as he listened. "There are many crosses in this building," he said.

"That symbol is how I'll know I'm in the right place."

"The right place for what?"

Ibra wasn't making this easy. "I'm searching for a message. Left by a Roman military leader who was a Christian in a time when Rome persecuted Christians. I believe this man risked his life to leave a message." Ibra still didn't react, so Harry played his ace. "This military leader lived when Christianity was still young. His message tied to the very beginning, when Christianity began."

He guessed that kind of prize would interest this young man studying to be a priest. A man for whom religion was the center of his life, who seemed to ascribe his survival to good works in his god's name.

"You are serious," Ibra said. Harry assured him he was. "This message, what would it say?"

Harry shrugged. "I won't know until I find it."

"How do the crosses help you?"

"I found a message from that Roman general in the Colosseum earlier tonight. Carved on the wall. It told me to come here and look for either an image of those medicinal crosses or a caduceus. I found a set of crosses in the crypt here. There wasn't anything else down there."

"You are sure."

Harry bit his lip. "I'm sure. I haven't seen any medicine boxes, so I suspect the crosses are what I'm looking for. Any idea if there are more here?"

Ibra looked beyond Harry, up to one of the windows. He rubbed his chin. "I am thinking," he said.

Time passed. Harry clenched his hand into a fist over and over as Ibra stood there, unmoving. "Ibra, these guys are still after me. I was attacked at the Colosseum. One of them died." He raised his hands, palms outward, at Ibra's reaction. "He had a gun," Harry said. "He fell on it and shot himself after he tried to shoot me."

Harry looked at his hand and realized his knuckle dusters were on full display. He jammed that hand in a pocket.

Distant sirens sounded outside. First one, joined a beat later by more. "Hear that?" Harry asked. "They've found the body. I swear, I didn't kill him." He held his arms out wide, clenching his loaded hand into a fist. "Check me. I don't have a gun. I'm trying to stay alive while I find this message."

"The man who tried to shoot you is dead?" Ibra asked. Harry confirmed he was. "Then you do not need to worry. It was self-defense. You should turn yourself in."

"There was a second man," Harry said. "He was wounded. I can't turn myself in. These guys have friends everywhere, remember? I'd end up dead in a holding cell. The way to stop them is find the message first. Once that happens, they have no reason to chase me."

"What will you do when you find it?" Ibra didn't react to Harry's predicament. He stood still, rubbing his chin.

"Depends on what I find," Harry said. "I have no idea if there's even anything still hidden. It could be another message telling me to look somewhere else. Or it could be gone. Chances are anything the general left behind is gone."

"Your path has not been empty up until now," Ibra said. "Perhaps the message remains."

"Perhaps." He looked toward the front door. The sirens still blared, just at the edge of his hearing. "Ibra, I don't have much time."

Ibra didn't move. *Fine. He wants to play it this way, so be it.* Harry could distract him somehow, then pop him on the back of the head. Not too hard. Just enough to take him down, no more. Then Ibra would spend a few hours locked in a room while Harry searched.

He'd let him go as soon as he was done. Harry's fingers flexed.

"Follow me." Ibra pointed toward a hallway across the room. "I have seen the medicine crosses before. In the crypt and in another place. I will show you."

Harry loosed a sigh. "Thank you." He took a step and nearly ran into Ibra's back as the man stopped.

"If you find anything here, it is the property of the Church. You cannot remove it from this place. Do you agree?"

"Deal," Harry said. "I won't try to take it."

Ibra nodded. "*Sawf 'athaq bik.*" I will trust you.

Which worked for now. Harry would figure out if he could keep his word after checking the other crosses. Ibra's powerful flashlight pushed the darkness away as they walked behind the altar, past stone pillars topped with sculpted cherubs and fronted by the painting of Mary and baby Jesus. The gold Latin letters encircling the apse glittered. Ibra pushed on a section of the wall to reveal a concealed doorway, likely how the priests came and went between services. Christianity's dazzling brilliance vanished as they stepped into a short, functional hallway.

Ibra turned through an open side door. "These are the priests' offices," he said. "Through here is our supply area." This shorter hallway had open doors on either side, revealing small offices with little more than desks and chairs. Harry flashed his penlight over each as they passed, mentally logging the route. The hallway ended in another doorway, which opened to a larger room. Shelving and more doors lined the walls. A set of wooden offering bowls rested on the closest shelf.

"This is storage?" Harry asked. "What does it have to do with the crosses?"

"In here." Ibra aimed his light at one of the bi-folding doors, four panels wide. "These are closets."

Harry gave Ibra a wide berth as he stepped past him, his penlight revealing a thoroughly uninteresting closet. Mops, a large recycling bin, bottles of cleaning products and a leaning pile of papers half-filled the shelves. He noted a curved brick arch above it all. "This used to be a doorway," Harry said. "Someone turned it into a storage closet."

"Centuries ago, this was a passageway," Ibra said. "I do not know where it led or when it was changed."

Harry noted the plaster wall's rough nature, the gaps where it didn't quite fit the curvature. "Is that a fresco?" His light brought the colors in the archway to life; muted red and blue and yellow lines faded to a soft glow, all surrounding more intricate designs. Harry leaned closer.

"Yes," Ibra said. "Painted in Roman times. It is the oldest painting we have."

"And you turned this place into a *broom closet?*"

Ibra laughed. "I did not. But you must keep the brooms somewhere."

Ibra stepped closer, and Harry flinched. Ibra merely played his light over the closet's right wall. "Pull the recycling container out," Ibra said. "This is what you must see."

Harry tugged the plastic bin aside to reveal artwork running down the wall. The bricks were bigger here, their rough surface making it hard to see the designs inscribed on them, though he spotted another ichthys. His gaze fell to the floor, and he dropped his penlight.

He fell to the ground, scrabbling to pick it up, breaths coming fast as he fumbled and knocked the penlight away. "Crosses," he said. He finally scooped it up. "Two crosses. Ibra, those are *medicinal* crosses. Look, right here. Below them." He touched the large brick immediately below the crosses, set one row above ground level. "Latin letters. No, not just letters – *initials*. My God, Ibra, this is it."

Three initials were inscribed on the brick. *L.A.C.*

"They have meaning to you?"

"Ys. *Lucius Artorius Castus.* He's the Roman general who left this path, whose messages I followed here."

"Why medicinal crosses?" Ibra asked.

"It's the same symbol that I found in the Colosseum. These two unique cross designs are how I knew to come back to this basilica. Artorius was a Christian. He would have been killed if the Romans found out. He had something to hide, and he left a trail showing where to find it: a series of messages hidden in the open where no one would think to look."

"What was so important for him to hide?" Ibra asked. "To keep his religion a secret is not hard. Practice in secret. God will understand."

"It wasn't just his religion. There's some sort of *truth* he had; whether it's a final message or an object, I don't know. The two men who wanted to kill me in the Colosseum followed me to Rome. Although the path has been here since Artorius died, no one's ever followed it this far. I had information no one else did." Harry stopped for air. "Nearly a thousand years ago a Welsh cleric provided the initial clue in Wales, and that's where the men chasing me first appeared. The cleric, a man named Geoffrey, called these men *three forces*. I think the *forces* are some kind of religious group, men who are willing to kill to find whatever it is Artorius hid." Harry stuck his light into a pocket. "They'd still shoot me if they knew where to find me."

"It is a good thing you lost them," Ibra said.

A crash echoed across the room. Ibra's light flashed wildly until it settled on a rolling wooden bowl. The same kind of offering bowl Harry had passed on their way in here.

An explosion of light filled the room as a new voice spoke from behind them. "Don't move."

Harry started to turn. A cool metal circle pressed against his neck. Roughly the size of a suppressor. Harry stopped moving.

"You didn't quite lose us, Daniel Connery. Or is it Harry Fox?" The pressure on Harry's neck vanished. "Turn around. Both of you."

Harry turned to find a man he'd never seen before holding a suppressed pistol, the barrel aimed at Harry's chest. A shadow beside this new gunman stepped forward. Harry's heart sank. Yarmulke man.

"Harry Fox," yarmulke man said. "I owe you my thanks." He grimaced, one hand going to his chest where the bullet had wounded him. A bandage encircled his torso. "You would have been better off killing me."

"The night's not over yet," Harry said. He looked at the second man, the one holding the gun. This new gunman didn't match with yarmulke man. The beard, the bare head – none of it jived. "You were on the phone with him in the Colosseum." Harry said to the new guy. "Yarmulke here was giving you a play-by-play the whole time."

"Two men were on the call," yarmulke man said. "We are *three* forces." He removed the yarmulke, which disappeared into a pocket. "Jewish." He nodded to the other man. "Muslim."

The last piece was obvious. "And Christian," Harry said. "Your partner in the Colosseum." Then he frowned. "And the one in Glastonbury. He was Christian too."

"I am Hiram." He inclined his head. "This is Mo. Our brother in Glastonbury was Aaron. Our organization is larger than any one of us."

"Yet it doesn't sound like you know what's out there," Harry said. "All these years and you can't even say what you're after."

Hiram turned to Mo, who lowered his weapon.

"A brother of ours uncovered the trail long ago," Mo said. "He fell ill on his journey to modern-day Croatia. As fate had it, he sought aid from a fellow cleric, a supposed follower of Christ."

"Geoffrey of Monmouth," Harry said. "The old priest who got sick and died was one of your group."

Mo's eyebrows lifted. "Yes."

Harry spread his arms. "Okay. So, *what is it?* You're saying it is so terrible. What are we searching for?"

Hiram's lips set in a hard line. Mo glanced at his partner, then sighed. "We believe it is knowledge. Information the world was not meant to know."

A spark flared in Harry's chest and he realized that he was angry. Mad as hell. Dom and countless others had died, and for what? If what Mo said was true, Harry had to know. The answer could be mere feet away right now, so he played a hunch. "You'll kill to get it? Fine." He stepped back and raised his hands. "I'm done. Have at it. Find the path, keep anything you find at the end of it. I'm going home." He stepped toward the door.

Mo leveled his pistol at Harry. "You can't leave."

Harry's teeth flashed. "You going to shoot me?"

"No." The pistol pointed at Ibra. "If I have to, I'll shoot him. Tell us what you know. Five seconds."

Mo didn't count. He kept his eyes on Harry the whole time. *Three. Two.* He was bluffing. *One.*

The pistol cracked.

"Jesus!" Harry jumped as Ibra fell to the ground. "Stop it," Harry shouted. "I'll tell you. Put the gun down." He darted to Ibra's side as his ears caught up with his brain. Wood had splintered on the wall behind Ibra. A cabinet, now sporting one new bullet hole. Mo had missed on purpose.

"Next shot is in his chest," Mo said. "Talk."

Hiram lowered his light to Harry's chest, and Harry looked up in puzzlement as a ghostly golden aura played over the wall behind Hiram. *Was there writing up there?* No, not writing. A reflection from his amulet. Harry had an idea.

"I didn't start out looking for whatever it is you're after," Harry said. "I was looking for a book, the original manuscript Geoffrey of Monmouth wrote."

"*The History of the Kings of Britain,*" Hiram said.

"You're right. I realized Geoffrey had tried to follow the trail. Only you guys kept coming after him. From Wales to Diocletian's Palace in Croatia. I found another message there."

"In the woman's tomb," Hiram said. "It was opened, the body disturbed."

"I didn't have much choice," Harry said. "After Croatia Geoffrey traveled to Trier, Germany." Hiram and Mo both let their mouths fall open. "Didn't know that? That was his last stop. I think someone got too close and scared Geoffrey, so he left a trail for another person to continue searching. It's not all bad, though. I think them scaring him off led him to create one of western civilization's enduring legends."

Mo frowned. "King Arthur? What does Geoffrey's hunt have to do with that myth?"

"I have a few ideas." He ignored their questioning looks. "Next, Geoffrey pointed me from Germany to Glastonbury, where I found the Roman sword with a message in the handle. That message led me to the Colosseum."

"You sent the sword to America," Hiram said. "Where?"

"Where you can't get it." Harry nodded to Mo. "You've been following me, and here we are."

"Correct," Mo said. "Whose sword did you find in Glastonbury? What did the message say?"

"It belonged to a Roman military leader named Lucius Artorius Castus." Both men started. "Yes, Artorius. As in Arthur." Harry paused, willing his voice to remain steady. "This is what the message said."

He moved with exaggerated slowness, reaching up to his neck to grab his amulet, which he lifted up and over his head. Mo kept the gun steady, though his eyes finally left Harry's face, following the amulet. Harry held it with both hands. His neck seemed cold and barren where the leather strap holding it should have been. Other than when he slept, he hadn't taken it off since his father died.

"I didn't know what it meant until I came here." He was making it up on the fly. None of it had to make sense, as long as it got Mo within striking distance. "Artorius wrote directions on it. In Latin, pointing to a symbol in this basilica."

Mo's gun wavered along with Hiram's light. Both stepped closer. Harry kept the amulet close to his chest, forcing them to approach.

"Is it in Latin?" Mo was a step away now. "Do you know what it says?"

"I do," Harry said. "It's telling me to—"

Harry whipped the amulet at Hiram's face and jabbed Mo square in the nose, ducking out of the line of fire an instant before the gun went off beside his ear. He grabbed the silencer and pivoted, ripping it from Mo's grip. He flipped it to his right hand and promptly lost it, the knuckle dusters making it impossible to hold. Mo had both hands on his face, blood pouring from his nose, when Ibra screamed, shouting to the heavens as he rushed Hiram, crashed into the man and slammed him to the ground amid a flurry of elbows and fists.

Mo's fist brushed Harry's cheek. Harry feinted low, and Mo ducked down, his chin skimming past Harry's knee as Harry brought it up. *Damn.* Harry lost his balance and fell back, crashing into a table as Mo charged. The busted nose threw him off just enough for Harry to turn aside, landing an elbow sharply against Mo's ear. Mo sprawled onto the table top and didn't get up.

The sounds of grunting and the thick *whack* of knuckles on flesh filled the room. Hiram had Ibra trapped beneath him, though as Harry took a step over Ibra managed to get a leg free and kick Hiram off, sending him tumbling. A metallic *clang* made Harry's ears perk up. *That's where the gun landed.*

Hiram realized it too. He scrabbled, came up with the pistol and turned to level it at Ibra. Both men were in a sitting position, Hiram leaning his weight on one hand, the other holding the gun. Hiram looked at Harry and kept the pistol on Ibra.

"Don't move. I'll shoot him if—"

Hiram's voice broke off as his hand slipped out from beneath him. Ibra reacted before Harry could blink, diving at the armed man with another chilling war cry, covering the distance too fast to see. Fast, but not quicker than a bullet. The suppressed pistol barked. Ibra grunted, his momentum carrying him forward to fall on Hiram and pin him to the floor. Ibra's head bounced off the floor with an audible crack. Hiram still held the gun.

Harry dove for it. The pistol flashed fire as Harry pounded Hiram's wrist, knocking the weapon loose. Harry grabbed for it, missed, then reached out and got hold of the grip. He threw the dusters off as he trained the barrel on Hiram, who scrambled from beneath Ibra's weight and stood. He stayed still, his eyes glittering in a shaft of moonlight.

Harry's chest heaved but the gun remained steady. "Back up," Harry said. "Get away from him." Hiram stepped back, too fast for Harry's taste. "Get down on your stomach." He looked to Mo, still sprawled on the table top, as Hiram followed orders. The bearded man hadn't moved.

Where was the amulet? His chest thumped, stomach roiling, as Hiram slowly lay prone on the ground, arms stretched out, watching Harry. Ibra hadn't moved. "Hands behind your head," Harry said. He pulled the penlight from his pocket, flicking it on to scan the ground near his feet. The amulet should have landed over here. Even if Hiram had knocked it out of mid-air, it shouldn't have gone far. His light revealed nothing. He turned, half looking back at Hiram, scanning the floor without luck. Was it behind furniture? The beam bounced back and forth across the floor, over Ibra's body and past Hiram as he lay on the ground. He couldn't leave it, not here, not with so much still to—

Gold reflected in the light. He'd nearly stepped on it. Harry bent and scooped it up, looping the leather cord over his neck, the metal still warm as it settled on his chest. Harry flicked the pistol at Hiram. "Scoot back. Away from him."

Hiram did, and Harry knelt beside Ibra, fingers flitting across the Sudanese man's neck until he found his pulse, strong and steady. No blood on the floor. Harry's stomach churned. Ibra had been shot. His chances weren't good if the bullet hadn't passed through his body.

Harry pushed and prodded, lifting Ibra's torso as he searched for a wound. None revealed itself until he grabbed Ibra's arm to find it warm and wet. A furrow scorched across Ibra's bicep where the bullet had grazed him. A flesh wound, the blood flow already slowed to a trickle.

He nearly sagged with relief as he got to his feet and stepped over to Hiram. "Face down," he told him. He kept the barrel on Hiram as the man obediently laid his forehead on the floor. "I will shoot you if you move." He grabbed a length of fabric from inside the closet he'd meant to search momentarily, used his teeth to rip a hole in the end and pulled off enough to bind Hiram's hands and feet. Only after sitting on top of the man did he start tying, going heavy on the knots – as though he had any idea of what constituted a secure one. He finished with Hiram's hands and then bound his feet, and after that he tied Hiram's hands and feet together with another loop. That left enough to secure Mo's hands behind his back, then lash him to the heaviest table leg in the room. Made simpler as Mo remained unconscious, though he moaned a time or two. Harry pulled on the knots, hard, and they stuck. Harry slipped the pistol in his waistband and headed for the broom closet.

Hiram finally spoke. "What does the amulet say?"

"No idea. I made it up. You already saw what told me to come here. It was the two medicinal crosses, symbol for Saints Cosmas and Damian, whom this basilica is named for. I came to find a matching set." He removed a mop and bucket from the broom closet and knelt, shining his light inside it. "You'd never think to look in here for the crosses. Unless you were Ibra. He pointed them out to me. Look at this." He nodded to them as though Hiram could see. "Artorius carved his initials here in the wall. Makes me wonder what's behind it."

"You will bring darkness to the world," Hiram said. "This is a power far beyond what you understand."

"I'll take my chances." Harry snapped an image of the wall,

grabbed a hammer from one shelf and attacked, pounding the stone with all he had, again and again. The lowest stone went to pieces. Another blow, and suddenly half the wall collapsed with a roar and a shower of dust, crushing whatever was inside. Harry fell back as his throat tightened. *Oh god… I destroyed it.* He dropped the hammer and flashlight, scrambling to pull stones and rocks out of the way, unable to see anything. All this way and he'd destroyed what Artorius left behind.

Harry froze, mid-scrabble. *It's an opening.* He picked up the light to find that what he'd done hadn't destroyed the entire wall. He'd actually torn down the stones that were *hiding an opening.* An opening Artorius had carved in the wall, the perfect spot to store a message. Like in a jar sealed with wax, perhaps. Like the jar Harry's light washed over now.

Dusty, made of red clay, about the size of a flour jar, the jar sat in a recessed portion of the stone wall. Harry reached in, dust filling his nose as he lifted the jar. The thing was *heavy.* Its wax seal looked intact, even after so many years.

Hiram stared as Harry pulled it out, setting it on the floor so the bound gunman could see it. Harry paused. He looked to Ibra, who was still out on the floor, his chest moving steadily. He'd be awake soon, same as Mo, though the bonds around Mo's hands and feet should hold him. Harry laid a hand on the jar. He'd promised Ibra anything they found would stay here, with the Church. That didn't work for him any longer. He'd come this far, lost a friend, dodged bullets, blades and an ancient order set on uncovering whatever this jar held. Still, he'd made Ibra a promise. Harry Fox could have ended up dead on the floor, overwhelmed by Mo and Hiram, if Ibra had cowered instead of turning into a human battering ram and taking Hiram down.

A soft rumble sounded in Mo's throat. He was coming around. Hiram heard it too.

"You cannot take that," Hiram said. "You have no idea what it can do."

"You don't even know what it is," Harry said. "So stop telling me what to do with it." Still, he wavered. A man was only as good as his promises. And a man did what he must to survive. Harry Fox was a man who found treasures and sold them for money, same as his father. He closed his eyes, searching for the answer, trying to divine from the darkness what to do. Without thinking, he reached for the amulet, rubbing his fingers across the now-warm gold. His eyes opened. He knew what to do.

Making certain Hiram could see, Harry unscrewed the silencer from Mo's pistol, unloaded the weapon, then used the gun's front sight to break the seal on the jar. The wax resisted momentarily before the metal notch ripped through it. He pocketed the weapon and put both hands on the lid, looking to Hiram as he lifted it off and set it aside. His penlight flashed on, lighting up each crevice and curve. Then he reached in.

The jar held a scroll, tightly wound, no thicker than his wrist. Papyrus, which suggested this truly was from the time of Artorius. Harry touched the scroll and found it sturdy. He could open it here without much fear of it disintegrating. At least that was what he told himself. He clamped the penlight between his teeth, shone the beam on the scroll, and got to work.

The outer page slipped in his hands when he started to unroll it, and he stopped breathing. Had he ripped it? The scroll should have been one continuous piece. It shouldn't fall apart in his hands unless it had been damaged or had deteriorated over time. He grabbed the center part, which fell out like a bullet from a shell casing. It was a single, long piece, rolled up, while the outer part was hollow. He shone the penlight beam on it and looked inside. *Writing.*

The outer shell was a second sheaf. He returned the inner scroll to the jar before turning his attention to the single sheet. He unrolled it. And frowned.

A single line of handwritten text ran across the top. He couldn't read it, though he recognized the language as Aramaic, the language of the Ancient Middle East. Below this single, horizontal line ran two rows of writing, each one stacked vertically and running from top to bottom, like two columns supporting the roof of Aramaic writing along the top. He squinted, turning the sheet to get more light. Those weren't sentences running vertically. They were *names*. The first column was mostly Aramaic writing, though near the bottom it switched to Latin and stayed that way for the second column. Perhaps ten names in each column, none of which he recognized. Save one. The last name listed.

L ARTORIVS

Harry let go of one side, allowing the sheet to fold back on itself. He set it back in the jar before removing the inner scroll. Harry took a deep breath, looking to Hiram, then over to Mo and Ibra. None of them moved, though Hiram watched with maniacal, silent intensity. Harry blinked and another face flashed across his mind's eye. His father's. *I did it, Dad. Because of you.*

He opened the scroll, just enough to see the first few lines scrawled across the papyrus. Neat writing, the words tightly grouped, letters small, economical in size. Aramaic again. Harry closed the scroll and set it back in the jar. An idea took shape in his head. He reached into the open broom closet and removed a single plastic garbage bag.

"Want to see?" he asked Hiram, nodding over at the jar.

The man nearly jumped off the floor. "You must show me." Sweat beaded on his forehead and his breaths came rapidly. "Please."

Harry reached back into the jar, grabbed the outer sheet of papyrus and moved closer to Hiram, then knelt in front of him. "You have any idea who I am, Hiram? I mean, do you really know?"

Hiram looked as though Harry spoke in tongues. "What? Yes, you are Harry Fox. From America." His teeth glowed white in the light. "Now show me the scroll. What does it say?"

"I'm from New York," Harry said. He didn't open the scroll. "I'm in the artifacts business. I acquire them, buy them sometimes, find them other times. Then I sell them." He waved the sheet at Hiram. "That's what brought me here. It's what I do. Now, I've read this." He nodded to the jar. "That other one too. I'll let you see this one, then I'm leaving. With my friend. I'll wait thirty minutes before I call the cops. You're a resourceful man. I bet you can get out of here by then."

"You cannot take it!" Spittle flew from Hiram's lips. "We will hunt you down, Harry Fox. Do you want to spend every day looking over your shoulder, waiting for the knife or bullet?" His eyes threatened to burst from his skull, the sweat flowing now. "We will never rest—"

"—until you find this. Yeah, I get it." Harry waved the scroll again. "Here's the thing. I'm a businessman and I have something you want. You have powerful friends, connections all over the world."

"More than you can imagine."

"*Rich* friends, I bet." Harry pointed the rolled-up sheet at him. "I don't want to keep this, so what am I going to do with these papers? I'm going to *sell* them. To you, if the price is right. I'll even give you first dibs."

Hiram failed to muster a response.

"Tell me how to contact you and we'll meet in two weeks. You can inspect the merchandise, see if you're interested, then hopefully we make a deal. Now, you should know I have friends who take threats seriously. Don't think you can muscle in and take these without paying. My friends have friends, the kind who hold grudges. Blood feuds, vendettas, the whole bit. You want these documents? You pay for them."

Hiram growled under his breath. Harry let him. "You won't sell them to someone else?" he eventually asked.

"I like doing business with people I know," Harry said. "We know each other now. I'm serious when I say I don't want these. You think I want to worry about your group coming after me? No thanks. I'd rather sell these and we part amicably."

Hiram's tone softened. "Perhaps we have a deal. Now let me read the scroll."

"Only this page," Harry said. "Trust me, what it says proves you want the whole thing." He had no idea what it said, but Hiram didn't need to know. "One thing. Can you read Aramaic?"

Harry was unsurprised when Hiram said he could. He turned the sheet toward Hiram, focused the penlight on it, then unrolled it. His hands were steady as Hiram's eyes flashed over the sheet. Five seconds into it he started murmuring in Hebrew. The words cut off abruptly an instant later.

Harry pulled the sheet back. He opened his mouth, saw Hiram's face, and closed it. Tears streamed down the bound man's face.

"Be careful with what you have. It is more valuable than you can imagine."

Strange thing for a potential buyer to say. He re-rolled the sheet with care. "How do I contact you?"

Hiram rattled off a phone number that Harry memorized. "I'll call," he said. Hiram didn't say another word as Harry replaced the single sheet back around the larger scroll and slipped both items into the garbage bag, which he tucked into his shirt. Ibra had started moving. Harry leaned over him, touched his shoulder and shook gently. Now for the hard part.

"Ibra, wake up." He threw a note of urgency into his words. "Get up. We have to go."

Ibra blinked, looked around, then bolted upright. He immediately fell to his backside and grabbed his bicep. "My arm. I have been *shot.*"

"I know," Harry said. He didn't tell Ibra it was a flesh wound. "We have to move. Right now. You need a doctor. Hurry up."

Harry didn't give the poor guy a chance to ask about Hiram or let him think about what Harry had him doing. The guy was half-concussed and had lost blood, and Harry was able to walk Ibra quietly outside, through the front door and out to the Via dei Fori Imperiali. He hailed a cab and told the driver to take them to the nearest hospital.

Ibra looked up as the car sped away. "Did you find anything in the closet?" he asked.

"I did." Harry paused. Ibra gasped. "A clay jar. It was beautiful. Empty, but a wonderful piece. I hid it back in the closet after I tied those two up." He patted Ibra's knee. "You're brave, Ibra. Crazy, but brave. You saved my life."

Ibra actually blushed. "It is my honor to help you in your quest. You are a good man, Harry." Ibra stretched out his hand.

Harry shook it. "I owe you."

"I believe in the power of good deeds. Do good, Harry. That is how you pay me back."

Any more of this and Harry would hand over the scroll, Mo and Hiram be damned. "Ibra, are you feeling okay?" Ibra said he was, all things considered. "Because I have to get out here and leave you. I'm sorry."

Harry told the driver to pull over on a corner with plenty of pedestrian traffic. He put a pile of euros in Ibra's hands, twenty times more than the cab fare would cost. "Take care, Ibra. I'll be in touch."

"God bless you, Harry. And Godspeed."

Harry found his voice wasn't working as he got out. The cab buzzed away, leaving Harry on the sidewalk with people flowing around him and a cold plastic bag in his shirt. Harry stood still. He let the thoughts rattle in his head, tugging loose a flood of emotions he'd never thought he'd feel. Cars rumbled by, people pushed past him, and life carried on outside the world of Harry Fox. After a minute, he drew a deep breath, turned and started walking.

Epilogue

New York City
One Week Later

Rose Leroux had hosted any number of meetings. This was one of the stranger ones, with more than double the normal number of guards. Six privately contracted security specialists stood around the room, in an office she kept in the heart of Brooklyn, large enough to fit several dozen people comfortably. Three of the specialists had fully automatic weapons looped around their necks. All wore bulletproof vests and kept a respectful distance from the table in the room's center around which Rose and three men sat. None blinked when one of the seated men opened his briefcase to reveal the contents.

The seated man wore a yarmulke. He pushed the briefcase across the table to Harry Fox, who took a jeweler's loupe from his pocket and began inspecting items from the case at random. After a few moments, he turned to Rose, who nodded her approval. Harry looked across the table at the two men who had tried to kill him a week ago. Now they were closing a deal.

"Satisfied?" Hiram asked.

"I am," Harry said. He opened the messenger bag at his side and took out a circular metal case, which he handed first to Mo along with two pairs of white cloth gloves.

Hiram took the case from Mo, put his gloves on before unscrewing its lid and removing the scroll he'd last seen in Rome.

232

The smaller sheet of papyrus covering it came out as well. Lines creased Hiram's forehead as he read. Ten minutes passed before he unrolled the scroll to its full length. Then he looked at Harry. Hiram wiped at the corner of one eye. "It is a gift from the heavens."

Harry wasn't so sure about that but said nothing. "What will you do with it?"

"Keep it safe," Mo said. He'd been studying the scroll along with Hiram, though his face remained impassive. "The world should not see this. I assume you read it?" Harry said he had. "Then you understand this message would cause immeasurable harm if released. People will interpret it to fit their beliefs. This could tear our world apart."

Hiram held the scroll with reverence a moment longer, then carefully put it back in the container and replaced the lid. "Mo is right. We do this for the good of all men, regardless of faith. It's too dangerous to let this message get out. Some would embrace it. Others, reject it. And there are those who would use it to further their own ends with no regard for the damage they caused. To me, this is imperfect. Yet it secures the foundation of my existence, one more unsteady rock placed on another until a solid, immovable base exists. A base that protects us all."

Rose and the three men at the table all stood. Mo eyed Harry a moment longer, then looked to the armed men standing guard. "I underestimated you in Rome," he said. "I won't make that mistake again."

"I'll be in touch if I find anything else you might want to buy," Harry said.

"You have my number." Mo nodded to Rose. "Ms. Leroux."

Hiram and Mo departed, two of the security guards escorting them out to a waiting car. Rose turned to Harry as they both headed for the door. "Care to join me for a drink?"

"I'll take a rain check." Harry checked that the briefcase was locked before picking it up and following Rose to the door. The two security men waited outside when it opened, ready to escort their employer and her guest home. "I need to share this news with Vincent."

"I believe this will surprise even him." Rose laughed. "Ten million dollars in diamonds." They stepped into the sunlight and into the back of an armored SUV built to withstand anything short of a bomb. Rose laid a hand on Harry's arm as the vehicle rolled into traffic. "Would you care to share what was on that scroll? Those were hard men, Harry. Whatever you had made Hiram emotional."

Harry's lip curled up. "I will later. First I need to see Vincent."

Rose let the matter rest as her security men drove them to Vincent's headquarters. The car waited at the curb as Harry got out and walked inside, then pulled away and rumbled down the street. Harry hurried upstairs, clutching the briefcase so hard his hand ached. Vincent's door was open, with both father and son waiting inside.

"Harry." Vincent waved to a chair. "Join us. All went well?"

"It did," Harry said.

Joey settled into the chair beside Harry. "What does a first-century scroll sell for these days?"

In the most recent unexpected development of this adventure, Vincent and Joey Morello had agreed without reservation to let Harry handle the negotiation and sale of the scroll. Normally Vincent laid out parameters for what he expected to receive in terms of payment for anything Harry found, and Joey was even more apt to step into a negotiation. However, neither Morello had intervened after Harry returned from Rome. Instead, embracing him as one of their own, Vincent and Joey gave Harry carte blanche to negotiate a price.

He did not tell Rose what the scroll contained, even as she facilitated the deal.

He did, however, give Joey and Vincent a general summary of his find, outlining what made the two-thousand-year-old scroll valuable. Written in Aramaic, the ancient language of Syria, this scroll provided the only contemporary account of a first-century Christian prophet ever found. It detailed the teachings and visions of a man who claimed to commune with God, a new God whose influence would sweep across the world and change the course of history.

Harry did not tell them who had written it; nor did he provide any more detail about its message than was necessary. He couldn't, not after he had come to understand what was on the rolled papyrus. Mo and Hiram were correct: the scroll should never be let loose on the world. Humanity wasn't ready for the story it told.

In some ways, it was a familiar story, one of visions and sermons, parables and promises. A story known around the globe. However, this account differed from all others in two ways. First, it had been written around 28 A.D., an eyewitness report on the birth of Christianity from what was now called the Middle East. Second, the scroll wasn't a retelling of what one man had seen. It was autobiographical.

The scroll had been written by a man named *Yeshua*. Or in Greek, *Iesous*. In English? *Jesus*.

Harry hadn't believed it at first. Then he had translated the single sheet on which Artorius had inscribed his name. The listed names were those of devout Christian men who had secured the writings after their prophet's death. Artorius was one of them. All had recorded their names, an act that would have been their death warrant if discovered. What made a believer out of Harry was the single line written across the top. A statement more profound than any of the men who kept it safe could ever have known.

Enclosed are personal writings of the prophet Yeshua, retrieved from the Romans after his death upon the cross. I swear upon God Almighty to protect these writings with my life.

The oath of those who swore to save the personal writings of a man they called the Son of God. A man whose death the first protector had witnessed. A death none of them refuted, even hundreds of years later.

Harry set the briefcase on Vincent's desk. "It's unlocked." Vincent lifted an eyebrow as he reached for the clasp. "Wait," Harry said. He dug in his pocket. "You'll need this."

The lines on Vincent's forehead deepened when Harry gave him a jeweler's loupe. Joey stood and went to his father's side. The clasp *snicked*, the lid came up, and their eyes went wide at the sight of all the black velvet bags lined up in a row. Joey opened one and stones slid out. Flecks of light in brilliant shades of every color bounced off the walls. A string of soft Italian slipped between Vincent's lips as Joey's mouth formed an O. He looked to Harry.

"How much is in here?"

"Ten million dollars' worth. No diamond under two carats."

Vincent emptied a second bag, picking a stone seemingly at random and studying it under the loupe for a moment. He beckoned Harry to come around the desk and stand beside him.

"Harry." Vincent stood, opened his arms, and wrapped Harry in an embrace. "Well done." He didn't smack Harry's back, didn't do more than give a gentle squeeze. To Harry, it couldn't possibly have meant more. "Your father is proud."

Harry bit his lip. The words wouldn't come out. He settled for dipping his head, once.

Vincent let go of Harry. "Joey, take this briefcase to the bank. One of the deposit boxes should have space." He reached into the briefcase before Joey closed it and removed one black velvet bag. The bag went into Harry's hand. "For your hard work."

Now Harry couldn't speak for another reason. There had to be half a million dollars in there. Joey seconded his father's words and left the room before Harry found his voice. He knew better than to protest. That would be disrespectful. "Thank you, Mr. Morello. You honor me."

"It's Vincent," he said. "You deserve it." He gestured to the chair

Harry had just vacated. "Have a seat. Harry, I think it is time I told you the story about how your father and I met."

Lightning may as well have struck him. First, the diamonds. Now Vincent wanted to pull back the curtain on a part of Harry's life he'd never fully known. It seemed as though currents of air pushed him into the chair; Harry blinked and found he'd fallen into the seat without engaging his brain. For as long as he could remember, his father had worked for Vincent Morello, traveling the globe for antiquities to be sold. Often Fred Fox had tracked down missing artifacts, recovering them and working with Rose to broker a sale, all of it profit. At other times he had located items for sale that he could buy low and sell high. His father had rarely spoken of the time before he worked for the Morello family.

"He never told me how you met," Harry said. "He didn't talk about the past much. Other than about my mother."

Lines crinkled around Vincent's eyes. "A wonderful lady. Your father never let her memory fade."

Harry pushed those thoughts aside. "Was there a reason my father never told me about how you met?"

Vincent chuckled. "Yes, there was. However, you can be the judge of whether his reticence was necessary." The old gangster peered at Harry with an unnerving intensity. "Your father and I met inside the Metropolitan Detention Center in Brooklyn."

The floor dropped from below Harry's chair. "You met in *federal prison?*"

"We did. I was being held on charges that were later dropped, charges trumped up by one of our rival families and intended to confine me in an area without protection. Your father was serving a ninety-day sentence for trafficking in stolen cultural artifacts." Harry's mouth flew open. Vincent raised a hand. "He was framed. Your father's academic expertise was requested to facilitate the sale of stolen Greek artifacts. He was set up. The sellers lied to him about the provenance. The buyer was an informant working with federal agents. Everyone at the sale was arrested, including your father."

Harry grabbed his head in both hands. He knew his father had once been an academic, but had never learned why he'd left scholarly life. He had eventually accepted Fred Fox didn't want to talk about it. Now it made sense. "I can't believe it."

"He was innocent," Vincent said. "Though I am personally grateful for his misfortune." Harry's head popped up and he looked quizzically at the old man. "I would be dead had your father not been framed."

Harry touched the amulet under his shirt. After coming back from Rome, he had had it secured to a metal chain, one that kept it out of view. A leather strap wouldn't do any longer. "What happened in prison?" Harry asked.

"Your father was assigned as my cell mate. I had no idea who he was, nor he me. I did not speak to anyone. The people who framed me had contacts among the guards. I suspected the charges had been crafted specifically to assure I went to MDC Brooklyn. This proved correct two days after your father's sentence began."

Vincent twisted in his chair to look out the window. "They tried to kill me in the exercise yard. I walked during exercise time, staying away from everyone. As I walked that day, I realized no guards were around. Everyone was near the doors, far from where I walked. A group of prisoners gathered between the guards and me, blocking me from their view." His eyes narrowed. "One man peeled off from the group and came for me. He had a shiv and cornered me by the fence, behind a set of benches. I would have died had your father not been sitting on one of those benches."

Harry leaned closer, his hands finding the edge of Vincent's desk.

"Fred saw the man coming at me. Your father had no idea who I was. He only knew I was in trouble. He intervened."

"How?"

"He tackled the assassin, wrestled away the knife, and in the struggle he stabbed the other man. He saved my life."

Harry ricocheted off the back of his chair. "He *what?*"

"He stabbed the man who would have killed me. Fortunately, the man survived. I would have hated for him to die and deprive me of vengeance."

Vincent Morello could be as hard as they came. "What happened to my father?" Harry asked.

"The guards were forced to intervene. My personal attorney defended your father. The judge found he acted in self-defense. I was released two days before your father, when the charges against me were dropped. When Fred walked out of prison, I had a car bring him here and offered him a job for life. The rest you know. It's *your* history."

It would take a long time to unpack that story. Harry fell back in the chair, not knowing what to think. His father had had a side Harry had never seen, or even guessed at. He pondered that, sitting in silence, until he found himself absentmindedly rubbing the amulet once more. A memory sparked. *The scarab.*

He sat up. "Vincent, I'd like to search for a very specific artifact next."

"Whatever it is, the answer is yes."

"Thank you." Harry pulled the amulet from under his shirt. "This was my father's."

"I have seen it before. Is it part of your new quest?"

"It is." Harry recounted how the Egyptologist in Germany had not only read, but recognized the inscription as matching those on a series of scarab medallions created by Mark Antony and Cleopatra. "I want to find the scarabs."

He waited a beat. That was not all he wanted. "Then I'm going to find out who framed my father and clear his name."

Vincent stood from his chair. "We will start today."

Author's Note

Much of this story draws from real life, from true historical facts, though these facts are interspersed with fiction in certain places. In others, fiction overtakes fact, always in the pursuit of one goal – a better story. I have tried to detail these parts below to provide a view into what is true and what is part of my imagination.

Lucius Artorius Castus (Chapter 2) is real. He was a Roman military commander who lived in the 2nd century A.D., and served the empire in many capacities, including that of *Dux Legionum*, a title which indicated a soldier serving above his commissioned capacity. Castus has widely been considered as a possible inspiration for the Arthurian legend, though in truth he is but one of many and the widely accepted view is that Castus is not the most likely man to have inspired King Arthur. This is mainly due to Arthur's existence being pegged to the 5th or 6th century A.D., as well as the earliest accounts of the legendary Arthur fighting battles against invading Saxon hordes, which did not occur until the aforementioned timeframe, at least three centuries after Castus died.

The true location of Geoffrey of Monmouth's grave (Chapter 2) is unknown, as is much about his early years. Geoffrey was born sometime around 1100 A.D. in or around Wales. He referred to himself as *Geoffrey of Monmouth* in his writings, which accounts for the moniker by which he is widely known today. Scholars believe Geoffrey spent most of his life outside of Wales in service of the church, often in what became Britain, which is the basis for his most famous work, *The History of the Kings of Britain*. For centuries after its publication around 1136 it was regarded as factual, though by the 16th century it became regarded as inaccurate, and is now recognized as being wildly so. However, the book is valuable in other ways – it popularized the legend of King Arthur, whose exploits still capture our imagination today. As for Geoffrey's grave, no one knows where it is.

St. Mary's Prior Church truly was founded in 1075 (Chapter *5*), but the current building dates from the 18th century. Anything which existed during Geoffrey's lifetime has been lost to history. On the matter of graveyards, one does exist on the grounds, though unfortunately there is no crypt in the basement. If Geoffrey was buried at St. Mary's Priory, his grave is now lost.

Lucius Artorius Castus served in the Roman military in the late 2nd to early 3rd century A.D., rising to the rank of *Dux Legionum,* or "Leader of Legions" at the end of his career. His true religion (Chapter *7*) is unknown, as inscriptions found on his tomb have been found on both pagan and Christian tombs around the time of his death in the early 3rd century, around the year 205 A.D. He was likely not living during Diocletian's time as Emperor of Rome, which lasted from 284 A.D. to 305 A.D.

Diocletian's Palace is located in Split (Chapter *11*), a town on the Adriatic Sea in Croatia, though to be fair it is better described as *the* town of Split. A palace built in the fourth century for Emperor Diocletian, it now covers half of the Old Town section of Split, the fortress covers over seven acres of the city and is recognized around the world, having been featured on the television show *Game of Thrones*. However, Castus is not buried within the Palace. The true burial site of Lucius Artorius is near Podstrana, on the Dalmatian Coast in Croatia, approximately seven from Diocletian's palace. Artorius's tomb is not actually beneath the streets of Split. Cathedral of St. Domnius is real and actually does date from 305 A.D.

The Roman empire had a fluid relationship with various religions, often changing with the times in order to capture public sentiment or maintain power in times of need. The plight of Christians is well-documented, with thousands of their faithful having met horrific ends in the Colosseum and elsewhere beginning during the reign of Nero, and continuing until the end of Diocletian's reign in 305 A.D. Ill treatment at the hands of Roman leaders continued sporadically for several years until Constantine recognized Christianity as a legal religion in 312 A.D., leaving Diocletian as the last Roman emperor to fully persecute Christians.

The memorial to Diocletian's daughter Galeria Valeria *(Chapter 11)*, does not exist. Galeria married her father's co-emperor, Galerius, in 293 A.D. The marriage was meant to strengthen the bonds between their families. However, with both Diocletian and Galerius dead by 311 A.D., Galeria was left under the care of emperor Licinius, though she fled his protection to seek that of yet another claimant to the seat of power, Maximinus Daia – this was a turbulent period in Rome's history with rival men seeking to control the empire. Galeria refused Maximinus's offer of marriage, so of course he had her imprisoned. Maximinus soon died, putting Galeria under the control of his rival Licinius, who promptly ordered her beheading. She managed to evade the executioner's sword by running for over a year, though she was eventually captured and beheaded, her body thrown into the sea. The memorial is entirely of my own creation for narrative purposes in this story.

Trier Cathedral *(Chapter 15)* is real. However, it is not dedicated to St. Bacchus, a deity who is the Roman version of Dionysus, the Greek god of many things, including wine, fertility, insanity and festivity. The Romans repurposed Dionysus into their god Bacchus, down to the stick or wand he often carried, topped with a pine cone. The first building of what became Trier Cathedral was built in 270 A.D., though over the centuries it has been destroyed or demolished time and again, first by the Franks, then by Vikings, as well as having updates or modifications made based on architectural styles of the time. I adjusted the true timeline for purposes of this story.

The *Basilica of Saints Cosmas and Damian (Chapter 20)* is located a stone's throw from the Colosseum on Via dei Fori Imperiali. The exterior is much as I have described it, though the image of medicinal crossed spoons is not present on the exterior. Right down the road, the famed Colosseum truly has 76 numbered entrances *(Chapter 20)*, though numbers are no longer painted, they used to be and were instrumental in getting upwards of fifty thousand spectators to and from their seats in an orderly fashion.

The interior of the Basilica *(Chapter 21)* is as described, though I took creative liberties with the layout. And, in one of the more amazing true stories I have ever heard, the painting in a broom closet is real. However, in truth it is only a thousand years old, not two thousand. I was fortunate to receive a personal tour of the Basilica during my honeymoon – if you're reading this, thank you Brother Mark! He was a fantastic tour guide, taking several hours out of his day to share the basilica with my wife and I. As Brother Mark told us, "We really do need somewhere to put the brooms".

Excerpt from *The Next Harry Fox Adventure*

Visit Andrew's website for more information and purchase details.

andrewclawson.com

Athens, Greece

Harry Fox was going to clear a dead man's name. He just had to be sure he didn't get himself killed in the process.

"*Próseche!*"

A motorcycle running between the curb and traffic nearly clipped his elbow when Harry strayed too close to the road. The man ripped ahead, cutting across three lanes of traffic to make a turn before disappearing between a row of white-washed buildings. No one so much as honked a horn the entire time.

"These people are nuts," he said to no one.

Harry was used to crazy drivers. He lived in Brooklyn. His fellow Americans had nothing on the motorists in Athens, who took lane markings and traffic signs as suggestions at best, invisible more often. He pushed between pedestrians to get further away from the deadly traffic buzzing past his elbow and then barreled on, keeping a tight grip on the messenger bag looped around his neck. He couldn't show up without a bag. No artifacts smuggler ever carried his purchases out in the open.

Exhaust scraped his dry throat. Sweat trickled down his neck as the Grecian air wrapped him in a smothering embrace. People filled the sidewalk, giving Harry cover to start and stop, duck into shops, and perform other countersurveillance measures as he walked. He looked for familiar faces, people paying him too much attention. Anything that might give away somebody on his tail. No one stood out.

Harry waited under the awning of a food market. He studied a warehouse down the street, the place where he was meeting the seller in thirty minutes to complete their transaction. The sale of a cultural artifact with questionable provenance. A statue of Zeus, King of the Gods in Greek mythology. The statue dated from before the time of Christ and would have been welcomed by any museum around the world. Such a piece was enough to draw attention across oceans, to attract an American buyer to Athens, determined to get his hands on this one-of-a-kind piece.

That's exactly what Harry wanted the sellers to believe. His demand to see the artifact before completing the sale went unchallenged. A week after learning where to find it, Harry was on the ground in Athens and headed for the rendezvous. The buyers didn't know his identity, not unusual in deals such as this. They had no reason to be alarmed, to suspect this was anything but a chance for them to make money. They had no idea what was coming.

His watched showed fifteen minutes until the meet. Harry reached into his bag and touched the cool metal inside. His phone rang. He closed the bag again and checked his screen, did a double-take when he saw the country code for Germany. *Why was she calling?*

"Sara?

"Good morning, Harry. Hope I didn't wake you."

It was early back home in the U.S. "I'm in Greece," Harry said. "Is everything okay?"

"Are you buying antiquities?" she asked.

Something like that. Sara knew he did something with cultural artifacts, which was partially true. She didn't know the specifics, and Harry intended to keep it that way. "If the price is right," Harry said. He changed the subject. "Is this about my amulet?"

Harry reached for his shirt, his fingers brushing across the amulet beneath his shirt. An Egyptian artifact that used to be his father's, and which Harry never went anywhere without. A piece which gave Harry more questions than answers, one of which Sara Hamed had helped answer.

"I certainly don't call for the conversation," she said.

Harry laughed, caught off-guard. "I didn't know Egyptologists had a sense of humor."

"Spending your days with three-thousand-year-old mummies isn't funny. You living people are better for that. But you're busy. Is later today better?"

"I'm not busy," he said hurriedly. The Zeus statue could wait. This was more important. "What's going on?"

"Your amulet. I learned more about it."

Harry's chest tightened. "Did you find something?"

"I believe so. Do you remember what I told you about the scarabs?"

"That the same writing on my amulet was on scarab medallions given out by Mark Antony and Cleopatra. It's not the kind of thing you forget."

"True," Sara said. "I confirmed the scarabs did say that. The reason you had such a hard time finding out what's written on your amulet is because no one has seen any of these scarabs for hundreds of years."

"You only knew it from a drawing, right?"

"Yes. There aren't any around now. Lucky for you I remember things."

When Harry had met Sara in Germany several months ago, she'd done two things which he'd never forget. The first was going toe-to-toe with a bunch of drunken skinheads who targeted Harry for how he looked. The second, and far more important, was telling him what the Egyptian hieroglyphs on his father's amulet actually *said*.

"That's the truth," Harry said. "What else did you learn?"

"I need a few more days to sort through all of it. Can we connect later this week once I'm certain of what I found? I don't want to give you bad information."

Harry clenched his hand into a fist. "You can't tell me now?"

"I just need a few days," she said. "I'm a professor. I need to be certain of this." He could hear the smile edge into her voice, remembering what it looked like without trouble. "Come on, Harry Fox. That amulet has been around for thousands of years. A few more days won't hurt anything."

She was right. As badly as he wanted to know, a couple days wouldn't matter. "I'm holding you to this promise," he said. "Call me as soon as you're ready to talk. Day or night, it doesn't matter."

"Will you still be in Greece?"

Harry's gaze went to the warehouse across from him. "I hope not."

He clicked off, slipped the phone in his pocket, then opened his bag and removed a pistol, quickly hiding it in his waistband. Harry dodged cars as he crossed the street, first circling the entire warehouse before stopping outside a side door where he'd been told to wait. All thoughts of the amulet faded, though when a buzzer sounded and the door lock clicked open, he reached up and touched the Egyptian piece beneath his shirt. Whether or not it would bring him good luck was hard to say.

Harry pushed the door open. A shadow waited in the murky depths inside. A man's voice sounded, the words English. "Murderer's Row."

Harry breathed a silent sigh of relief. "1927 Yankees."

"World Series champs."

"Four game sweep over Pittsburgh." Their agreed upon code words exchanged, the shadow stepped forward so the light caught his face. "This way," he said, pointing into the darkness behind him.

Harry stepped through the door, squinting in the darkness. The other man was taller than Harry, not unusual, and he moved around behind Harry to shut the door. His white shirt was practically fluorescent in the dim warehouse.

"I can't see anything," Harry said. He turned to keep the man in view. "Where are the lights?"

A switch clicked, and far overhead a series of lights flashed to life, some more brightly than others. "Follow me," the man said.

White shirt didn't mind Harry bringing up the rear as they walked up an ascending concrete ramp which brought them to the main open floor. Judging from what he'd seen outside a metal wall ran down the center of this rectangular building, parallel with the two longer sides. A separate wall ran perpendicular to the longer one near the back, above which rows of glass windows stretched the length of the interior. Offices, from the look of it, accessed by steel grated steps which switch backed up in front of them. Instead of taking them the man veered away, leading Harry to a door in the perpendicular wall.

Light spilled out from the open door. Harry stopped walking. "How many of you are here?" he asked. "We agreed on two."

"We are only two," white shirt said. "I see you are alone."

"My associate is outside," Harry lied. "In case I don't come out on time."

The man offered Harry an oil grin. "We are businessmen. There is no trouble here."

His accent sounded Greek. These were local boys. Which jived with what his broker told him. "Glad to hear it," Harry said. "You don't want to upset my boss."

A tremor cracked white shirt's rictus grin, then vanished. "I see," he said. "Follow me."

One of the overhead lights buzzed as they entered the room. Thin lines of sunlight outlined a door at the rear, which would open to the street. An easy escape if needed, for any of them. A single table had been placed in the room's center, though no chairs were around it. An old television hung in the corner. Harry's attention went to a new man, this one standing beside the table, though this guy had a mustache. He looked an awful lot like the one who had led him inside. A metal case sat on the table.

Mustache man raised his arms as Harry followed white shirt inside, who quickly stepped to one side. "Welcome," mustache said. "I have—"

White shirt gave it away. He had nearly jumped aside, waiting for Harry to pass by as they entered. Harry's hands tingled as he stepped in. His vision focused, everything coming into clear focus, so much that he didn't miss the flash to his left, away from where white shirt stood. Nearly hidden behind the open door, he'd have missed it if he weren't on edge.

Harry ducked, lashing a kick out at the first man as he went low and twisted. White shirt cried out as his knee buckled. Harry stepped toward the shadows to where he'd seen a flash of movement, closing the distance and getting inside the third man's reach before he sprung up, his fist headed for the guy's chin.

On the walk over Harry had reached into his pocket and found the ceramic knuckledusters he carried everywhere. His weaker hand slipped into them, then stayed behind his back until now, when his fist smacked dead into the chin of a man stepping out to ambush him. Teeth cracked, the man toppled, and the gun he'd been holding out fell at Harry's feet.

Harry kicked it away and pulled his pistol out, aiming at mustache man. "Get down on the ground. Hands where I can see them."

Mustache hesitated. White shirt tried to stand, screaming when he put weight on his wounded leg, then collapsing. Harry stepped out, away from the guy who'd ambushed him. Who was now down for the count. "On the ground," Harry said. Again the man hesitated, and Harry played a hunch. His pistol now aimed at white shirt. "Or I shoot him."

"*érchomai se!*" White shirt screamed it twice, and the mustached man got down. Harry moved his pistol back to aim at him as he lay on the ground. "He's your brother, isn't he?" Mustache nodded. "Thought so. Hands behind your back."

The fight had gone out of him, and mustache kept still as Harry put a knee in his back, pinning the man down so he could remove the man's belt and use it to bind his hands together. He dragged the one who'd tried to ambush him into the open, then used that man's belt to tie his hands together. The man was breathing, though he didn't make a move the whole time. He'd be up soon, missing a few teeth and with one heck of a sore jaw, but he'd live.

"You." Harry waved his gun at white shirt, who still clutched his knee. "Take your belt off and tie it around your hands."

The man spat Greek words from between gritted teeth, none of which Harry understood. "Yeah, your knee hurts. Shouldn't have tried to ambush me. Now do it, or I'll tie your legs together. How do you think that will feel?"

White shirt took the hint, looping his belt around until Harry warily came over to finish the job. With all three men tied up, he tucked the pistol in his waistband and turned to the mustached man. He glared at Harry from the floor. "Are you in charge?" The man said nothing. "If you don't talk, I'm taking everything I can find and shooting all of you." Not quite the truth, but this guy didn't know that. Harry gave him a blank stare.

Mustache swallowed, hard. "We can make a deal. What do you want?"

"This was a business deal. Your man over there had a gun. He was going to shoot me."

"No," mustache said quickly.

Harry raised an eyebrow. "So it was a robbery."

Mustache hesitated, then nodded. "We were not trying to kill you."

Harry shook his head. "You guys are idiots. How long do you think you'll be in business if you pull stunts like this? And what happens when I leave and then come looking for you?" He went to

251

the table and reached for the square metal box. Latches clicked open, the lid flipped up, and Harry pointed inside. "You think this statue is worth robbing me for? Vincent Morello isn't worried about losing half a million dollars. You'll spend the rest of your life running, and that much money won't get you guys very far."

The guy's eyes went wide. "You work for Vincent Morello?"

Harry paused, his hand still over the open metal box. "That's right."

Mustache man went very still. "From New York."

Harry nodded. Vincent Morello ran the most successful Italian crime family in New York City. He didn't have many enemies, because his enemies didn't live very long. That this crew of punks knew Morello's name wasn't that surprising. "You trying to pick a fight with the Morello's?"

"No. We are not. Please, I'm sorry. We had no idea."

"What's your name?" Harry asked.

"Luke."

"Okay, Luke. You tried to rob me." He grabbed the pistol and aimed it between Luke's eyes, which shut. Harry counted to three. "I forgive you."

Luke risked opening one eye, and he saw Harry put the pistol away. "You do?" he asked.

"I do, because I need something from you. Information."

Luke couldn't muster a response to that.

"This statue." Harry tapped the metal box. "How did you get it?" The man sputtered. "If you don't want to talk, I can change my mind about the forgiveness."

"No, I'll tell you," Luke said. "A long time ago. Almost twenty years."

Harry fought to keep his face neutral. That lined up with what he'd hoped. "Tell me how you got it. I want to know everything."

"I bought it from an American," Luke said. "He needed to move it quickly. No provenance."

"Why quickly?" Harry asked. "It's stolen, but so is everything you buy." Luke didn't argue. "The police must have been after them."

"I don't know, but I heard these men had almost been arrested a few months before I bought it. One person at the deal was an informant."

"For the federal government?" Harry asked.

Luke shook his head. "No. I don't touch anything the American government is after. I heard it was a local police force."

"Local as in New York."

Luke shrugged. "I suppose. I didn't ask questions."

"Who did you buy this from? Names, Luke. Give me names."

The guy Harry had knocked out groaned. Harry waited for him to roll around, realize he was tied up, and start struggling. Then Harry whistled. The pistol was in his hand again. "Hey, you. Don't try anything stupid. Your buddy Luke and I are talking."

Luke said something in Greek. "What'd you say?" Harry asked.

"I told him to listen," Luke said, then spoke again in English. "He works for Vincent Morello."

The formerly unconscious man stopped struggling. "But he is not Italian." The man squinted. "Are you?"

"Your eyes work. Congratulations," Harry said. His pistol disappeared. "Those names, Luke."

"I don't know them, I swear. I only saw one of them during the deal. That's it. No names."

Harry grunted. What he said made sense. "What else can you tell me. Anything." He kept his voice level, though it was an effort. *This was the best lead to clearing Fred Fox's name.*

"The only thing I ever heard is that these guys all disappeared. The one who sold it to me and all his friends."

"How do you know?"

"I tried to find them again the next year. To buy more artifacts." The man's eyes went to the metal box, then back to Harry. "More statues. No one I talked to had heard from them since my last buy. They disappeared."

"You mean someone killed them," Harry said. Luke agreed. "Why kill them?" Harry studied the flickering light overhead. "The statue's not fake, is it?"

Luke didn't respond. Harry looked down to find the fear had returned. "You were trying to sell me a fake statue, weren't you? You didn't think I'd notice?"

"The statue is real." Words rushed out of Luke's mouth. "It's real, I swear. Except it's not here."

"You don't have it here?" Harry looked to the box. "Then what the hell were you going to sell me?" Harry didn't need an answer. "Nothing. You wanted to steal my money."

Luke's eyes kept going to the metal box and back to Harry. One of the men behind him muttered something which Harry didn't catch. He turned, but they weren't moving. Both white shirt and the guy who ambushed him were looking at the box too. Harry's gaze followed suit.

"What's in this thing?" Harry pulled the box closer to him. Metal screeched, and the flickering bulb cast dim light inside. The box was felt-lined. And heavy. It sure wasn't empty. Harry removed the knuckledusters and reached inside where he found a rectangular object, smooth around the sides, and solid. It took him a second. "You brought a stone *tablet*?"

He lifted it out. Solid stone, about the size of a shoebox lid. "There's writing on it," Harry said. He angled it under the light. "What language is this?" Then he realized the back was smooth either, and he flipped it over to find the rear covered with writing. He couldn't make heads or tails of it, but one thing was clear. This table was old. "What is this thing?"

"A royal Persian decree," Luke said. "Written five centuries before Christ."

"Why did you bring it?" he asked. Luke didn't respond. "You

254

want to steal my money, not sell this to me. What is this, a prop? Damn, but you guys are stupid. You bring a real artifact when you're trying to rob me."

It looked real. Harry had no idea what it said, though the wedge-shaped letters and repeated slashes resembled other ancient Persian texts he'd seen before. Luke and his co-conspirators had given him what he truly needed. Not the statue. Information, which brought him one step closer to clearing his father's name. This tablet was a nice bonus.

"I like this tablet," Harry said. "Tell you what. You tried to rob me. I forgave you. Now you're going to sell this to me."

Luke stared at him, dumbfounded. "Sell it to you?" he finally managed.

"Yes. Instead of the statue. Same price, minus a fee for my trouble." Harry pulled out a black felt pouch from his messenger bag. He removed two of the larger diamonds inside and pocketed them. "There. Almost half a million in diamonds. Now you didn't lose everything and I got what I needed." He didn't bother explaining what that meant. "We never see each other again. Deal?"

Luke didn't hesitate. "Deal."

"Try to follow me and I'll shoot you." Harry slipped the Persian tablet into his bag, went back to the door he'd walked through and left, flicking off the lights before he went out. None of the men made any noise by the time he made it across the warehouse and back outside, checking every direction before he slipped into the foot traffic and headed for safety, holding his bag tight. He needed to talk to someone about an artifact deal that went bad over twenty years ago. After that, he had a tablet to decipher.

To continue the story, visit Andrew Clawson's website at andrewclawson.com

GET YOUR COPY OF THE PARKER CHASE STORY
A SPY'S REWARD, AVAILABLE EXCLUSIVELY
FOR MY VIP READER LIST

Sharing the writing journey with my readers is a special privilege. I love connecting with anyone who reads my stories, and one way I accomplish that is through my mailing list. I only send notices of new releases or the occasional special offer related to my novels.

If you sign up for my VIP reader mailing list, I'll send you a copy of *A Spy's Reward*, the Parker Chase adventure that's not sold in any store. You can get your copy of this exclusive novel by signing up here: DL.bookfunnel.com/uayd05okci

Did you enjoy this story? Let people know

Reviews are the most effective way to get my books noticed. I'm one guy, a small fish in a massive pond. Over time, I hope to change that, and I would love your help. The best thing you could do to help spread the word is leave a review on your platform of choice.

Honest reviews are like gold. If you've enjoyed this book I would be so grateful if you could take a few minutes leaving a review, short or long.

Thank you very much.

Dedication

For Rose, whose laughter brightened every room and whose kindness changed lives.

Also by Andrew Clawson

Have you read them all?

In the Parker Chase Series

A Patriot's Betrayal

A dead man's letter draws Parker Chase into
a deadly search for a secret that could rewrite history.

The Crowns Vengeance

A Revolutionary era espionage report sends Parker
on a race to save American independence.

Dark Tides Rising

A centuries-old map bearing a cryptic poem sends Parker Chase
racing for his life and after buried treasure.

A Republic of Shadows

A long-lost royal letter sends Parker on a secret trail
with the I.R.A. and British agents close behind.

A Hollow Throne

Shattered after a tragic loss, Parker is thrust into
a race through Scottish history to save a priceless treasure.

A Tsar's Gold

Parker follows a trail through the past toward a lost treasure
which changed the course of two World Wars.

In the TURN Series

TURN: The Conflict Lands

Reed Kimble battles a ruthless criminal gang
to save Tanzania and the animals he loves.

TURN: A New Dawn

A predator ravages the savanna. To stop it, Reed must be
what he fears most – the man he used to be.

TURN: Endangered

Tanzania's deadliest gangster is after everything Reed
built – and will stop at nothing to destroy him.

Harry Fox Adventures

The Arthurian Relic

When a forgotten manuscript suggests Great Britain's
most famous king may not be fiction, Harry plunges
headlong on a dangerous path to uncover the truth.

Check my website AndrewClawson.com for
additional novels – I'm writing all the time.

About the Author

Andrew Clawson is the author of multiple series, including the Parker Chase and TURN thrillers, as well as the Harry Fox adventures.

You can find him at his website, AndrewClawson.com, or you can connect with him on Twitter at @clawsonbooks, on Facebook at facebook.com/AndrewClawsonnovels and you can always send him an email at andrew@andrewclawson.com.

Printed in Great Britain
by Amazon